W9-AVB-070

"I want you to sleep here tonight," Meg said.

Tye opened his eyes lethargically.

"Those stairs aren't too easy to climb, and that floor up there is too hard. You'll sleep here."

Her damp fingers touched his lips before he could form a protest. The intimacy startled them both, and she drew her hand away.

Her touch remained on his mouth. She backed away, took the cooled towel from his thigh and gently dried his skin.

And then she touched him. She held a bottle of liniment in one hand, and with the other she worked the greasy salve into his puckered skin without a qualm. His leg absorbed the warmth, and he relaxed even more, once again allowing his eyes to close.

He sensed when she'd left the room, for the heat and the light seemed to leave with her. He experienced the softness of the mattress beneath him, the gentle brush of cool night air from the open window, and wearily tried to recapture the glow of her presence....

Dear Reader,

Entertainment. Escape. Fantasy. These three words describe the heart of Harlequin Historicals. If you want compelling, emotional stories by some of the best writers in the field, look no further.

This month, we are delighted with the return of Cheryl St.John, who is known for her emotional stories set in America's heartland, all with strong yet tender heroes. Cheryl made her debut with Harlequin Historicals in March of 1994, and has gone on to write five more historicals and three contemporary romances for Silhouette. *Joe's Wife* is extra special.
Tye Hatcher, the town bad boy, returns from the Civil War to prove his worth. He marries the widow of the once most popular man in town, Joe, and must live up to the memory of him. Keep a hankie close by!

My Lord Protector by first-time author Deborah Hale is an ultraromantic English tale of a young woman who is forced to wed. She marries her fiancé's uncle, who vows to "protect her" until his nephew returns—but the two fall in love....
Margo Maguire is also making her debut with *The Bride of Windermere*. In this captivating medieval tale, a rugged knight succumbs to the charm of the woman he has been sent to protect on her journey to see the king.

And don't miss *Silver Hearts,* a delightful new Western by Jackie Manning. Here, a doctor turned cowboy rescues an Eastern miss stranded on the trail, and their paths just keep crossing!

Whatever your tastes in reading, you'll be sure to find a romantic journey back to the past between the covers of a Harlequin Historical®.

Sincerely,

Tracy Farrell, Senior Editor

Please address questions and book requests to:
Harlequin Reader Service
U.S.: 3010 Walden Ave., P.O. Box 1325, Buffalo, NY 14269
Canadian: P.O. Box 609, Fort Erie, Ont. L2A 5X3

CHERYL ST. JOHN

JOE'S WIFE

HARLEQUIN®

TORONTO • NEW YORK • LONDON
AMSTERDAM • PARIS • SYDNEY • HAMBURG
STOCKHOLM • ATHENS • TOKYO • MILAN • MADRID
PRAGUE • WARSAW • BUDAPEST • AUCKLAND

If you purchased this book without a cover you should be aware that this book is stolen property. It was reported as "unsold and destroyed" to the publisher, and neither the author nor the publisher has received any payment for this "stripped book."

ISBN 0-373-29051-9

JOE'S WIFE

Copyright © 1999 by Cheryl Ludwigs

All rights reserved. Except for use in any review, the reproduction or utilization of this work in whole or in part in any form by any electronic, mechanical or other means, now known or hereafter invented, including xerography, photocopying and recording, or in any information storage or retrieval system, is forbidden without the written permission of the publisher, Harlequin Enterprises Limited, 225 Duncan Mill Road, Don Mills, Ontario, Canada M3B 3K9.

All characters in this book have no existence outside the imagination of the author and have no relation whatsoever to anyone bearing the same name or names. They are not even distantly inspired by any individual known or unknown to the author, and all incidents are pure invention.

This edition published by arrangement with Harlequin Books S.A.

® and TM are trademarks of the publisher. Trademarks indicated with ® are registered in the United States Patent and Trademark Office, the Canadian Trade Marks Office and in other countries.

Printed in U.S.A.

Books by Cheryl St.John

Harlequin Historicals

Rain Shadow #212
Heaven Can Wait #240
Land of Dreams #265
Saint or Sinner #288
Badlands Bride #327
The Mistaken Widow #429
Joe's Wife #451

Silhouette Intimate Moments

A Husband by Any Other Name #756
The Truth About Toby #810

Silhouette Yours Truly

For This Week I Thee Wed

CHERYL ST.JOHN

is the pseudonym for Nebraska author Cheryl Ludwigs. Cheryl's first book, *Rain Shadow*, received nominations from *Romantic Times, Affaire de Coeur* and Romance Writers of America's RITA.

She has been program director and vice president of her Heartland RWA chapter, and is currently a liaison for Published Authors' Network and a conference committee chairman.

A married mother of five and a grandmother several times over, Cheryl enjoys her family. In her "spare" time, she corresponds with dozens of writer friends from Canada to Texas and treasures their letters. She would love to hear from you.

Send a SASE to:

Cheryl St.John
P.O. Box 12142
Florence Station
Omaha, NE 68112-0142

This book is lovingly dedicated to
Erin, Ryan, Zachary, Adam, Jaden, Alexis and Eric,
the most precious grandkids a Bama ever had.
I love you.

Chapter One

Aspen Grove, Colorado, 1865

"I'm tellin' ya the same thing I told ya last week an' the week before—there ain't no job for ya here." Uncomfortably, Emery Parks glanced past Tye Hatcher as if he wished he'd disappear before any respectable customers discovered the town pariah in his store.

Even though Emery'd had a help wanted sign in his front window since the first time he'd inquired, Tye didn't argue. It wouldn't do any good to challenge the mercantile owner. It had been the same everywhere he'd gone in the five months since he'd been back in Aspen Grove.

The only one willing to give him work had been Jed Wheeler, and Tye had taken the position of part-time bartender, part-time piano player with the intention of getting out of the Pair-A-Dice Saloon as soon as he found something else. Roundup was growing near; one of the ranchers would need him, even though they couldn't afford an extra hand right now. "I'll take some papers."

Emery reached behind him and impatiently tossed the packet of cigarette papers on the counter.

Tye plunked down a coin. "Thanks."

Sometimes he wondered why he'd come back here after the war. He could have ridden anywhere in the country and started his life over where no one knew him, where he didn't have a past…or a reputation hanging over his head. Sometimes he wondered why he'd chosen instead to return to the town he'd grown up in, the place where he'd never been accepted. His mother was dead now, and there was nothing physical binding him.

More than once he'd lain on his lumpy bed at the boardinghouse and wondered what had drawn him here. Something more than sentiment or lack of? Something less tangible probably. Something like pride.

The bell over the door clanged, and Emery glared at Tye. Tye leaned insolently back against the counter, crossed his ankles and watched three women enter the store and pass through a dusty patch of sunlight streaming in the window. Edwina Telford, hair as steely gray as iron, her stiff black skirts rustling up dust motes, led her two daughters-in-law into the mercantile. Tye had rarely seen Edwina in any color but black. She'd worn it after the death of her parents and after the death of her husband. And now she wore black following the death of her eldest son, Joe.

Joe's widow, Meg Telford, and her blond sister-in-law, Gwynn, trailed behind the stalwart woman like ducklings on their way to a morning swim.

"Good morning, Mr. Parks," Edwina called.

"Morning, Telford ladies," the shop owner called, addressing the trio. "What can I do for you today?"

"We're shopping for Forrest's birthday celebration," Edwina said with pride.

"How old is the little fellow?"

The woman had reached the front counter, and Edwina skirted Tye as though he were a barrel of rat poison. Her powdery verbena scent made him want to sneeze. "My grandson will be four tomorrow. His father is surprising him with the pony he's been asking for. Harley went to great pains to find a well-trained Shetland."

"The little guy will like that, won't he? He must be glad to finally have his daddy home from the war." Emery spoke conversationally, as though Tye weren't standing there.

Gwynn, too, stepped deliberately past Tye and replied, "We're all grateful to have Harley home safe."

Meg reached the spot where Tye stood, but instead of pretending he didn't exist, she nodded and gave him a hesitant smile. "Morning, Tye."

Her use of his first name caught him by surprise, but he held securely to his nonchalant expression. A knot of humiliation burned in his gut, and he resented feeling it. No reason why this woman seeing him spurned should make any difference. "Morning," he returned.

Meg received a scathing look from her mother-in-law and hurried to join her.

Tye studied her straight back in the plain black dress and remembered her in vivid colors, remembered her dancing with Joe at socials, remembered her as a young and smiling girl. She still had the curviest figure in town. And though her hair was bound in a knot shaped like a figure eight, he recalled the rich tresses the color of dark honey that had flowed down her back in her school days.

The women gave their list to Emery and chattered among themselves.

Tye replaced his hat after tipping it to the ladies. ''Nice chattin' with ya.''

Meg smiled apologetically, embarrassed for him and for her rude in-laws who didn't acknowledge he'd spoken.

Emery looked up from the list with a scowl.

With a discernible limp, Tye sauntered from the store.

''Of all the impertinent men,'' Edwina huffed, pressing her hankie to her nose as if she could keep Tye Hatcher's taint from entering her bloodstream through her nostrils.

''Been in here ever' week askin' for a job,'' Emery said. ''Think he'd take the hint by now that nobody wants him in town and head out.''

Meg studied their disapproving faces, then glanced at the door Tye's tall form had disappeared through. Why had he come back? Surely the rude treatment he received had discouraged him long before now. Even in school the kids had snubbed him because of their parents' attitudes toward his illegitimacy and his mother's questionable vocation.

He was regarded as a troublemaker; whenever there'd been a brawl in one of the saloons, he'd reportedly been present. In Meg's company he'd always been reserved and mannerly, so she had a difficult time relating the solemn-faced young man with the haunted eyes to those tales of carousing and drinking.

Edwina was going over the list of things they'd need for baking that afternoon. Meg's attention wavered to the jars of hard candy lined across the counter, and an acute ache stabbed through her chest. She would never come in here without remembering her Joe's fondness for peppermint sticks.

It had been nearly a year since she'd received news of his death at the battle of the Potomac. But the reality of him never coming home hit her afresh at every turn. Why him? Why her Joe?

She steadied herself against a rough barrel exuding the sharp smell of salted meat and tried not to wonder what was going to become of her without him. It was the same quandary she faced every day. Even her well-meaning in-laws and her own family added to her dilemma with their constant insistence that she sell the ranch and move in with them.

"Meg? Are you all right, dear?"

At Gwynn's gentle touch on her sleeve, Meg blinked away her oppressive thoughts and conjured up a smile. "I'm fine."

"You sure?"

"I'm sure." She busied herself with looking at skeins of colorful yarn in a nearby bin. *I'm fine. Just fine. I've never been so fine.* A tear fell on the back of her hand, and quickly she brushed it away. "I just need some air. I'll be outside."

Not caring what her in-laws might think, she hurried out the door, the bell clanging behind her.

The rustle of clothing and a scrape on the wooden floorboards alerted her to someone's presence. She turned, just as Tye Hatcher flicked a cigarette butt end over end into the dusty street. The mellow smell of tobacco drifted to her.

His dark gaze met hers. "Ma'am," he said politely, thumbing his iron gray hat back on his head. He took an awkward step forward. "I never had a chance to tell you how sorry I was to hear about Joe. He was a good man."

Silence stretched between them. A buggy clattered past on the deeply rutted street.

"I'm sure you saw a lot of good men die," she said softly.

His dark gaze revealed no emotion. "Yes, I did, ma'am. On both sides."

For some reason it sounded odd to hear him call her ma'am. She'd known him since she could remember. She hadn't known him well, but he'd always been there, always been a part of Aspen Grove. "We had to send for his body after the war, you know."

"I know." He looked out across the expanse of the street, offering Tye the opportunity to study his face, his smoothly shaven square jaw. His brows and sideburns were as black as the waves that curled over his collar. He was a man now; a handsome one, regardless of the unsmiling slash of his full lips. The sadness she sensed had always been there. But now it was more, more than just the disillusionment of a young boy.

Would Joe have looked that much older, too? Would the war have etched similar years on his face?

"I've always wondered if we really got the right one," she blurted. "If the man we buried was Joe." She hadn't expressed that doubt to anyone before, and she wondered why she'd revealed it now. She looked away, but she felt him swing his gaze back to her face.

She realized then she had no reason to feel embarrassed in front of this man. Somehow she knew he understood her apprehension. She raised her chin and met his eyes. She could have sworn she recognized a measure of vicarious emotion this time.

"They tagged 'em the best they could," he said. "Long as the body was identifiable and someone knew him, they should have been certain. Did you get his things, too? I mean the things he had on him. His saddlebags?"

She nodded.

"You can be certain, then."

Meg closed her eyelids briefly, a considerable flame of comfort warming her at his words. "Thank you." *Even if it was a lie, thank you.*

The bell clanged a warning and Edwina plowed her way across the boardwalk, Gwynn behind her. "Meg! What *are* you *doing* out here?"

"I needed a little air, Mother Telford. I feel much better now." She glanced up at Tye. His deep blue gaze held their secret, and a touch of appreciation. "Much better."

"You shouldn't stand out here alone. The riffraff is lurking along the streets, even in broad daylight." She handed Meg a paper-wrapped package and towed her away.

Tye tugged his hat brim back over his eyes and watched them cross the street. Meg lifted her hem and delicately traversed the riveted road. She followed her in-laws into the post office.

No doubt she'd marry again. Damned shame Joe Telford had died and left her a widow. A woman like that deserved happiness. A husband. Children. She was too young and pretty to spend her life grieving. Some lucky fellow would snap her up before much longer.

He tried to think of any young unmarried men in town or on the surrounding ranches, but he couldn't come up with one who'd make a suitable husband for Meg Telford. The war had pared the possibilities down to nothing.

He discarded the thoughts and headed to the livery for his horse. A good ride would clear his head and prepare him for a long night in the smoke- and perfume-filled saloon. He needed a lot more money than he made there in order to carry out his plans.

The land office had nothing he could afford until he multiplied his meager savings. And Aspen Grove was makin' that possibility difficult.

The birthday boy, Forrest, and his older sister, Lilly, had eaten their fill of cake and now led the Shetland pony around the newly green rosebushes in the dooryard. Harley Telford and his younger sister,

Wilsie, had spent hours supervising rides on the pony Forrest had named Cinnamon, and now engaged in a bickering game of checkers. After washing and drying the Sunday china, Meg, Edwina and Gwynn joined them on the shaded porch Edwina called a veranda.

Meg studied the tree-lined street and neighboring houses, feeling sorry for the pony, who would have to spend all but Saturday and Sunday afternoons at the livery stable. Children and animals needed wide-open spaces. She'd been so glad to move to the ranch with Joe. From the very beginning, the hills and fields, the wide sky in all directions had appealed to her dreams of escaping town life. After growing up in a house full of siblings, and helping her father in his accounting business, she'd been eager to have the space and the freedom.

"Meg, I've prepared a room for you," Edwina said. "You'll be quite comfortable in the front bedroom that overlooks the street. There are two windows, and it stays quite pleasant even in summer."

"Mother, that's your room," Wilsie said in surprise.

"It was *our* room when your father was alive," Edwina corrected. "Meg will need the space to keep some of her things she doesn't want to part with."

"That's generous of you, Mother Telford, but I can't impose on you."

"Nonsense. It's just Wilsie and I now, since Harley and Gwynn have their own home, and we ramble around in this big old house. Before long Wilsie will marry and leave me, too."

"Not unless some prospective husbands show up," Wilsie said with a petulant pout.

"I am afraid the war has left us short of eligible young men, my dear," Edwina sympathized. "In any case, Meg, the house has plenty of room, and it's high time you gave up your silly notion of staying out there on that patch of dirt in that rustic house and moved in with us."

"Mother's right," Harley said. "It's highly improper for you to be living out there with only a couple of ranch hands who should have been put out to pasture long ago. They can't keep up the work, and neither can you."

Meg drew a steadying breath and lifted her chin a notch. "I have Hunt and Aldo, too."

"They're boys," he scoffed.

"We've done all right so far."

"All right? Talk around town is you've had to sell Joe's guns and your silver to pay the help, make the mortgage payments and buy feed. What will you sell next?"

Meg resented the question because it was time to buy garden seed and another banknote was due, and she'd been pondering the dilemma herself for weeks. She'd learned how to run a business from her father; keeping the books and managing was no problem, but she couldn't handle the physical work alone.

Thirty years ago Gus and Purdy had traveled the Chisholm Trail. They knew cattle and they knew horses. They worked hard and were as loyal friends as she'd ever had. But they were old men. The banknotes came due regular as clockwork, and the stock had to eat. Since Joe'd been gone, she hadn't been able to cut and rake hay.

Meg pursed her lips and refused to get angry at Joe for leaving her in this predicament. It wasn't his fault that the war had broken out and he'd gone and lost his life honorably. It wasn't anybody's fault. And that's what made accepting her situation all the harder. She had no one to blame. No one to get angry at.

And no one who understood her desire to keep the ranch and hang on to something she knew and loved.

The ranch had been Joe's dream. It had become hers, too, and she wasn't about to let another dream die. She'd sell the furniture if she had to. She'd sell her bed and sleep on the floor. As a last resort she'd sell some stock. But she wouldn't sell their dream.

"I've started asking around at the bank and the land office, seeing if anyone's in the market to buy," Harley said. "Niles can get you a good price for the place."

Niles Kestler, junior owner of Aspen Loan and Trust, had been Joe's best friend since childhood.

"You can do your own dealings on the stock," Harley went on. "You'll get enough money to live on for a good many years."

Meg closed her eyes against the Telfords' manipulations. A good many years. Years of sleeping in the room upstairs, taking her meals with her widowed mother-in-law and passing the days doing needlepoint and volunteer work. The stifling idea horrified her. She'd feel like that Shetland was going to, cooped up in a confining stall.

Meg's widowed mother had remarried and moved to Denver several years ago, and her brothers and sisters were married and scattered from Colorado to Illinois. There wasn't a one of them she'd want to live with or impose upon.

The whole worry was so unfair. This wasn't supposed to be happening. She and Joe should have been stocking the Circle T by now, having children and seeing all their plans come to pass.

"Meg," Harley said. "You can't keep the ranch going with no man."

"Harley," Gwynn cautioned her husband gently.

His words were not a revelation. They were simply a fact Meg had been unwilling to face.

"Well, it's the truth," he said. "And a truth she'd better take to heart before she has nothing left to sell. A woman can't run a cow ranch alone."

Meg strengthened her resolve. Harley was only looking out for her interests. He thought he knew what was best for her. The life he had planned for her would have been best for Gwynn if he hadn't returned. It would have been best for a good many women.

But it wasn't for her, and she knew it. "I appreciate your concern, Harley. Yours too, Mother Telford. But I can't sell our ranch."

They exchanged a look she couldn't quite decipher. Out of breath and giggling, Forrest and Lilly scrambled onto the veranda. "Papa, come give us rides again! Watch us, Nana!"

Edwina turned her attention to her grandchildren. The subject was not forgotten. Meg would hear

about it each time they were together. Nothing short
of a miracle would keep them from chipping away at
her until she conceded. And she wasn't willing to do
that.

But Harley was right. She thought about it as she
drove her wagon and team home before dark. She
couldn't keep the ranch going without a man.

Someone to shoulder the workload. Someone
strong and capable and willing to put in the long
hours and backbreaking work required. Someone she
didn't have to pay.

Meg almost smiled at that one. Where would she
ever get an able-bodied man willing to work without
pay? She could barely keep Gus and Purdy and two
young hands fed, and she paid them only a meager
salary.

The man she was imagining sounded like a husband. A man to take on responsibilities and have a
stake in the ranch's success.

A year hadn't passed since Joe's death. Since the
war, many widows had already married again to provide for themselves and their children. Meg didn't
have children, which she saw as a mixed blessing. It
would have been comforting to have something of Joe
left behind. But she wouldn't have wanted the added
burden of raising and feeding them alone.

Ranch was a glamorous word for ten thousand
acres of grass, several holding pens and barns and the
modest house she glimpsed as she topped a rise, but
the sight gave her the same warm sense of accom-
plishment and belonging it always did.

Joe's mother had been chagrined over the fact that

Joe had concentrated on the stock and the outbuild-
ings before building an acceptable home.

But Joe'd convinced her that all they'd needed was
a place to cook and sleep while they got the ranch on
its feet. A more stately house was something they
could build in the future. With affection, Meg studied
the corrals, the barn and efficient house where she
lived. She and Joe had spent their wedding night in
the tiny bedroom. They'd eaten their first meals as
man and wife in the long kitchen. They'd planned and
dreamed as they walked the land, and lastly they had
prayed beside the back door before he'd gone off to
fight.

So much of Joe was in this ranch. They would have
to drag Meg off this land. If finding another man was
what it took to keep it, she'd do it. Nothing would
stand in the way of her keeping the Circle T. Nothing.

Chapter Two

Tye woke to the weekday sounds of horses' hooves and clattering wagons on the street below his second-story window at Yetta Banks's boardinghouse. The dry scent of dust filtered through the open window of his rented room. In the distance the ring of the blacksmith's hammer punctuated the light tap at his door.

The knock came again, assuring him he'd actually heard it. He sat up in surprise. "Hold on."

He threw his legs over the side of the bed, immediately grimacing at the pain that shot through his thigh. Awkwardly stepping into his pants, he wondered who'd be calling. The only townspeople who spoke to him were the regulars at the Pair-A-Dice, whom he doubted would be up this early, Jed Wheeler himself, the Reverend Baker and Tye's landlady.

Pulling on a rumpled Calcutta shirt and leaving the laces loose, he ran a hand through his hair and squinted at his dark-whiskered cheeks in the mirror before opening the door.

A young boy stood in the hall, threadbare knees in

his trousers, his cap askew. "Message for you, mister."

Tye stared at the envelope. "For me? You sure it's for Tye Hatcher?"

"Yes, sir." The boy thrust it forward with an important flourish.

Tye accepted the envelope with a frown. "Here, wait up."

He found a nickel on the stand beside his bed and flipped it to the boy, ignoring the fact that he'd regret it later.

"Thanks, mister."

Tye closed the door and tore open the envelope. Unfolding a piece of paper, he read the words scrawled in black ink.

Hatch, I need to see you. I'm at Rosa Casals's house.

Lottie

He had wondered if Lottie still lived in Aspen Grove. No one spoke of her, and since he hadn't seen her in the time he'd been there, he'd assumed—or hoped, for her sake—that she had found a husband and settled down.

Rosa Casals and Lottie Prescott had both been saloon girls at the Pair-A-Dice before the war. He and Lottie had enjoyed a satisfactory relationship, nothing serious, but something that took the edge off the loneliness.

Tye shaved and dressed in his good clean shirt. He needed a haircut, but he was saving every penny.

He'd discovered years ago that the custom of eating three times a day was merely a habit that could be modified, too.

Tye added his wide-brimmed hat to his ensemble. A morning exercise usually took the stiffness out of his leg, so he determinedly walked to the house on the edge of town where Rosa had grown up with an aging father.

Like most of the houses he'd seen on his travels home, the outside needed a coat of paint, a new fence and several boards replaced on the porch.

Tye rapped on the door and waited, hat in hand.

The door opened, and Rosa Casals smiled a familiar smile, one front tooth overlapping the other and giving her a girlish look, even though silver had appeared at her temples. "Hatch," she greeted him. "Come in."

He glanced at the street behind him. "You sure it's all right?"

She grabbed his wrist and pulled him forward. "It's a little late to be concerned about my reputation," she said teasingly, taking his hat and hanging it on a rack in the hallway. She waved him into a neat parlor that smelled sharply of lemon wax and candles.

Tye met her round, brown-eyed gaze and smiled. Rosa had always been fun-loving and impetuous. Working in the saloons hadn't been conducive to finding a decent husband, however. "Are you still working somewhere?" he asked out of curiosity.

"Nah. Papa, the old coot, died three years back and left me enough to live comfortably. He was such a penny-pinching old miser. I never had a decent dress or a cent to spend on myself the whole time I was growing up. Then I find out the skinflint was hoarding it all those years.''

Tye glanced around. "I had a note from Lottie."

Rosa's face grew serious. "I know. I sent the boy for you."

"She's here?"

"Yes. She's been with me for a little over a year now. She wants to see you, Hatch."

"Okay."

"She's not well."

"What's wrong with her?"

"Consumption. Doc says he's done all he can."

And she wanted to see him? "Oh."

"Ever since we heard that you were back in Aspen Grove, she's been wanting you to visit. She has some good weeks and some bad weeks, and this is one of her better times, so we decided to send for you now."

Tye stood waiting, uncomfortable, but unwilling to turn aside a friend's request.

"Come with me," she said. "I'll take you to her room."

He followed her down a hallway where several candles flickered, though the day was bright, and he soon realized they were meant to dispel the cloying smell of the sickroom.

Rosa swept into the room ahead of him. A frail, strawberry-haired woman rested against a bolster of pillows on a lofty four-poster bed. Tye had to step close before he recognized Lottie's warm brown eyes. Their luster was gone, as was the shine of her unruly hair. Her pale skin seemed paper-thin and drawn too tightly over her fragile bones and pallid face.

"Hatch. Come sit by me. Let me see you," she said, patting the spread. Only her voice was familiar.

She took his hand, and her skin felt powdery smooth against his palm, her fingers thin and bony. "God, you feel good. You look good. You look older. Not a bad look, mind you, just older."

He perched on the edge of the bed. "Yeah, well, it's been a while, Lottie."

"Yes." She looked deeply into his eyes. "We had some good times back then, didn't we?"

They'd kept each other company for a while, was all. But he wouldn't spoil her enhanced memories when she had so few and no time left to make more. So he nodded. "Yes."

"Where were you?" she asked. "During the war. I mean."

"I was with General Thomas."

She frowned as if she were trying to remember. "Chattanooga?"

He nodded. "And Chickamaugua. We held off Braxton Bragg's army."

"I knew you'd be one of the strong ones who came home."

"How did you know that?"

"I don't know. I just did. You're a survivor. Strong inside, where it counts."

Lottie'd always seemed strong, too. Full of life and energy and big plans for the future. The antithesis of the ghostly pale woman in this bed before him. Life sure took some unfair twists. "I thought you'd have found a man by now. Be living in the city in that big house you wanted.''

''Yeah, well...'' She gave him a sad-sweet smile. ''I had hundreds of offers. Just that nobody ever measured up to you.''

She was teasing him. Theirs had never been a passionate relationship. She'd had plans for a rich man and a house in the city. He'd wanted a patch of ground and some livestock to call his own. He gave her a warm smile.

''I'm not here for much longer,'' she said simply.

Tye didn't know how to reply.

''I need you to do something for me,'' she said tentatively.

''You know I will.'' He leaned forward, and she placed her palm on his chest as though touching him gave her strength. ''I'll do anything you ask.'' Did she have last-minute debts to repay in order to go to her resting place in peace? Damn! He couldn't help her if she needed money. ''What is it?'' he asked.

''I have a child,'' she said, and tears welled in her eyes.

''You do? Where is he? Do you need me to go get him for you?'' Perhaps she needed to say goodbye.

''No. She's here. What I need you to do is...''

''What?''

''I need you to take care of her for me.''

Tye stared at her. ''I don't have much, Lottie. I can help, but—''

''Not money,'' she interrupted. ''I mean take her. After I'm gone,'' she clarified, and blinked back the moisture in her eyes. ''Raise her.''

Was she all right in the head? Had her sickness gone to her mind? Tye glanced behind him but Rosa had left them alone. Lottie was asking him to take responsibility for a small person! A kid he didn't even know. "I don't know the first thing about a kid. I'm sure she'd be better off with someone else."

"No!" she said firmly. "She wouldn't. Nobody else would have her, you know that. She'd end up in an orphanage or worse, and I can't die afraid of that happening to my Eve."

"What about Rosa?" He glanced over his shoulder again, as though he could conjure up some help.

"No. She's getting married. Emery Parks has a brother-in-law whose wife died, and Rosa is marrying him. He already has five children. He wouldn't take another one."

"Well..." Tye glanced about the room helplessly. "Surely there's *someone*."

"That's what I've been believing all along. I've been praying that someone will want her before it's too late. Before she goes to an orphan asylum." She pierced him with a steady gaze. "She's a child born out of wedlock, Hatch. Folks consider her trash, just like they do me. She'll grow up just like me, too...unless somebody takes her. Unless you take her and give her a different life. And a name."

She knew exactly what she was saying to him, and exactly how he'd react. Tye's own father had been a rancher right here in Colorado. He hadn't married Tye's mother, and he hadn't claimed Tye as his son. More than anyone, Tye knew the stigma of being a bastard. And Lottie was using that against him.

"Nobody'd want my name, Lottie," he argued. "My name's no better than hers would be."

"At least it would be *somebody's* name," she said, her voice stronger than her appearance dictated. "It would show that somebody wanted her. That *you* wanted her. You're a good man. I know you'd take care of her, and you wouldn't let anything happen to her."

Her urgent pleas hung in the air like the unpleasant smell of sickness and the cloying scent of wax.

"You said you'd do anything for me," she said softly. Unfairly. And she knew it. But she was dying, and she had a child to look out for.

A trapped sensation made him want to bolt for the door. But he couldn't. He wouldn't. She had to have been desperate to have called on him.

"Go see her," she urged. "She's in the room next door to mine."

He stood slowly, releasing her hand. Her eyes held so much hope. So much fear. So much love for her child. With uncertainty bombarding his mind and a sense of human duty harping at his conscience, Tye walked out of the room to the next one like a man walking toward an uncertain fate.

He took a deep breath, his head not understanding why his feet were going ahead with this monstrous demand on the rest of his life. He didn't know the first thing about a kid. Sure, he wanted one or two someday, but not until he had a place to live and a wife to give him his own.

What if he didn't even like her? The door stood ajar, and he tapped his knuckles against the wood.

He didn't know what he was expecting. Certainly not the fragile, dark-haired angel who sat beneath the window holding a rag doll and looking for all the world like a porcelain doll herself. She raised wide eyes the shade of deep blue pansies and blinked.

Something in Tye's chest contracted painfully. She looked so small and helpless. "Eve?" he asked softly.

She nodded, and her midnight black ringlets bounced against shoulders he could span with one hand. "Are you Mr. Hatcher?"

"Yes."

She merely stared at him.

What should he say to her now that he was here? He didn't have any experience with kids. "Did your mother tell you I'd be coming?"

She nodded again. "I stayed clean till you got here. Me an' Molly was getting kind of tired of staying clean an' all."

"Well, you look very clean to me."

"Thank you. You look clean, too. Them's my manners and Mama said I best mind 'em."

Her piping voice and serious expression enchanted him. He found himself wanting to hear her say more. "How old are you?"

"Five and a half. My birthday's behind Thanksgiving."

"Oh."

The tiny creature hopped to her feet and placed the doll on the bed. Her wrists and hands were as delicate and frail-boned as anything he'd ever seen. A stiff wind would blow her clean to Texas.

He crossed to sit on the corner end of the mattress,

wondering what to say next. He glanced at the cloth doll. "Is that Molly?"

She bobbed her head. A smattering of pale freckles across her golden skin reminded Tye of Lottie, but her dark hair and lovely wide eyes were a mesmerizing combination all her own. No wonder Lottie adored her. No wonder she feared for this child's welfare being placed in the hands of strangers.

Not that *he'd* ever laid eyes on her before. But the unknown was often more frightening than the familiar, and Lottie'd known Tye for many years. He was the only person she could turn to. The only person she trusted.

How pathetic.

"My mama's bad sick," she said, adjusting the doll's dress and arranging her against a pillow.

What must she think of this frightening situation? She'd grown up over a saloon and only now moved to a house so her mother could die. "I know."

Eve climbed onto the bed and dangled her feet over the side.

"Sometimes I'm scared to go to her room and see her." Her silvery voice and tiny chin trembled.

Oh, Lord, what if she cried? What if she asked him something he didn't want to answer or didn't know how to answer? "That's okay," he said to reassure her.

"She don't look a whole lot like my mama anymore, but she sounds like her, and she loves me like her."

Her observation seemed too mature. But he'd noticed Lottie barely looked like herself. Her dreadful appearance must be frightening to her daughter. ''She loves you very much.''

''She said someone would come for me before the angels came to get her.''

Tye's throat closed up tight. He didn't know how to handle this. He'd seen so many people suffer and die, he shouldn't have had any feelings left when it came to death. He'd fought and killed with his own hands. He had blocked out recrimination and sorrow. What did he know about a child losing a mother?

Nothing. But he knew a lot about being a kid without a father. It wasn't really the cruelty of classmates and townspeople that hurt so much at this age; a kid didn't have anything to compare his experiences with. It was the memory of those humiliating slurs years later that ate at a person's gut.

What kind of burden had Lottie asked him to carry? What kind of mess would he make of it, of this kid's life, if he went along with her request?

Nothing worse than life in an orphanage. Unwanted kids didn't even get to eat the foods they needed to grow healthy. They got the scraps, the dregs. And it was never enough.

Tye had learned to use his fists and his wits for survival. But this little girl? He didn't even want to think about it. He had only to look at Lottie to see what would become of her.

Unless someone stepped in.

''Did you come for me, Mr. Hatcher?''

Tye looked up. Knowing what was happening, yet unable to do anything to prevent it, he fell headlong into her black-lashed, blue-violet gaze, eyes that reflected trust and innocence and waited for him to make the decision that would shape the rest of her life. She had no one in the world. No one but him.

Heaven help her.

"Yes, Eve. I came for you."

Chapter Three

Before dark, Gus and Purdy returned from the hills with the welcome news that others who'd been fighting a brushfire since yesterday had been successful in quelling it and that they'd be following. Meg had a hearty stew and corn bread warming, as well as rice pudding with raisins and currants in a milk pan in the oven.

Freshly washed, his thinning gray hair combed back in streaks on his sun-browned head, Gus entered the kitchen without knocking, as was customary on the Circle T. He did as much cooking as Meg did, coming in early each meal to grind the beans and start the coffee.

"Fire's out?" she asked.

"Yup. Got a big patch of brush up by Lame Deer and was spreadin' to the Anderson place, but we stopped 'er."

"I could smell it on the wind this afternoon." Meg had kept herself busy, the thought of the fire spreading this far licking at her already edgy nerves.

"Seen you got the cows milked," he said, opening

the oven and stirring the rice pudding, which had turned a smooth caramel brown.

She nodded. "Thought Patty was going to kick me good, though."

Joe's Newfoundland "puppy," which he'd brought home from a buying trip, only to watch rapidly grow to the size of a Shetland pony, had slipped in behind Gus and now stood with a chunk of firewood in his mouth.

Meg propped the door open with the wood. "Good boy, Major. Get more."

The dog immediately bounded for the woodpile, returning several times and dropping the wood into the firebox. Gus had taught him the trick, perhaps with the idea of saving his own steps, and the dog had caught on the way he did to everything.

After several trips, Major sat before Meg, his snout quivering in anticipation. She rewarded him with a lump of sugar, and he found a place in the corner of the long room to settle. He caught much of his own food: rabbits and squirrels. Meg had thought the practice disgusting at first, but had since grown appreciative due to the fact that she couldn't afford to feed another mouth.

The rest of the hands arrived minutes later: Purdy, along with the "boys," Aldo and Hunt Eaton, brothers in their teens, who'd been too young to go to war and needed to work to eat. Their parents lived on an acreage near town with several younger children. For lack of grown men, Meg had hired the brothers on as reps a couple of years ago.

Joining them as the day progressed came reps from

nearby ranches, stopping to eat before heading to their own places. She fed them gratefully, this bedraggled bunch of cowboys who'd been too young or too old to fight, or who'd only recently come home to ranches in need of more attention than they could afford.

All were respectfully solemn in deference to her widowed state and her mourning clothing, and they soon headed out.

Purdy was shorter and wirier than Gus, a long gray handlebar mustache his distinguishing feature. He walked with a hitch now, and lengthy stretches in the saddle enfeebled him for days. Tomorrow he probably wouldn't be able to do much around the place, and the others would work harder to make his slack unnoticeable.

"I'm gonna take care o' the horses now." He grabbed his hat.

"I'll do it," Gus offered.

"No," Meg said immediately. "Aldo and Hunt, will you see to the horses, please? You two—" she shooed Gus and Purdy with a flour-sack towel "—hit your bunks. I'll finish up here."

"Yes, ma'am." The boys got up from the bench and headed for the corral. Gus and Purdy followed.

Another hour passed before she had the dishes washed and beans soaking for tomorrow's noon meal. If she weren't so tired from checking the stock and doing all the chores while the men fought the fire, she'd have filled the big tin tub that sat in the space beside the pantry. The prospect sounded too exhausting for this evening. She'd settle for a tin basin of water in her room and sponge herself off.

At the sound of a horse and buggy, she paused in scooping warm water out of the stove's well. She peered out the back door, but the rig must have continued to the front.

Meg walked through the house and opened the seldom used front door. Niles Kestler stood on the grouping of boards that could only be called a porch in the broadest of terms. "Niles! How nice to see you."

She probably smelled like cows and lye soap. Belatedly, she whisked off her spattered apron. "Won't you come in?"

"I don't know if I should," he said, stepping from one foot to the other uncomfortably.

He'd been to their home many times when Joe had been alive; Niles and Joe had been pals since their youth. But her widowed state changed that situation. For propriety's sake, she shouldn't have asked him in.

Which was ridiculous. Gus and Purdy and the Eaton brothers had the run of her home, with nary a thought to impropriety. But to meet his standards of decorum, she stepped outside. "What brings you?" she asked.

"I thought I'd pay a call and see how you're doing."

"I'm doing fine."

"Good."

"How is Celia?"

"She's well, thank you."

Niles's wife was expecting a baby, but men and women didn't speak of such delicate things.

"Harley spoke with me this week," he said.

So that was why he'd come. Harley'd gone ahead with it.

"I can get you a sizable price for this land, Meg. There are investors who will snap it up in a minute."

Her civility fell to the wayside. "Oh? And would they be among those select few Northerners who got rich off the war?"

Niles bristled. "The point is, Meg, you need the money. You can't keep going without some help."

"Well then, how about a loan until I get this place back on its feet?"

"You must know I can't do that."

He could probably do it out of his own pocket. He would have done it for Joe. The thought angered her. As Joe's wife she'd had respect because he'd been respected. As his widow she had sympathy and little else. She'd known Niles her whole life, yet he wouldn't consider an investment in her.

Exasperated, she turned and gazed across the expanse of dirt and grass to the corrals, where several horses stood outlined in the moonlight. "And you must know I can't sell. You know what this place meant to Joe."

"I *do* know," he said quickly, and then added, "but Joe's not here anymore."

"And what a nice commission you could make off the sale of Joe's ranch." She didn't bother to withhold the derision in her tone.

She turned back to look at him.

"You know you have to do it sooner or later," he said. "Don't be a foolish woman. Why not do it be-

fore you've sold everything that means anything to
you?''

"The ranch is what means everything to me," she
replied. "And it's worth any sacrifice."

He stepped back and placed his smart, narrow-
brimmed felt hat on his head. "All right. Do it your
way. But you'll be coming to me soon. And by then
you'll be in dire straits."

"Well," she replied matter-of-factly. "I'll do everything else in my power first."

"Good night, Meg." He climbed up to the leather
seat of his fancy buggy and guided the horse back
toward town.

Meg folded her arms beneath her breasts and
watched him disappear in the darkness. Her anger had
only been a temporary disguise for hurt and fear, and
as it dissipated, tears stung her eyes. She set her
mouth in a firm line to keep the desperation at bay.

Movement caught her eye. Gus stood silhouetted
in the doorway on the side of the barn where the men
slept in roughly finished rooms. She waved, knowing
he'd been checking on her visitor and her safety. He
returned the wave and closed the door.

Exhausted, she entered the house, dipped her water
and washed up in her tiny bedroom before donning
her cotton gown, extinguishing the lamps and climbing into bed.

She'd thought about her situation every day and
night since Mother Telford and Harley's insistence. It
wouldn't improve. Without a man to take on much of
the physical work, she couldn't keep the place going.

And the Telfords would keep trying to wear her down.

The more she'd thought about it, the more she'd resigned herself to the fact that a husband was exactly what she had to have. For the past several nights she'd gone over the limited possibilities. All the bachelors were too old or too young, except for three. Jed Wheeler ran one of the saloons, but just the thought of marrying him made her shudder. Besides, he wouldn't know anything about ranching.

Colt Brickey was a year or two younger than she, but had come home from the war teched in the head. He could probably work, but she needed more than that—she needed someone who could help her make decisions.

The third and last was Tye Hatcher.

Still not husband material in society's eyes, but the only prospect capable of working and planning. He limped, but that shouldn't keep him from riding. If Purdy could do it at his age, surely Tye could. He'd done ranch work since he'd quit school to take care of his mother. He'd worked as a rep and helped with roundups, and from everything she'd seen, he seemed honest and hardworking.

Once she had narrowed her options down to him, the thought of actually carrying out her audacious plan gave her pause. What would he think of a woman so bold as to propose marriage? Did it matter?

If he said no, it was doubtful he'd tell the town of her foolish plan. And even if he told, the townspeople wouldn't believe him. And if they did, what did she really care? Holding on to the ranch was all that mattered, and at this point, she didn't have any choice.

Meg recognized the bleak emptiness of this bed where she'd lain alone for the past few years. For too short a time a man's soft snore had accompanied the night. Now she lay awake listening to the sounds of the house and the wind along the timberline.

She was contemplating bringing a stranger to the ranch. To her home. To Joe's bed. Plenty of women married men they didn't know, she assured herself. Tye Hatcher had always been polite and respectful in her presence. He wasn't bad looking. Not at all. It wouldn't be like Joe, but maybe it wouldn't be so bad.

This was business, after all. Meg was a determined woman. She could bear a good many things to get what she wanted.

Tomorrow was Sunday. He didn't attend church, but she'd heard talk that Tye often called on Reverend Baker in the afternoon. She would seek him out. And she would ask him then.

Sunday visits were a custom carried from the East. As a boy, Tye had seen families gather for Sunday meals and an afternoon of visiting and play, and always on the outskirts, he'd wondered what that was like. His mother had never been accepted among the respectable residents of Aspen Grove. She and Tye hadn't even gone to church because of the rude treatment she received. But on Sunday afternoons she'd taken him to Reverend Baker's, where she'd had someone who treated her kindly. Apparently it was acceptable for the preacher to receive her calls; he was, after all, responsible for her immortal soul.

But Tye never remembered any talk of saving his mother's soul on those visits. He remembered only the tiny measure of acceptance and the pleasure that gave his mother, and he would be forever grateful to the preacher for that kindness.

The first time he'd run into the reverend upon his return, the man had greeted him warmly and extended an invitation to come by for pie and coffee. The preacher had been a widower for more than twenty years yet had the most well stocked pantry and cleanest house in the county, thanks to the dutiful parishioners.

As his mother had done, Tye always waited for the dinner hour to pass. Often the reverend accepted an invitation and returned midafternoon. Then Tye would wait for any "real" callers who might stop by to pay their respects. And then, when everyone had gone home to their families, he would call on Reverend Baker.

Today, as a late afternoon sun warmed the porch, they shared a peach cobbler Mrs. Matthews had dropped off and drank strong black coffee.

"Ah, nothing like a fresh pie and good coffee," the preacher said, leaning back in the wicker chair and folding his hands across his belly. "And then a bit of man talk."

With a grin, Tye pulled his tobacco from his pocket and deftly rolled them each a cigarette.

Reverend Baker took a drag and smiled a contented smile. "The only thing better than this would have been if Mrs. Baker hadn't gone 'home' quite so soon.''

"I barely remember her." Tye thought a moment. "She was tall, wasn't she?"

"Aye. With the face and voice of an angel. I think that's why God called her so soon. She's part of the heavenly choir right now." He gazed upward sheepishly and gestured with the cigarette. "This is just a little afternoon relaxation, my dear, and I still never do it in the house."

A buggy slowed to a stop on the street, and Tye moved to leave.

"Wait." The reverend held up one hand. "Don't go. This is our time." He handed Tye his cigarette, and Tye pinched the fire from both and slid them into his shirt pocket.

A lone woman stepped from the wagon and, with a dart of surprise, Tye recognized Meg Telford, a beaded reticule dangling from her wrist. She gathered her black skirts and agilely mounted the wooden porch stairs. Her light floral scent reached Tye before she did. Violets.

"Afternoon, Miz Telford." The preacher rose to greet her.

"Good afternoon, Reverend Baker. Mr. Hatcher."

The minister smiled in satisfaction at her acknowledgment of Tye.

"Mrs. Telford." Tye stood and addressed her properly.

She seated herself in one of the wicker chairs and removed her stiff black bonnet. A lock of her shiny hair snagged and caressed her neck for a moment before she caught it and tucked it neatly back into place.

"Would you like some cobbler?" the reverend asked. "I have coffee, too."

"I would enjoy a cup of coffee, thank you," she replied.

Tye turned toward the door. "I'll get it."

He filled a mug from the pot on the stove and wondered belatedly if she'd like cream or sugar. He carried it out and asked.

"Oh, no, just like this is good. Thank you." She took a sip.

She and the minister discussed the morning's sermon and a particular passage from the Book of John. Tye listened.

After nearly a half hour of pleasantries, he prepared to leave. "I'd best be on my way. It's been a pleasure."

"How did you get here?" she asked.

"Walked," he replied simply.

"May I give you a ride?" she asked. "I'll be leaving now, too."

Did she think he couldn't walk? His neck grew uncomfortably warm.

"Please?"

He met her eyes and found no pity. Perhaps she just wanted to extend a gesture of friendship. He wouldn't recognize the effort if it jumped up and bit him on the butt. "Thank you."

Tye carried their mugs to the kitchen and wished Reverend Baker a good afternoon, slipping him the remainder of his half-smoked cigarette.

He assisted Meg onto the wagon seat and sat beside her. She guided the team onto Main Street. "You're staying at Mrs. Banks's?"

"Yes."

"I hear she keeps a nice place."

"It's clean. She cooks daily meals for those who want the cost added to their room."

She didn't say anything for a few minutes. Perhaps he shouldn't have mentioned the cost of meals. Maybe she thought he couldn't afford them.

"Tye, I wish to speak with you about something," she said at last.

He looked over at her, thinking she had more questions about Joe. Or the war. "Go ahead."

Her cheeks were pink in the shade from her hat brim. "Is there somewhere we could talk alone?"

His mind raced. Alone? Surely she didn't mean alone. That wouldn't be right. She just meant where they wouldn't be overheard. On the Sabbath the parlor at the boardinghouse was generally filled with boarders playing cribbage.

The saloon wasn't open, but he had a key. Stupid thought.

There was a small pastry shop across the street, but it was never open on Sunday afternoons.

She seemed to be looking about with the same dilemma. She reined the horses to a halt and pulled the brake handle. She met his eyes directly. "Your room?"

Tye couldn't have been more shocked if she'd started to disrobe on Main Street. What on earth did she have to say that she couldn't have said on the ride here? And why did she want to say it to him? "What if someone sees you coming in?"

"I have a perfect right to visit anyone I like." She lifted her chin defensively. "I would hardly leave my horses and wagon here in plain sight if I planned on doing something shameful. Besides, we'll leave your door open."

Tye glanced from her sincere face to the practically deserted street. "If you're sure."

"I'm sure." She hopped down ahead of him, and he took a little longer, easing his foot to the ground without jarring his leg.

Tye stayed between Meg and the parlor door as they passed, preventing her from being seen, not that anyone looked up.

She walked ahead of him up the flight of stairs, and he struggled to keep his eyes from her shapely backside beneath the rustling ebony dress. A titillating glimpse of white eyelet petticoats caught his eye when he looked down. He concentrated on his hand on the banister, thought about placing one foot in front of the other. He was taking Meg Telford to his room.

In a million years, he'd never have even dreamed up this possibility. Unlocking his door, he pushed it open wide and ushered her in.

She glanced around. There wasn't much to see. His other shirt and trousers were at the laundry. His saddlebags and guns were pushed under the bed. The room looked just as it had when Yetta Banks had rented it to him months ago.

Tye picked up the straight-backed chair and moved

it in a direct line in front of the open door and gestured for her to be seated.

She did so, arranging her skirts and holding the
reticule in her lap. What did women carry in those
silly things, anyway?

Tye had little experience with women of quality,
and her presence in his room doubly confounded him.
He deliberately avoided sitting on the bed and stood
uncomfortably by the bureau.

"I have a business proposition to offer you," she
stated.

He waited, unable to imagine any business Joe Telford's widow would have with him, and not even
willing to guess.

"I'm having a difficult time with the ranch."

He hated that news. She'd seemed so happy when
Joe was alive. "I'm sorry. Can I do something to
help?"

She raised her head and looked him in the eye,
unsettling him, unaccustomed as he was to having
women meet his gaze. "There is. I just don't know
if you'll be willing."

"What is it?"

"The Telfords are putting a lot of pressure on me
to sell."

Damn! Her husband had bought a prime piece of
land, and if she was offering it to him, he hadn't a
snowball's chance in hell of coming up with enough
money.

"I won't sell, however." Her chin rose a notch
once again. "I'm determined to hang on to the ranch.
Joe and I bought that place together. He sank money

and time and all his dreams into making a go of it, and I'm not going to sell out just because things are a little tough. Not without a fight.''

''I admire that. I wouldn't sell it if it was mine.''

''That's what I want to talk to you about.''

''What?''

''I have two old men and two young boys besides myself. Last year I hired a few extra reps for roundup, but I can't do it again. I've had to sell several things to keep the place going.''

She knew he didn't have any money, so the only thing she could want from him would be labor. ''Are you asking me to work for you? I've tried to get work everywhere, but no one will take me on.''

''I couldn't pay you, Tye,'' she said plainly. She took a deep breath and hurried on. ''What I've decided I need is a husband. That way, you'd have a stake in the place. The work you did would be to your own benefit. As you know, when a man marries, his wife's property becomes his.''

He stared. Deepening pink tinged her smooth cheeks.

Slowly, he worked at assimilating her words and the idea behind them. He raised a hand to knead the back of his neck and took an unconscious step or two. ''I think I'm confused here. What is it you're asking me?''

''I'm asking you to marry me.''

He looked her over for some gross mistaken identity. This was Meg Telford, no doubt about it. Meg Telford in his room. Asking him to marry her. He shook his head to clear it. "You don't know what you're asking."

"Yes, I do."

"You can't. Nobody in Aspen Grove will even look at me or talk to me. You'd lose the respect of everyone in town if anyone knew you were here right now. You saw how your family acted when you talked to me in the mercantile! You can't want to marry me."

She stood abruptly. "I don't give a fig what anyone's going to say about it. I don't need this town's approval to do what I believe is right."

"You say that now, but you don't know what it's like. You don't know jack squat about how it is to have people look at you like you're dirt. You've never spent Sundays or holidays alone or seen women snatch their skirts aside so's not to touch you." He ran a nervous hand through his hair. "Trust me, you'd think differently after that happened a few times."

Primly, she moved back to the chair and sat. "Anyone who would treat me like that after knowing me all these years wouldn't be worth having as a friend."

Fine talk, but she hadn't lived it.

Tye studied her perched on the chair. *Marriage. To this woman.* He couldn't keep his curious gaze from sliding to her rounded breasts beneath her starched dress, and images of sleeping with her had him moving to stand behind her.

"Ma'am, you're talking of *marriage* here. I just can't believe you've thought this through."

"I'm not an innocent young girl," she countered. "I know what marriage entails."

A delicious surge of heat teased his body. He tried to let his brain do the reasoning. "I want children someday," he said honestly. She might as well know his concerns. He wouldn't saddle himself with a woman who could give him land, only to find she wasn't willing to see to his other wishes.

To his surprise, she didn't blink an eye. "So do I. There's no reason I can't give you children."

What more could he want? Meg was the most beautiful woman in the whole damned county. She was offering to turn her land over to him, marry him and give him children.

He didn't have to wonder, "Why me?" The privilege had fallen to the only able-bodied, unmarried man in the area. Not exactly flattering.

But promising.

Very promising. And as long as they were revealing their expectations, he had more. "There's something else I want," he said.

She turned her head, but not enough to see him. "What is it?"

Tye'd come back with a plan to prove his worth to this community. The war had shown him that when it came to wearing a uniform, picking up a gun and fighting, he was as good as any man. No one he'd fought beside had cared whether or not he bore his father's name. He'd fought prejudice and ridicule in this town since he was old enough to raise his fists, and these people would only see him differently once he proved himself an equal. "I want to start a packing plant."

"A—packing plant? Like in the East?"

"Yes." He abandoned his inhibition and moved to sit on the edge of the bed, where he could look directly at her. "I listened to cattlemen the last few years. I heard their stories of losing hundreds of head while driving them or shipping them by rail, about how the cattle lost weight and brought less money. If we could slaughter them here, we'd save the trip and the hardships. We'd ship the dressed meat right out. Think how much more meat will fit in the railcars already dressed."

"What kind of investment are you talking about?" She was listening!

"A big one. I've been saving because I needed to buy land. But if I already have the land, all I have to do is build pens, a slaughtering house, and then hire workers."

"There are no workers."

"There will be if there are jobs for them."

Thoughtfully, she studied him. Her gaze wavered reflectively to a spot over his shoulder, then back to his face. "But you'd still help me with the ranch? I need your word on that. And you have to promise me you'll never sell Joe's ranch."

"If I agree to marry you, I'll do whatever I can to make the ranch a success. But I would need the same promise from you."

"About the packing plant?" she asked.

He nodded. "It would benefit you. You wouldn't have to ship cattle."

"All right. If you'll marry me, I'll help you get your packing plant started. And—you won't ever sell?"

"I won't ever sell. Unless you ask me to." Something here was too good to be true. But then, he was her only choice. Belittling as that might be, her proposal was an end to his quest for land. He could have his dream.

"All right," he said. "These are the terms—I help you keep the ranch and get it going. You help me get the plant started. This will be a marriage in all respects."

She blushed noticeably, but she nodded.

"Then I agree to marry you."

She paused only momentarily before getting to her feet. "Very well, then. We'll arrange it as soon as possible. Next week sometime. Will that be convenient?"

"I'm not goin' anywhere."

"Perhaps Saturday?"

"Whatever you'd like."

"I'll let you know."

He walked her out the door, down the flight of stairs, and assisted her onto the wagon. This time when he extended his hand, she looked at it, and then up at him, before she placed her gloved one in it. It would have been much easier if he'd simply lifted her, but she obviously got up and down unassisted the rest of the time, and he wasn't comfortable with touching her in a more familiar manner.

Yet.

She raised herself up to the seat and straightened her skirts. She met his eyes and he could have sworn she was thinking the same thing. "We'll be in touch, then," she said.

He nodded.

She unwound the reins from the brake handle and flicked them over the horses' backs.

Tye watched her go and told himself that the anticipation already warming his blood was due to the stroke of luck in having a site for his innovative business dropped into his lap.

But the word *wife* echoed teasingly in his head. A thought entered his awareness too late. Perhaps he should have mentioned he'd soon be getting a child to raise. Lottie couldn't last much longer, and he'd promised her that he would come for Eve.

Maybe Meg wouldn't even mind; after all, she wanted children.

There would be time to tell her later.

Chapter Four

Tye Hatcher wanted children.

Meg turned the lamp wick down low, removed her clothing and pulled a snowy white linen night shift over her head and buttoned it up to her throat.

Of course he wanted children. Now that he'd brought it up, she might as well get used to the fact that this was going to be a marriage in all respects. She would follow through on her part of the arrangement. It wasn't as if she hadn't given a lot of consideration to bringing him here.

She fell to her knees beside the hide-upholstered trunk at the foot of the bed and raised the lid. Reverently, she ran her hands over Joe's shirts, fingered a hairbrush with a few fair strands still caught in the bristles, and took out a packet of letters held together by a faded ribbon.

Joe had wanted children, too.

These letters were filled with dreams for their future, plans for the ranch, words of caring and commitment. She didn't want to read them just now. She knew exactly how long it took to read them all, where

Joe'd been when he'd written each one, and the post from which each envelope had been mailed.

She knew, too, the bittersweet feelings of melancholy and heartache that swamped her when she allowed herself to open and read them. Those moments were best saved for nights when she could handle the feelings of abandonment and loss.

This wasn't one of them.

Meg replaced the stack of letters carefully, closed the trunk and, after blowing out the lantern, climbed into bed.

She and Joe had wanted a family.

Each month her body prepared for a baby, and each month came and went without hope for a seed being planted. She was still young though; her body was still firm and strong.

Tye Hatcher was the means to help her fulfill all of her and Joe's dreams. The ranch. The stock. The children to inherit the land.

That's how Joe would want it.

She snuggled deep into the coverlet and rubbed her feet against each other for warmth. She would tell Mother Telford tomorrow. Harley and Niles would have to spare her their condescending offers and their patronizing attitudes. She wasn't going to be put off her ranch now or ever.

Tye Hatcher would help her see to that.

A bolt of unease rocked her midsection and shot a shiver up her spine. She'd known Tye Hatcher since they were children. He was right about his treatment by the community. She'd told him she didn't care what the citizens of Aspen Grove thought of her. She wanted with all her heart for that to be true.

She would make it true.

Tye couldn't help who his parents had been. It was unfair of people to treat him cruelly because of things that were beyond his control.

She could help them see that.

Joe and Tye had never been friends exactly, but Joe had never treated Tye badly, either. This was what Joe would have wanted her to do. Assuring herself of that, she hugged a feather pillow to her breast.

Saturday.

In six days she would marry Tye Hatcher and bring him to the ranch.

Five more nights alone in this bed.

And then she'd be Tye's wife.

It hadn't gone well. Not well at all. But then Meg hadn't expected her announcement to be met with congratulations and hugs of encouragement. Edwina Telford had turned as red as a pickled beet and fairly exploded with indignation. "You can't be serious!" she'd screeched, bringing Wilsie on the run.

"I am serious, Mother Telford," Meg had said before Edwina could gather up enough steam to roll over her. "And nothing you can say or do will dissuade me. I've made up my mind that I'm going to keep the ranch, and this is how I aim to do it."

Wilsie brought smelling salts and waved the bottle under her mother's nose. "My poor Joe will turn over in his grave, God rest his soul," the woman moaned, wringing her lace handkerchief. "His wife taking up

with the likes of that—that good-for-nothing illegiti-
mate rakehell! O-oh! I'll never be able to hold my
head up in this town again.''

"Joe would want me to do whatever it took to hang
on to our ranch,'' Meg disagreed, refusing to be
swayed by her mother-in-law's histrionics. "It's not
you who's marrying Tye Hatcher—''

"Don't speak that name to me!''

"It's me, and you don't have to approve of what
I'm doing. I'm doing it no matter what anyone thinks.
There's no law against it. I'm an adult and a free
woman, and I'll marry whomever I please. Harley and
Niles will have to forsake their plans to disburse my
land. It's going to stay mine.''

"Yours! It's going to fall into the hands of that
man, and who knows what he'll do with it or what
will become of you after he's drunk and gambled
away your last dollar!''

"He promised me he would never sell.''

"Promised? What good is the promise of a heathen
like that? Meg Telford, you've lost your mind! He'll
make you miserable. He'll take you down with him!
Why, he spends his money and his time in the saloons. He drinks and consorts with floozies! I've a
notion to send you to the doctor in…''

And so it had gone, with Edwina ranting about Meg
dishonoring Joe's memory, and poor Wilsie trembling
and casting Meg fearful sidelong glances. Meg had
driven the team home, fully expecting Harley to be
close on her heels. He hadn't arrived until after the
accounting office where he worked had closed for the
day.

And then she'd gone over the same arguments with him. Mother Telford had a room all ready for her. Meg wouldn't have to bother herself with the running of a ranch. Edwina needed the company. Tye Hatcher was a sorry excuse for a man. He would ruin her good name and hurt her.

But Meg had stood her ground, firm in her belief that she was doing the right thing—the *only* thing— to keep Joe's ranch. Harley had ridden off, anger and disapproval leaving a dusty trail behind him.

It was too much to expect them to understand this soon, she could see that, but they would come around. They had to. Eventually they'd see that she'd made a wise choice in taking Tye Hatcher on to save her land. Tye couldn't possibly be as bad as they'd made him out to be. Why, it would take three men to do all the things he'd reportedly done and would soon repeat.

Meg had to concentrate on taking care of business. Preparing for this wedding certainly wasn't like anticipating the first. With no time to have invitations printed, she wrote several notes to her friends and family and posted them, but no one showed up to help her, and the only responses she received were regrets.

Their treatment hurt, but she refused to let it deter her. As soon as they saw that what she'd done was for the best, they would change their minds.

Saturday morning, she gave the house a last-minute cleaning before bathing and dressing, then Gus and Purdy accompanied her into Aspen Grove.

Only a pitiful handful of guests sat in the pews when she made her way to the front of the church. Glancing at them, she recalled her first wedding, the

freshly polished pews packed with friends and family
in their best clothing, the scent of chrysanthemums
drifting on the summer air. That had been the happiest
day of her life.

Meg recognized Gwynn immediately and breathed
a sigh of relief that at least one person from her family
had chosen to bless this union.

A dark-haired woman whom she'd seen in town
and knew only as Rosa sat several rows behind
Gwynn.

Jed Wheeler sat alone at the opposite end of the
hard, polished pew Rosa occupied. He slipped a finger
into his shirt collar and adjusted it.

Meg smiled at Aldo and Hunt Eaton's shy, grinning
faces, wondering if they'd asked their parents' permission or if they'd simply left her cattle long enough
to attend.

Reverend Baker smiled warmly and gestured for
Meg to take her place beside Tye.

Finally, she allowed herself to look at *him,* the man
she was about to marry. His deep blue eyes gave
away nothing of what he was feeling. He held his
solid jaw stiff and met her gaze squarely.

"Tye?" she questioned uncertainly.

Something behind his eyes flickered. Surprise?
Doubt?

She extended her gloved hand.

His unreadable gaze drifted across her hair, fell to
her crocheted collar and then to her gloved hand.
Without pause, he accepted it with both of his and
held it firmly between his large palms. Heat seeped
through the fabric of her gloves.

"Are we ready, then?" Reverend Baker asked softly.

"We're ready," Tye replied.

The reverend nodded, and to Meg's surprise, Fiona Hill, whom she hadn't noticed sitting behind the organ before, unskillfully launched into a wedding song. Meg gave Tye a smile, pleased that he had thought to add music to the hasty ceremony.

"Dearly beloved," Reverend Baker began, once the last harsh notes reverberated into the morning air.

Meg listened to the same words he'd recited over her and Joe that sunny morning so long ago. She didn't place the same naive hope in the vows as she once had. Her first marriage had held promise and had been a union of love.

Not that she didn't take this one seriously, for she did. She meant to adhere to her pledge. But this was a business arrangement, an agreement, and she in no way felt the same love and anticipation she had when she'd married Joe.

Tye understood that.

"And repeat after me, 'With this ring I thee wed.'"

Tye released her left hand, and Reverend Baker waited expectantly.

Meg stared in numb recognition at the silver band Tye held between his long thumb and forefinger. "Oh."

She hadn't been expecting a ring. She *had* a ring. Awkwardly, she tugged off her glove and glanced at the gold band she still wore. *Joe's ring.*

But of course, she wouldn't be able to wear the ring Joe had given her. Her face warmed in embarrassment. Without stopping to think about what she was doing, she twisted the band from her finger, dropped the ring into her pocket and extended her hand.

"With this ring I thee wed." Tye's voice sounded oddly distant as he repeated the words. He took her hand and slid the warm silver band into place, his fingers strong and hard. She stared down, finding the silver piece strangely out of place on her finger.

A new pain, deep and dull and laced with bitter resignation, expanded in her chest. She blinked back the humiliating prickle of tears and unthinkingly gripped Tye's hand hard. His other came to rest over the back of hers, its gentleness and warmth a much needed reassurance.

"I now pronounce you man and wife. You may kiss the bride."

Without a second's hesitation, as if he feared she might balk or bolt or burst into tears, Tye leaned forward and kissed her cheek, then quickly straightened.

With a characteristic lack of finesse, Fiona banged out the wedding march, and Meg allowed Reverend Baker and Tye to escort her to the back of the tiny building. One by one, the few guests offered congratulations and stepped out into the sunshine.

Gwynn gripped Meg's fingers. "I hope this is right, Meg," she said shakily. "I do wish you the best."

"Thank you for coming," Meg managed to say around the knot of distress in her throat. "I'm going to be just fine. Don't worry about me."

"Well, you come to me if you need anything." She glanced around. "Harley doesn't know I came. So I'd

best hurry home before he figures out where I went."
She pressed her cheek against her sister-in-law's. "I'll
see you in church tomorrow." She rushed down the
wooden stairs.

Her concern touched Meg.

"This is Rosa Casals," Tye said from beside her.

"Of course," Meg said, turning to greet the dark-
eyed woman. "Thank you for coming."

"I just wanted to congratulate you both. Here's a
little something from me and Lottie. It's not much."
She pressed a small, paper-wrapped package into
Meg's hands.

"Why, thank you!" Meg said with surprise. A
wedding gift!

"Well, goodbye and good luck," Rosa said.
"Hatch, I'll see you before I leave town." Hastily,
she left the church.

Meg looked at the package in her hands. None of
her Telford family except Gwynn had come to this
ceremony. None of the other church members. If her
hired hands and Tye's two friends hadn't come, no
one would have witnessed their marriage.

Tye stepped into the small cloakroom with Reverend Baker, and Meg realized he was paying him for
the ceremony. "Come sign the certificate, Meg," the
reverend called easily.

A few minutes later, they stood outside the building, and the surroundings seemed oddly ordinary
compared with the rest of this surreal day. "Well,"
she said. "Do we need to go get your things?"

Tye nodded.

Gus pulled up the wagon, Purdy riding in the bed,

then got down and climbed in beside Purdy, leaving Tye and Meg to climb onto the springed seat.

"You know Gus and Purdy?" she asked.

"Worked roundups with 'em," Tye said, nodding to the two older men. "Guess we'll be working the ranch together now."

Purdy leaned forward and shook Tye's hand, mumbling his congratulations. Tye took the reins and drove the team to Banks's Boardinghouse. Meg and her hands stood, preparing to get down, but Tye stopped them with an upraised palm. "I'll be right back."

"We'll help," Meg offered in bewilderment.

"Don't need help."

She exchanged a glance with Gus, then sat back down. Tye eased himself to the ground carefully. A few minutes later he returned carrying a saddle and saddlebags, a bedroll and two rifles. He wore his hat and had strapped his gun belt to his hips. He stashed the saddle and bags in the back, the rifles under the seat, climbed back up and took the reins.

Meg said nothing. She'd been in his rented room once, yet she hadn't realized he owned nothing more than these few possessions. A man didn't need much, she guessed.

He made another stop at the stables for his horse, tied it behind the wagon and led the team out of town. They didn't speak more than a few words on the ride home, Meg knowing that the two old men were seated behind them and that any awkward thing they might say would be overheard.

Tye couldn't get the image of Meg's shock and

confusion over the ring out of his mind. Had she planned to wear her first husband's ring even though she was marrying him? No, she must've just forgotten. But it bothered him.

She'd stared at that gold band on her hand, and he'd stared at it, too, knowing it was worth a lot more than the silver one he'd loaded fertilizer for four nights to earn.

And then, as if she'd been sacrificing an arm, she'd worked the ring from her finger and allowed him to replace it. No one in attendance believed theirs was an alliance of love and passion, so he had nothing to hide. But the fact that she'd worn Joe's ring to their wedding seared a new, yet familiar brand of humiliation into his previously callused hide.

Tye observed the land they reached and the meager assortment of buildings with mixed emotions. Legally this land was his now. Morally, it was Meg's. They'd struck a bargain. His entire life he'd never owned anything worth more than a rifle or a horse. He'd never had a place to call home or to sink time and sweat and energy into. He meant for this to be that place.

And he meant to do right by Meg and by their agreement.

Gus took the team and Tye retrieved his things.

Meg led him into the house.

The kitchen, smelling of warm bread, took up the entire back half of the structure. An enormous cast-iron stove stood at one end of the room. Two long trestle tables, lined end to end, occupied the center of the floor, benches along their lengths. The other side of the long room held a fireplace, a rocker and a few mismatched, overstuffed chairs. That area, which opened into an L-shape, shared the fireplace with whatever lay beyond the doorway.

Meg removed her bonnet and gloves and set the small package on the table.

Tye deposited his belongings near the door.

"I'll show you the rest of the house," she said matter-of-factly.

He followed her down the length of the room to the bottom of the L. The space around the corner held a sofa and chair, an oak cabinet of some sort and a glass-fronted china closet.

"That was my grandmother's. Joe and I planned to have a real house someday, with a porch and a dining room and a parlor. I have my mother's china packed away. No sense using it out here with only cowhands eating at my table."

"You can still have your house with a porch and your dining room," Tye said.

She didn't look at him. "Maybe someday," was all she said.

After a minute, she opened a door that led into a bedroom that smelled like violets—like her. He followed her uneasily.

He first noticed her chest of drawers just inside the door, a tall, hand-carved piece of heavy furniture. A comb and brush, a book and a few hairpins lay on the top. Meg's things. He had the crazy desire to reach out and touch them, but he kept his hand at his side.

A metal bedstead stood against the wall, the mattress covered with a star-patterned quilt, soft-looking, homey, inviting images of sleeping with her beneath its downy comfort. He refused to entertain those thoughts right now and let out a slow, self-disciplining breath.

At the foot of the bed sat a horsehide chest. The stand beside the bed held a pitcher and face bowl on an embroidered scarf. He pictured her standing there in her underclothes…or less…washing. A reprehensible tide of heat and longing engulfed him, and he reminded himself she'd brought him here to show him where he'd sleep, not to rip off his clothes and immediately sate his aroused body.

Whatever happened between them would have to happen naturally. Slowly.

He turned abruptly. A wardrobe stood on the opposite wall. Tye's attention was riveted on a pair of black polished Union boots standing beside it. Joe's boots.

Joe's room.

With a sinking feeling of disappointment in his gut, Tye pulled his gaze from the boots.

He didn't let himself look at the bed again.

Another man still occupied this room.

Inasmuch as they'd struck a bargain, he was a stranger to this woman. She'd been widowed barely a year. He'd seen the grief and pain in her eyes that day outside the mercantile when she'd asked him about her husband's body.

She wore a pale green cambric dress with darker green stripes, obviously not new, but nice, and he'd been pleased to see her appear in it that morning. Of course, she couldn't wear mourning to her own wedding ceremony, so this dress didn't mean anything, he realized. She was still wearing black in her heart.

She needed Tye to help her keep this ranch. But she didn't love him.

"Is there another room?" he asked without much hope. The house hadn't looked that big from the outside, and this seemed like the only space left behind the kitchen.

"A pantry," she replied. "A root cellar. And some storage space in the attic."

"Can I see it?"

"The attic?"

He nodded.

"Well...sure."

She led him back into the other room and pointed to a trapdoor overhead. "Pull on there," she instructed, indicating the dangling rope.

He did, and a narrow set of stairs extended. Grimacing against the pain in his thigh, he climbed the steps and surveyed the room above. It ran the width of the house and had a tiny window at each end. A few packing crates sat in a far corner, probably holding Meg's mother's china. The space wasn't tall enough to stand in, but the flooring was solid and there was room to stretch out.

"I'll sleep up here," he decided aloud.

"What?" she called from below.

He descended the stairs carefully, holding his expression firm. "I'll sleep up there."

Her wide hazel eyes rounded with surprise. "Why?"

"I can't sleep in the barn, because I assume your hands have rooms out there."

"Yes, but—"

"So, I'll sleep up there." He started to walk away from her, then decided he owed her an explanation and turned back.

She met his eyes, doubt clouding hers.

"We need a little time to get to know one another," he said. Besides, there was already one man sleeping in that bed with her, three would make a crowd. "Let's give each other that time."

Was that relief he saw in her expression?

A deep rose flush darkened her neck and cheeks. Her gaze moved to his shirtfront. If she had any feelings on the subject, she kept them to herself. But she didn't argue with him.

He'd known she wouldn't.

"Why don't you open your gift?" he suggested.

"Oh, oh yes, of course." She bustled into the kitchen. The small package looked pathetically alone on the enormous table. Meg approached it, reminded of her wedding to Joe and the reception that had followed at the Telford home, with guests spilling into the yard and gaily wrapped packages stacked atop a table on the veranda.

That had been before the war, when the citizens of Aspen Grove and the neighboring ranches had still been prosperous. Many of the items she and Joe had received that day had since been traded or sold.

Meg slipped the white ribbon from the package and peeled back the paper. The box held a set of carefully wrapped, cut-glass salt and pepper shakers with sterling silver lids.

"They're lovely," she said, and meant it. She'd had an entire set, much like them, consisting of spoon trays and berry bowls, jelly dishes and cruets, but those had been among the items she'd sold for feed last winter. "Rosa said it was from her and Lottie. Who's Lottie?"

He couldn't explain Lottie to her. Not just yet. "Lottie is…another friend of mine."

"Oh. Well, it was kind of them to send a gift. I'll be sure to send a proper thank-you."

"I'm sure you will."

She met his eyes uncertainly.

He'd have to tell her eventually. He'd given his word to take Eve and raise her.

Tye watched the mixture of expressions cross her lovely face, studied her straight spine as she turned and placed the salt and pepper shakers in her cabinet. The pale green dress was lovely on her. Its cinched style showed off the tiny waist he'd often admired and left him wondering about the softly rounded hips and legs so well hidden beneath the folds of the skirt.

A small, knitted purse with tasseled ties still hung forgotten from her elbow.

It had been all he could do in the time he'd had before today to earn the cash money for the ring. He would have liked to have given her something else, an heirloom or something meaningful, something a woman like her deserved. He'd never had much more than the clothes he wore. When he was old enough, he'd made enough to provide for his mother, and the rest…well, the rest he'd drunk and gambled because he was isolated and lonely—and because it was expected of him.

She wouldn't have wanted anything that had belonged to his mother, anyway, even if he'd had something.

Two solid thumps on the screen door brought him out of his thoughts.

Meg turned with a smile. "That's Major. He must have been out hunting when we arrived. He's probably curious to know who's here."

The door opened without her crossing to open it, and an enormous, long-haired dog nosed his way through. He carried a chunk of wood in his mouth, promptly crossed the room and dropped it in the wood box beside the stove.

"Good boy, Major," she said with a laugh.

The dog immediately zeroed in on Tye and came forward slowly, nose sniffing the air, tail wagging low.

Meg crossed to Tye and touched his arm. "This is Major," she explained, the touch obviously a sign for the animal that he was a friend.

The heat from her fingers seeped through his shirtsleeve, and Tye stopped himself from moving away from the temptation of her nearness. She moved away herself soon enough. "I'll change now. I was going to make a pie for our supper."

"I'll change, too. And then I'll acquaint myself with the place."

"I know it doesn't look like much right now," she said apologetically. "We've had to let some things go in order to care for the stock. The fellas try, but, well…"

"It's the best place I've ever lived, ma'am," he told her honestly. "I'll do all I can to take care of things now."

She smiled then, a genuine smile of reassurance. "I believe you will, Tye. If I didn't believe that, well, we wouldn't be here right now. Neither one of us."

Meaning she'd have been put off her ranch, and he'd still be trying to earn enough money to buy an acre or two. This way they each had what they wanted.

It would be a fine place to bring Eve to, as well. Maybe he should have told Meg about the child before they'd gotten married, but there just hadn't been the right time. Working extra hours for the ring and these clothes had seemed the imperative need at the time. He had no idea how he was going to find the words to tell her now.

Besides, there would still be a little time for her to get used to the idea—he hoped. He hadn't checked on Lottie for several days, so he really wasn't sure about her condition.

Tye picked up his belongings, stowed them in the attic and changed into work clothes. No time like the present to get down to business.

Meg hated herself for the sense of relief that had accompanied Tye's decision to sleep in the attic. She should have spoken up, shouldn't have allowed him to postpone the inevitable. But she'd gone along. And the fact that she'd been unable to fall asleep that night was likely due to guilt over his uncomfortable sleeping arrangements.

She rose early and prepared breakfast as she always did. Gus, probably allowing them privacy, hadn't ground the beans or started the coffee, which added another task to her routine.

Tye appeared from outside with Gus and Purdy. The two hands hung their hats and took their places beside each other on a bench. Tye stood awkwardly to the side.

Meg placed a hot plate of skillet cakes on the table, then realized he was waiting for her to assign him a seat.

"There." She gestured to a single chair at the end. The chair where she usually sat. The chair that had been Joe's.

Tye stood behind it.

Gus and Purdy dug into the food without hesitation.

"You don't have to wait for me to sit," she said, realizing his intent. "I jump up and down a half-dozen times during a meal."

Tye seated himself.

Meg poured coffee, then sat to his left.

No one said much as they ate together, their first morning in this new situation. Meg tried to make it seem natural but knew she wasn't fooling anyone.

Tye ate more slowly than the ranch hands. And he didn't eat half as much as most men she'd cooked for.

She tasted everything to make sure she hadn't made a mistake in her haste. It all tasted fine to her.

"Everything all right?" she asked hesitantly.

He looked up from his plate, his deep blue eyes vibrant in the morning light that streamed through the long kitchen windows. "Everything's just fine, ma'am. Thank you."

Meg glanced at Gus, and he met her eyes only briefly, then popped his last bite of ham into his mouth, downed his coffee and stood.

Purdy followed, going for his hat.

"We've just got enough time to change," Meg said, folding her napkin.

Tye laid down his fork and sat still.

"Tye?" she asked curiously.

Gus and Purdy tromped out the door with a screech of hinges.

"You don't want me to come to church with you," he said. It wasn't a question.

"But of course I do. I always go to church."

"I don't."

She had started to get up, but she eased back down on the bench. "Aren't you a God-fearing man, Tye Hatcher?"

"Yes, ma'am. But for your sake, I fear God's good people more."

"What do the others have to do with it?"

But she knew. She might not understand, but she knew how he'd been treated in town his whole life. She hadn't seen firsthand the rejection his mother had received after he'd been born, but she'd lived in this town as long as he had, and she'd seen the way he was snubbed.

"I warned you how people would react," he said softly. "No one came yesterday, did they?"

At that, she did stand, her posture rigid and perhaps a little defiant. "That is *my* church, Tye Hatcher. I've gone there since I was six years old. And you're my husband. I don't intend to let a few narrow-minded attitudes stop us from going." Those people couldn't ignore her forever. They hadn't shown up at her wedding, but she'd be hanged if she'd let them control her comings and goings in town or her attendance at her place of worship.

A few syrupy bites of a skillet cake remained on the plate he stared at. "I'll come if you ask me to."

Was it unfair of her to ask this of him? No. She wasn't about to leave Tye behind like one of the ranch hands. "I'm asking."

He stood, his long legs pushing back the chair. "I'll change."

Chapter Five

He stood near the wagon when she exited the house. He wore the same dark trousers and white shirt and tie he'd worn for their wedding, his revolver holstered to his hip and his hat pulled low. But even with his eyes shaded, she knew his gaze followed her from the back steps appreciatively. It warmed her to know he was looking at her in a way no man had looked at her for a long time. But it startled her that she liked the feeling.

"I'll take a step up," she said, when he appeared uncertain of how to assist her.

Immediately, he made a step of his laced fingers, and she pulled herself up to the seat. Tye brushed his hands together and seated himself beside her.

They didn't have much to say to each another, but she soon learned that theirs could be a comfortable silence if she relaxed her thinking. As man and wife they would have many rides like this, plenty of time together, and all the years ahead to get to know one another.

Tye pulled the wagon into a shaded area in the lot

near the church, and this time she allowed him to place his hands around her waist and lower her to the ground. Her gloved hand touched his upper arm briefly, and the thick, corded muscle beneath the shirt made her sharply aware of his reserved strength.

She glanced up.

He released her and didn't meet her eyes. His tight expression revealed his stoic determination to go through with this. *Because she'd asked it of him.*

Harnesses jingled, and Meg turned to see the Telfords' leather-upholstered buggy drawn into the lot. She started toward it, then realized Tye wasn't beside her, and paused. He joined her, reluctantly, and she continued toward her family.

"Good morning!" she called.

Harley assisted Mother Telford from the buggy, then turned for Gwynn. The children jumped to the ground and ran ahead with noisy enthusiasm. Wilsie hung behind Gwynn, her cautious stare fixed on Tye as if he were going to suddenly pull his gun and blast them all full of lead.

Edwina adjusted her stiff black skirts, cast a reproachful eye on Tye and said to Meg, "I don't know what you're doing, bringing him here like this. As if you haven't disgraced us enough, Meg Telford, now you're flaunting this shameful alliance before the whole town!"

Meg recovered from her shock immediately. "I'm coming to church like I do every Sunday morning. It just so happens that this particular Sunday I've brought my husband with me."

"Husband!" The way she spat the word indicated

she didn't consider Tye any such thing. "Joe is your husband and don't you forget it. This man is trouble, mark my words. I never thought my Joe married a stupid woman."

Edwina gathered her skirts and made a wide circle around the couple. "*Joe* wouldn't have worn his holster to church," she continued, looking Tye up and down with scorn.

"Joe wouldn't have been expecting one of the brethren to shoot him in the back," Tye said with an audacious grin.

Harley ignored him, took Gwynn's arm and led her behind his mother. Gwynn cast a regretful glance over her shoulder.

Wilsie scampered to join them.

Meg stared at the empty buggy, hurt and anger warring in her breast. Beside her, Tye waited in grim silence. Finally, she turned and met his gaze.

The hard blue stare beneath his hat brim revealed no emotion. He'd been expecting it. Had been braced for it. If a person bore insults a thousand times over, did the barbs lose their sting?

"Still want to go in there?" he asked.

Resolutely, she laced her arm though his and headed toward the building.

The drone of voices hushed as they entered the aisle. The Telfords were already seated in their pew, third from the front on the right, the pew where she'd sat with them every Sunday since becoming engaged to Joe seven years ago.

She couldn't sit with them now, she realized belatedly. She paused a few rows back and slipped into an available wooden seat. Tye sat beside her, his long thigh brushing her skirts, and stared straight ahead. He'd hung his hat on the row of hooks inside the door, so he had no brim to take refuge beneath.

A few whispered comments broke the silence.

Meg glanced around, taking note of the townspeople unwilling to meet her eyes. Friends who'd greeted her every Sunday morning since she could remember now avoided her. The ones who did look at her did so with disapproving stares.

Finally Reverend Baker walked to stand behind the pulpit, Fiona stumbled through the beginning hymn, and the congregation stood.

Meg opened the hymnal. The words and music blurred. Voices rose on all sides. She blinked, determinedly cleared her throat and joined them. Towering beside her, Tye remained silent. She extended the hymn book, and he took the other side obligingly but didn't sing.

Later, instructed to sit once again, she noticed his long fingers massage his thigh unconsciously. She glanced at him, and his hand stilled. Reverend Baker began to speak, and Tye met her eyes at last. He hadn't wanted her to see this. Hadn't wanted the same ill treatment to befall her. He'd said as much that first day in his rented room.

But she'd asked for it. She'd insisted. And she'd gotten what she'd asked for.

She couldn't help thinking that the Telfords would gather for dinner after this, as they always did, and afterward they'd sit on the wide front porch, and the children would play on the lawn. Even during the war, she'd eaten Sunday dinner with Joe's mother, sister and sister-in-law. And after his death, they'd been her strength and her only family.

Dinner! Her mind ran through the supplies she had to prepare a meal. She couldn't regret losing company for her Sunday meal. She'd gained a means to hang on to her life. They would come around, she told herself again. She hadn't changed. Nothing had really changed. They would see that.

The service ended finally, and she and Tye made their way to the back like everyone else. No one greeted them. Everyone carefully maintained a reproachful distance.

Reaching Reverend Baker, the couple received their first greeting and smile. "Meg, you're looking lovely. Hatch, I was pleased to see you in the congregation this morning."

"You're the only one."

The reverend grinned at Tye's low remark. "I hope this doesn't mean you won't be callin' on me Sunday afternoons anymore. I enjoy our talks together."

"I'll make it a point to visit," Tye replied. "Probably not today, though. I've got a lot to figure out around the place."

"Why don't you come to the Circle T for dinner next week?" Meg asked eagerly.

"I'll do that," the reverend said, and shook Tye's hand.

Meg smiled up at Tye. He settled his hat on his head, and they crossed the side yard, pointedly ignoring rude stares and whispers.

Tye made a step of his laced fingers, and she

climbed onto the seat and tied her bonnet beneath her chin.

She'd been the prettiest woman there, just as she'd always been the prettiest woman anywhere in Aspen Grove. Tye wished he could be proud to have her beside him. But she hadn't married him for any reason he could take pride in.

He'd borne the indignities of his birth and his mother's status his entire life, and he detested her observing it. He would have done just about anything to avoid her seeing how unkindly people could behave, and never for anything would he have allowed her to suffer the same if there was any way to prevent it. He'd come here for her.

Because she'd asked him. And, he admitted to himself, he knew he'd never deny Meg anything she asked.

She'd taken his arm in front of the whole town. She'd acknowledged him, sat by him and—Lord help her—married him. He perused her now and she surveyed him back.

She wasn't ashamed to have married him.

For the first time he allowed himself to look into the honeyed depths of her eyes without wondering what she was seeing when she looked at him. She had a peaches-and-cream complexion with a smattering of freckles across the bridge of her nose that she probably hated, but that were nearly unavoidable working every day on a ranch.

He loved the saucy turn of her nose and the bowed shape of her pink lips. Her hair smelled like violets, and its scent fluttered on every breeze within six feet.

Now, only a few errant curls were visible beneath the bonnet, but he knew the exact hue, like rich honey, and could only imagine the heady texture.

Tye realized he'd worked himself into an embarrassing state simply by looking at her, and he tore his gaze away and fixed it on the rumps of the plodding horses. He wanted a cigarette bad.

The Circle T, she'd called it, he remembered as they rode in. Not "the ranch," not "our place," but "the Circle T."

"T" for Telford.

He let the horses stand long enough to change his clothing, then led them into the barn, brushed them down, gave them grain and water and turned them into the pasture.

Tye stood with one boot on the bottom rung of the fence, watching them graze with the other horses, and rolled a smoke. A robust liver-colored chestnut in a separate corral caught his eye, and he couldn't recall ever seeing a horse like it before. He pinched out the match, slid it into his pocket and inhaled tobacco into his lungs.

His own horse, a black with speckled white hindquarters, galloped over to where he stood and nudged his shoulder. Tye stroked his forehead. He'd purchased the horse after the war and ridden him home.

"Don't let the missus catch ya doin' that," Purdy said, coming up beside him and indicating his smoke.

Tye acknowledged the advice with a nod. He hadn't imagined Meg would take too kindly to the vice.

"Slack season's nearly over," Purdy said, referring

to summer, with roundup and calf branding growing near.

"Plenty to do before roundup," Tye replied. "Thought I'd go up in the hills this week and get some pine poles for a fence to make a south pasture."

"Want help?"

"Be glad for it."

Purdy nodded.

"What breed is that dark chestnut stallion?"

"Don't know." Purdy shrugged. "Joe sent him and two mares home whilst he was gone."

A bell rang then, its clamor echoing across the pasture.

"Dinner on Sunday?" the old man questioned, his gray eyebrows raised.

"You don't usually have Sunday dinner?"

"The missus is generally gone until late afternoon. Gus cooks for us."

Of course. Her Sunday routine had been shot to hell by his presence. Tye squeezed off the fire from his smoke and dropped the cigarette into his pocket. "Well. Let's see what it is."

Tye was unaccustomed to so many meals and so much food. He'd already eaten her breakfast, so he prayed he could do another meal justice.

He and the hands washed at the pump outside, entered the kitchen, hung their hats...and stopped in their tracks.

The table had been spread with a pressed white linen cloth and set with vine-and-flower-bedecked china, the edges of the cups scalloped, the plates set neatly at the end where they'd eaten that morning. A clove-studded ham graced a platter, a bowl of creamy mashed potatoes beside it, and butter melted into a bowl of steaming greens. The cut-glass salt and pepper shakers with the silver lids had been filled and added to the setting.

"What are you gaping at?" she asked the gathering of men, carrying a bowl of gravy. "We're starting our own Sunday tradition."

Tye and the hands seated themselves.

"Tye, slice the ham and serve us, please."

He picked up the knife and serving fork and did as she asked, placing a thick slice of meat on each plate. The bowls were passed, and before long he had a plateful of food to work his way through.

He ate slowly, not remembering the last time he'd eaten ham, but he'd never tasted one so succulent. She'd made a thin, dark, salty gravy, pure pleasure to his unaccustomed palate.

The hands took seconds and dashed through their meal, Purdy excusing himself and Gus getting up to start scrubbing pans.

Tye glanced up to find Meg finished, watching him. He laid his fork down.

"Is everything all right?" she asked.

"Everything's good. Don't know when I've eaten so well."

"Well, don't stop."

He picked up his fork and endured her watching him finish the meal.

"Coffee?"

He nodded, and she brought the pot from the stove and filled the delicate china cup. Tye's finger didn't fit in the handle, so he picked it up by holding the brim between his thumb and forefinger and drank the delicious black brew. "Thank you."

He studied her as she sipped her coffee, her small fingers holding the handle just so. Her warm tawny coloring reminded him of nature, of a beautiful mountain lion or an autumn hillside streaked with ore. Her eyes were bright and gemlike, lit from within like a smoldering fire.

He thought of how he'd lowered her from the wagon twice that day, and how his hands had spanned her tiny waist. That harmless touch had been enough to inspire his lusty nature into more dishonorable thoughts. His fingers had recognized the bone shelf, and he wondered how she tied that corset herself, and if she wore it only beneath her Sunday clothing and had cast if off for the day dress she wore now.

What else did she wear beneath those modest dresses? Her skirts didn't rustle like she wore stiff crinoline, but they were full and swayed as she walked, so layers of petticoats were evident. Were they dyed? Red or black? He'd glimpsed a white one that day at the boardinghouse. White seemed to suit Meg.

Those thoughts reminded him she was Joe's wife. Joe Telford had married her, had known what sort of underclothing she preferred, and had initiated her to a man's touch. Those images disturbed him, so he blocked them from his mind.

She turned those wide, tawny eyes on him now. "Tye?"

She was the only person besides his mother and

one or two schoolmasters who'd ever called him Tye. It made him sit up a little straighter and cast the errant thoughts aside. "Ma'am?"

"Last year the Eaton boys and I cut two hay fields, but it got wet and rotted before we could get it into the barns. We spent this spring raking it so the new would grow. I had to buy feed over the winter, and it's gone now."

"The fields look good," he said. "We should get two or three cuttings this summer."

"I just want you to know where things stand. I told you right off I couldn't keep going alone. I need your help in figuring out what to do."

"It'll probably be a spell before the first cut," he said. "But we really only need to feed the teams. The cattle are on their own until roundup, anyway. And we can move the rest of the horses from this pasture to another farther south as soon as I can get a new fence up. There's plenty of land here, plenty of grass and water. You got them through the winter, and they'll make it now."

"We need seed for the garden, and the banknote comes due every three months. That's just a few weeks away."

He considered her words and the pending situation. "Do you have any horses you can sell?"

"We could sell one of Joe's horses, maybe one of the Welsh. He was going to breed them. That would be the last resort, though. I'd rather sell the furniture first."

"Maybe we can make some money studding

them,'' he suggested. He wouldn't allow her to sell her furniture.

"Maybe,'' she replied. "If we found someone interested.''

"Let me take care of that,'' he said.

Meg nodded her agreement and let her glance fall across his hair and face, grateful for someone to share the burden at last, someone who wanted to keep the ranch as badly as she did. Someone who wasn't trying to get her to sell the place off and move to the city.

He was an anomaly, this blue-eyed man with the intent expressions. He was all bottled up and inside himself, and her only glimpses of his feelings were in the shadowy nuances of his expressive eyes when his barriers were down.

Everything he did, he did purposefully and with calm control: eating, walking, speaking.

Meg refilled his coffee cup and the unfamiliar scent of tobacco flitted against her nostrils as she leaned over him. She glanced down at the spare planes of his tanned face. "Do you like dried-apple pie?'' she asked.

"Yes.''

"I'll make one for tonight.''

His expression didn't reveal pleasure in her offer, but rather an almost pained look of resignation.

Behind her, Gus clanged a skillet on top of the hot stove to dry.

"I can't drink any more coffee,'' Tye said. "Thank you for the meal.''

He stood, catching his balance on the leg he didn't favor, and grabbed his hat from a peg. Major stood outside the door and sniffed at Tye's pant legs as he exited.

A strange man, to be sure. A very strange man. But a man she trusted to help her.

A few days later, Meg hung the laundry Gus had helped her wring. The clank of hammer against iron echoed across the space between the house and the barn, a few choice words following a prolonged silence. She didn't like swearing, and the men never did it in her presence, but often the wind carried the colorful phrases to her from the corral.

Meg was grateful for Gus's help with kitchen and household chores, for she found them tedious, and once she worked her way through them, she preferred outdoor tasks.

The hammering sound came again, and she followed it to where Tye had a mare tied to a post, her hoof bracketed between his knees. He bent over the task of pounding a shoe into place.

He clipped the nails and filed them as methodically and with as much concentration as he did everything, not noticing her presence even after he'd clipped the last nail, filed it smooth and straightened, catching his balance. He loosed the mare and swatted her rump to watch her gallop surefootedly across the enclosure. Apparently satisfied with his job, he went after the horse, his limp more pronounced than Meg had ever seen it.

He spotted her then but looked away quickly and opened the far gate to release the mare into the pasture.

"The Eaton boys haven't been in since day before yesterday," Meg said when he neared. "They usually at least come at noon. I thought I'd better ride out and check on the herds, take the boys a sandwich. They probably just went home for dinner, but I'd like the ride."

"I'll ride with you," he said.

"I'll change." She hurried toward the house.

She removed her petticoats and pulled a pair of Joe's knickerbockers on beneath her skirt. Returning to the corral, she found two horses saddled.

The red dun bearing her saddle didn't shy as she approached. He accepted her weight and stood placidly.

"You took the buck out of him," she said to Tye, who led a sturdy gray mare with his saddle.

"Yes, ma'am." He raised his good left leg to the stirrup and swung the other up over the back of the horse with a grimace.

Neither Gus nor Purdy was up to gentling the horses for her, and she was unaccustomed to the courtesy. Since there were no gentle horses left—she'd sold the tamest ones for profit—she'd had to handle them on her own each time she wanted to ride. Sometimes she feared she'd knock a hole in her chest with her chin before they settled down enough to command.

Tye opened the gate from where he sat and closed it behind them. Meg kicked her horse into a gallop.

They rode along the stream that meandered through the southeast section of the Circle T, wild rosebushes lining its banks. Tye climbed down from the mare and dipped water in his palm to drink. Before mounting again, he plucked a rose from one of the bushes, snapped off the thorns and handed it to her.

Their gloves brushed as she accepted the delicate pink flower. "Thank you."

Their eyes met only briefly before he adjusted his hat and turned away. Without a word, he climbed into his saddle, and her red followed his lead. Not knowing what to think, Meg studied his broad back. She lifted the flower to her nose, inhaled its delicate fragrance, then carefully placed it in her skirt pocket.

They came across a small herd grazing in the afternoon sun. Tye looked them over, pointing out a familiar brand. "Double Oarlock. Mitch Heden's brand."

"That one's Bar Sixteen," she said. "Belongs to the Wheaton outfit."

"Worked for him one summer," Tye replied.

The next herd they located was larger, with at least thirty calves. Aldo spotted them and rode over.

Meg handed him the bag of sandwiches. "Have you eaten?"

"Nah, we was just fixin' to move these cows into the valley," he said. "Hunt is chasin' a fractious calf."

"We'll lend you a hand," Tye said. They separated and started the herd eastward.

Meg rode the outskirts of the herd, watching carefully for separated calves. On the opposite side, a cow broke loose from the others and charged toward Tye.

He took off his hat and swung it at the bellowing

mother with a whoop of his own. Her calf loped behind her, lowing pathetically.

Tye's horse stood its ground, and Meg's heart felt as though it dropped into her stomach. Finally Tye's wild machinations turned the animal back to the herd.

They reached the valley without mishap. Meg rode up an embankment and joined Tye and the Eaton brothers on the bluff that overlooked the cattle.

At her approach, Tye ground the lit end of a cigarette stub between his thumb and forefinger and slid it into his shirt pocket.

The boys ate their sandwiches. "That cow might be a mother, but she sure ain't no lady," Hunt said with a laugh, hitting his hat against his thigh.

"No love-light in that cow's eyes," Tye agreed, a grin edging one side of his mouth up. He blew smoke from the same corner and met Meg's eyes.

"Let's bring that small herd we saw earlier down here, too," she suggested.

They turned back the way they'd come, the Eatons accompanying them. The afternoon grew late by the time they had joined the smaller herd with the one in the lush valley.

"Hunt's stayin' with the herd tonight," Aldo said. "I'm gonna sleep in my own bed."

Meg waved a goodbye and she and Tye headed back.

Cooking smells drifted from the kitchen when they reached the yard. Knowing his nature, she fully expected Tye to dismount ahead of her and help her from the saddle. She didn't need the assistance, or prefer it, but she expected him to make the effort. Instead, he rode a little behind her, slowing.

Meg rode up to a stump Joe had left outside the corral for that very purpose and dismounted. Tye remained seated but reached to take the reins from her. "I'll take care of the horses," he said.

She stretched her legs and headed for the house.

It hit her then, the reason he'd stayed in his saddle.

She stopped before she reached the porch and turned back.

He sat in the dust inside the barn doors, a cigarette dangling from his thinly drawn lips, his leg extended. Smoke curled past the starburst of lines at the corner of his squinted eye.

"Why didn't you say something?" she said, hurrying toward him.

He started to put out the cigarette, but she interrupted. "Don't waste it on my account."

He took a drag instead, held the smoke in his lungs and released it through gritted teeth. She crouched beside him, her skirt hem trailing the dirt floor, and started to reach for his leg.

His hand lashed out, grabbing her wrist.

"Can I do something?" she asked.

"No."

"I'll unsaddle the horses, then."

"Suit yourself."

At his uncharacteristically surly reply, she wrenched her wrist free and stood, taking the mare's reins and leading her to a beam, where she tied her.

She unbuckled the saddle and, knowing she couldn't raise it as high as a stall, left it against the wall, where one of the men could put it away later. She found a gunnysack and wiped the horse down, then turned him into the pasture.

Returning, she found Tye on his feet, the saddle removed from the other horse and both saddles hung over the racks.

"You don't have to do everything, you know."

"Yes, I do," he replied.

"Tye, when your leg hurts you, give yourself a chance to—"

"To what?" he interrupted. "The only thing my leg needs is time. And that passes quickly enough." He took the sack she'd hung on a nail and wiped the horse down.

"You'll let me tend to that leg tonight," she said, brushing past him.

"There's nothing to be done."

"We'll see about that." She left him in the barn.

She had no idea what had happened to his leg, or where or how badly he'd been injured. Sleeping on the hard attic floor these past nights couldn't have helped his discomfort, and physically pushing himself to the limit undoubtedly added to the strain.

Meg felt responsible on both counts. He'd chosen to sleep in the attic to spare her, and she hadn't opposed his decision. She'd also asked him to help her, and she'd explained just how bad things were and how much work there was to be done. He was driving himself too hard, and it was partly her fault.

Gus had supper waiting, and Meg kissed his grizzled cheek. Then, she quickly changed clothing and helped him place the food on the table.

* * *

That night Tye returned to the house after a few chores. He hadn't said no last night when she'd pressed another warm slice of her apple pie on him. He'd eaten it, drunk the coffee she'd poured and promptly chucked it up into the tall weeds behind the outhouse.

His stomach had pained him the duration of the night. He wasn't used to so much food. But he couldn't refuse her.

He hadn't said no to her request to accompany her to church that morning, and he hadn't refused when she'd asked him to come back to the house early this evening. He entered the kitchen, praying she wasn't going to ask him to eat again.

"What happened to your leg?" she asked, and he turned to find her coming from the pantry.

"Took some shrapnel."

"Thank God you didn't lose it."

"Yes," he agreed.

"Let me have a look at it."

He tensed instinctively. "It's not something you'd want to look at."

"There are plenty of things I don't want to do that are necessary."

Like marrying him?

She poured steaming water from a kettle into a teapot and placed the lid on it. Turning, she picked up a tray. "Follow me."

He followed her through the rooms, hesitating when he saw she planned to lead him into her bedroom.

She turned and waited expectantly, and he grudgingly followed.

"Take off your pants and lie down," she instructed.

Tye stopped dead in his tracks. "Ma'am?"

Chapter Six

Tye didn't know why those words from a woman's mouth should draw him up short, but they did.

She reached to take his hat and hang it on the metal bedpost. "I can help you with your boots. I gave the jack to Gus."

He'd consorted with women since he was old enough to shave, but he'd never been with a woman like Meg. His dignity demanded that he take control of the situation. "I can take off my own damned boots."

Her gaze narrowed, and she paused in the midst of unfolding the crisp white sheet she'd brought from a drawer. "Very well then, do it."

She left the room.

Tye forced himself to move and sat on the edge of the soft mattress. Her violet scent emanated from the bedding and triggered a spiral of unease through his chest. He could have used her help. Bending his leg to pull the boot off brought cold sweat to his forehead. He managed it, removed the other and unbuckled his pants.

She'd left the sheet for a purpose, he realized gratefully, wrapping it around his waist to protect her modesty and easing back onto the bed.

She returned with an oilcloth and two cups of tea. "Drink this."

He accepted the cup. The pale liquid had a bitter minty smell, and he sipped it, grimacing. She reached for the sheet and he steeled himself for her reaction. She folded it away from Tye's upper leg, and he knew the instant his thigh became visible. A distressed expression crossed her gentle features. "Oh my," she said softly on a gust of breath.

Mercifully, the bone had only been nicked, but the muscles had been laid back and the skin shredded. The doctors had told him it was a miracle he'd never contracted gangrene. They wouldn't have been able to save his leg—possibly his life—if he had.

But pieces of flesh had been missing, and the remaining muscle and skin had been left to rejuvenate on its own. It had taken months for much of the area to fill and scab over, and now, even nearly a year afterward, the tight scar tissue tormented him, and the muscle, when strained, shot anguish throughout his leg.

"Can't say I didn't warn you," he said, though her reaction hadn't been what he'd expected.

She eased the oilcloth beneath his leg. "I just feel bad for how painful this must have been," she said, her voice thin and reedy. "Or still is."

"I'm alive," he replied.

Her hands stilled.

"And I've got my leg."

Joe had stepped into the room as surely as if he were flesh and blood.

She got to her feet, swept from the room and returned with a basin of steaming water. She placed the basin on the floor and wrung a piece of toweling gingerly. Holding it over his leg, she met his eyes.

"Go ahead," he said with a curt nod.

She draped the hot cloth over the scarred tissue, and he clenched his teeth against the searing agony.

"I'm sorry," she said softly, needlessly. She wouldn't have deliberately caused him anguish.

After a few minutes, the heat seeped into the muscle, and Tye relaxed, once again sipping the special tea she'd prepared.

The hot packs did a miraculous job of extracting the pain and easing the muscles. Meg changed them with regularity, going once for a fresh basin of hot water and even bringing a cool cloth to gently wipe the perspiration from his face.

She stroked the cloth over his forehead, his temples, down his nose and across his cheeks. She ran it over his rough jaw and chin, then over his lips. Her hand stilled and she studied his face for a moment too long, her gaze lingering on his mouth.

He couldn't help a slow smile.

Her tender aid moved Tye in a deep and unfamiliar way. No one had ever touched him like this. The doctors and nurses who'd tended his injuries had been perfunctory and terse. The women he'd bedded had been paid to take care of his needs.

This woman touched him as if she cared.

That notion didn't go to his head. She was a good

woman, a lady, and she would care about any hurting creature. And for some unknown reason, she apparently didn't see the shame of his birth in the same light that everyone else did.

Tye relaxed his body and closed his eyes, blinking them open when she took the cup from his hand.

"Go ahead," she said. "Rest."

He obeyed her gentle command as he did every other, not knowing why he did, only knowing that he didn't have it in him to refuse. Behind his closed lids, he saw her rich hair, shot with golden fire from the lantern. He saw her hands, so small and yet so strong, arranging the steaming towels on his unsightly thigh. He recalled the feel of the cool cloth on his face, soothing and sensual, and remained awed at her graciousness.

Wafting through the strong tea smell, her violet scent wrapped around him and comforted him as much as the heat penetrating his aching muscle and flesh.

He saw her as she'd been that day in her saddle, her shoulders straight, her cheeks flushed from the sun and the wind, a pair of men's knickerbockers visible beneath her hiked skirt.

He'd wanted to kiss her.

His mind's eye conjured up the slope of her breasts beneath her dress, the curve of her cheek, the way she sipped her coffee and how her tongue darted out to touch her lip.

"I want you to sleep here tonight."

He opened his eyes lethargically.

"Those stairs aren't easy to climb, and that floor up there is too hard. You'll sleep here."

Her damp fingers touched his lips before he could form a protest. The intimacy startled them both, and she drew her hand away.

Her touch remained on his mouth. Her sweet smell enveloped him on this pillow. His body had a strong, immediate reaction.

Tye raised his good knee and held her gaze.

She backed away, took the cooled towel from his thigh and gently dried his skin. He closed his eyes and ached in a wholly pleasurable new way.

And then she touched him. The nerve endings on his leg weren't sensitive, but he sensed the pressure and opened his eyes. She held a bottle of liniment in one hand, and with the other she worked the greasy salve into his puckered skin without a qualm. His leg absorbed the warmth, and he relaxed even more, once again allowing his eyes to close.

He sensed when she'd left the room, for the heat and the light seemed to leave with her. He experienced the softness of the mattress beneath him, the gentle brush of cool night air from the open window, and wearily tried to recapture the glow of her presence.

He didn't remember falling asleep, but he woke to the sounds of water splashing and the smell of freshly ground coffee beans. Early morning light streamed through the lacy curtains.

Tye glanced at the other side of the bed and found

no evidence of her having been there. Of course she hadn't slept beside him. Where *had* she slept?

He swung his legs over the edge of the bed and, to his surprise, found that much of the stiffness and soreness in his leg was gone. The memory of her care the night before pierced him anew.

He tugged on his pants and boots and frowned at his rumpled shirt and the dark growth of whiskers he discovered in the oak-framed mirror that hung over her bureau.

To his consternation, a fresh shirt lay at the foot of the bed. He picked it up and looked over it. It had obviously been Joe's. It still had plenty of good workdays left in it, though, and beggars couldn't be choosers. A basin of warm water had been placed on the stand, along with his razor and shaving soap.

He shaved, shrugged into the shirt and found the sleeves too short. He rolled the sleeves back, then carried the basin of water to the front door and dumped it on the ground. In the kitchen, Gus shuffled back and forth between the table and the stove. He looked up only long enough to nod a good-morning.

Meg entered from outside, pails full of milk in both hands. Major followed her and plopped on the floor beside the stove. "Morning, Tye," Meg said with a bright smile.

"Ma'am."

She covered the pails with wet towels. "How's your leg this morning?"

"It's much better. Thank you."

"You're welcome."

He poured himself a cup of Gus's coffee. "I have to make a trip into town."

She nodded indifferently, having no idea where her new husband was off to. Maybe he should tell her now.

Meg, I'm going to see Lottie. She's a whore. Well, she used to be a whore, back when we were friends. She's dying. And Meg, I've promised to take her little girl to raise. I hope you won't mind.

She set a plate of eggs and biscuits on the table for him. "Will you be here to eat at noon?"

Maybe this wasn't the best time to tell her. He sat and picked up a fork without enthusiasm. "I don't think I'll be back in time. I have another stop to make, too."

"Hunt and Aldo plan to be here. I'm going to bake some potatoes and slice the rest of yesterday's ham. I'll save a plate for you." She turned and busied herself at the sink.

Gus sat across from Tye and motioned for him to place one of the eggs on his plate. Tye did so quickly.

"Those hens are laying more than we can eat," she said without turning. "Do you want to sell some eggs in town?"

"Sure."

She turned around then and checked their coffee cups. "Gus, you must have dropped a biscuit."

Major licked crumbs from the floor, then sat and looked at Tye expectantly. Tye ignored the dog and placed his fingers over his cup before Meg could fill it.

Gus didn't say a word.

Major's tail thumped against the floorboards.

Meg set the pot back on the stove.

Tye and Gus exchanged a conspiratorial look.

Purdy came through the doorway, and Tye stood and grabbed his hat. "I'll see you this afternoon."

Meg watched him leave. "Does he think we're so poor he can't have seconds?" she thought aloud.

"Meg, you're shovin' so much food on the poor fella, he's stuffed to the gills, and he can't tolerate it."

She turned to Gus. "What do you mean?"

"I thought he'd turn hisself inside out pukin' that apple pie the other night."

"Oh my...is there something wrong with him?"

"Nothin' a little time won't cure. Somebody what ain't used to eatin' three squares needs to go slow. He was a soldier, and he probably didn't get much more'n hard tack and beans toward the end."

Meg thought about all the food she'd pushed on him, and remorse washed over her. "I had no idea...."

"'Course you didn't. Now ya do." Gus finished his breakfast and ambled out the door.

She glanced at Major licking biscuit crumbs from between the floorboards. Tye had eaten everything she'd placed in front of him—except maybe that biscuit. Why hadn't he said something?

Pride? He did have an abundance of that, she thought, remembering him sitting in the dirt in the barn because he refused to let her see how badly his leg hurt.

Courtesy? Was it that he didn't want to hurt her

feelings? He'd been more than polite, to the point of calling her "ma'am." He could have refused the food. Look what it had cost him not to.

Her thoughts drifted back over the last couple of days, back to Sunday mornings. He hadn't refused to attend church with her, either. "I'll go if you ask," he'd said, and without considering the consequences for him, she'd asked. What had that cost him? Never before had he attended. He'd done it for her. He'd made the sacrifice for her and had been snubbed and insulted. She'd let that happen—no, she'd *made* that happen.

Shame and repentance washed over Meg, and she regretted her callousness. Why had he gone with her? Simply because she'd asked? Did he think he had to do her bidding as part of their bargain? She couldn't grasp his thinking. But she'd be mighty careful what she asked of him from now on.

Lottie was worse. Much worse. She didn't seem to recognize Tye. He sat beside her for half an hour, not saying much, feeling inadequate and helpless. Finally Rosa relieved him, and he entered Eve's room.

Her wide, violet-hued eyes followed him as he crossed to where she sat on the window seat holding her rag doll.

If possible, she seemed even smaller and frailer than she had the last time he'd seen her. "How's Molly?"

"Molly's scared."

"What's Molly scared of?"

"She thinks I'm gonna leave her."

Her tiny voice and revealing words pierced that vulnerable place inside him—a reaction he thought he'd toughened himself against, until she'd come into his life. "You wouldn't leave Molly if you could help it, would you?"

"Won't never leave her. She needs me."

How did a person comfort a child losing her mother? Maybe she shouldn't be here for this ugly and terrifying end. But Rosa had informed Tye that Lottie still had a few lucid hours now and then when she asked for Eve. The child was all Lottie had in the world, and she seemed to need her there.

Lottie needed Eve. And Eve needed Tye. He would be there for her. He'd promised Lottie.

"Eve, you know your mama wouldn't leave you if she could help it," he said.

"Can't help she's sick," she replied.

"That's right. And she's done all she can to make sure you're taken care of. She doesn't want you to be afraid."

"Can't help she's gonna die," the little girl said somberly.

Did she even understand what that meant? "I'm going to take care of you, Eve," he promised her. "You don't have to be scared 'cause you'll be just fine with me."

He stayed with her for an hour, watching her play, listening to her lilting voice and losing his heart to her every mannerism and word.

"I'll be back," he promised.

"When?"

"As soon as I can." He moved closer, willing

strength into her with every ounce of his being. "If you need me sooner, Rosa will send for me."

"Where are we gonna live—when you come for me for good, I mean?"

"On a ranch, Eve. It's a wonderful place with lots of room to run and play. And a dog."

"A dog?"

He nodded and she smiled. "Are there any other kids?"

"No. But there's a nice lady. And lots of horses."

"Can I ride the horses?"

He slid to his knees, ignoring the resulting stab of pain, and took her slender shoulders in his hands, noting her diminutive bone structure and running his palms down her arms to her hands. "I'll teach you to ride. We'll eat together every night. We'll go to church and have Sunday dinner afterward. And sometimes we'll even go on picnics."

"What's that?"

"That's when you pack food in a basket and take it somewhere nice, like under a tree, to eat it."

She tilted her head, and her eyes widened. "How do you carry milk in a basket?"

Tye grinned and wanted to hug her. "In a jar, I guess."

She smiled. "That sounds fun. Is it fun?"

"I'm sure it is." He'd never been on a picnic himself. Tye realized he was promising her all the things he'd only dreamed of doing as a child. "Of course it is. It's lots of fun."

"Will the nice lady come, too?"

He nodded.

"What's her name?"

"Meg."

"Is she pretty?"

"She's the prettiest lady I've ever seen."

Her smile turned to a frown. "My mama's the prettiest lady."

"Of course, you're right. Meg is the second-prettiest lady."

She grinned. "I can't wait to go for the picwic."

"Me, neither."

He never left Rosa's house without a deep feeling of sadness and melancholy eating at his insides. Fear crept in around the edges of that, making him question his ability to care for Eve, making him wish he'd told Meg up front and not waited until the day was imminent. He would tell her tonight. He had to. She'd need some time to prepare.

Tye stopped at the saloon and picked up his last pay, had a shot and questioned the few ranchers who'd stopped for a drink. One of them mentioned a neighbor who might be interested in breeding his mares, so Tye rode west and paid a call on the rancher.

It was late afternoon when he returned to the Circle T. True to her word, Meg had left a plate on the trestle table. Tye lifted the towel and discovered a sandwich, cut neatly into four squares. He ate two of them and washed them down with cold coffee he found in a pot on the stove.

"I could have heated that up for you."

He turned to find Meg carrying a basket of folded clothing in the door. "No need."

Her eyes flickered to the plate and back. "How was your trip?"

"It was good. I found someone willing to pay to have three of his mares bred."

"Why, that's wonderful!"

"Yeah. He'll send for me when they're in season."

Her expression fell. "Oh, of course. That could be a while."

"Yeah." Meanwhile the payment had to be made to the bank. "There's money from your eggs." He laid the coins on the table, knowing they were barely enough to buy a few staples.

Meg glanced at them.

He'd tell her about Eve later, after supper, after Gus and Purdy were in the barn for the night and everything was quiet.

She placed a few towels beside the money and carried the rest of the laundry into the other room.

At supper all the food was in serving dishes and Meg didn't place anything on Tye's plate, allowing him to select his own portions. She even raised one eyebrow in a question before she poured him more coffee. He exchanged a look with Gus but, never having discussed the matter with the old man, had no idea what was going on in his head. Or Meg's, for that matter. At least he wasn't forced to politely stuff himself and suffer the consequences later.

After dinner, he rolled a smoke in the corral, checked on the animals and milked the cows. He found Meg had pulled the rocker into the cramped sitting room. A basket of mending sat at her feet, a shirt in her lap. The front door stood open, and she sat in the line of the chilling breeze. The sun had gone down behind the mountains and the temperature had dropped quickly. He carried a comfortable chair in and sat a few feet from her.

"You'll let me see to that leg again tonight," she said.

The leg hadn't bothered him near as much that day, and he knew her nearness would be a test of his resolve. But the heat and the liniment had helped, and her tender care was an exquisite torture he'd endure at any cost. His silence was his acquiescence.

His heart beat a panicked rhythm. "There's something I need to tell you."

Her fingers didn't halt their progress with the needle and thread. "All right."

"I probably should have found a way to tell you before, but there never seemed to be a right time."

"Tell me before what, Tye?"

"Before we got married."

"We didn't have a before."

"Yeah, that's right."

"What is it?"

"You asked me who Lottie was, and I told you she was a friend."

"Yes." Her fingers paused, then continued.

"She used to work in the saloon. Years ago."

"I see."

"She's sick now. Dying of consumption."

Meg raised her tawny gaze. "I'm sorry to hear that."

A calf they'd been doctoring bawled from the pen. Meg shivered.

Tye got up, closed the door and lit the fire he'd already laid in the fireplace. "She has a little girl. Her name's Eve."

Meg just looked at him as if she were wondering when he was going to get to the point.

He watched the flames catch and grow, then sat back down. "Lottie and I used to be friends. There was never anything serious between us. Just— friends."

Still she waited.

"I must be the only person she really knows— besides Rosa—that she feels she can trust."

Meg gave up on the sewing and let her hands rest in her lap.

"She asked me to take care of her little girl."

Meg lifted a brow at that. "You? Did that strike you as unusual?"

"I guess so. But like I said, she doesn't have anyone else."

"Who's her father?"

"She wouldn't know."

She couldn't look at him. Even Tye felt a wash of embarrassment at saying something so obviously shocking to this genteel woman before him. "How long does Lottie want you to take care of her for?" she asked finally.

"Forever."

Meg was pretty good at keeping the astonishment from her expression. "She just wanted to *give* you this child of hers?"

He nodded.

"When did this take place?"

"The same week you came to me with your... proposal."

Finally, she picked up the material again and started the chair to gently rocking. "What a preposterous thing to do. What did you tell her?"

"I told her I would."

Her hands stilled. The chair stopped.

"You'll love her, Meg. She's a beautiful child."

She leaned forward and placed one hand on the arm of the rocker. "We can't take someone else's child just like that!"

"Why not?"

"Well, I don't even know this woman, or her child."

"That doesn't change the fact that Eve needs a home."

"This Lottie worked in the saloon, you say?"

He nodded.

She leaned back. "I didn't fall off the cart yesterday, Tye. I know what that means."

"Eve can't help what her mother is, what she did."

"That doesn't mean we have to take her."

"I gave my word."

"Without asking me!"

"Lottie asked me to take Eve before you asked me to marry you. Even if she'd asked afterward, I would have done the same thing. The kid will go to an orphan asylum if I don't take her. Lottie made me promise I wouldn't let that happen. I don't *want* to let that happen."

"Can't you find someone else to take her?"

"There isn't anyone else."

"There must be someone."

"There isn't. No one wants a bastard child. No one." His revealing words hung in the brisk evening air between them.

Meg pulled the shawl from the back of the chair around her shoulders.

"I really thought that you, above all others, would understand," he said softly. She'd never treated him as though he were tainted. He fought disappointment over her reaction.

"Do you feel that you owe this woman something?"

He studied the floor for several minutes, then met her eyes. "I guess I do. Compassion. Kindness. Friendship."

"My family won't speak to me already," she said just above a whisper. "This will only make it worse."

"I warned you about that from the beginning," he said honestly. "But you were willing to risk that. You said if the good people of Aspen Grove snubbed you, they weren't worthy of being your friends."

Her beautiful eyes filled with tears and he immediately regretted putting them there. He wished he could take her in his arms and comfort her, somehow make it better. Eve was his responsibility, and he certainly didn't mean to place Meg in an awkward or embarrassing position.

Quickly, she lowered her gaze to the shirt in her lap.

"I don't want you to be sorry," he said, barely above a whisper. "I don't want you to lose your family and friends. We could still change our minds."

Her head snapped up. "Are you saying if I want you to keep our agreement I have to accept this?"

"No, I'm just saying it's not too late. We can get an annul—"

"No!" She tossed the mending to the floor and sat up straight. Meg stared into Tye's eyes, unfathomably dark and blue in the lamplight. She'd vowed she would do anything, endure anything to keep Joe's ranch. She'd already married this man she barely knew. What was so unreasonable about taking in an orphan, too? What choice did she have now? "We'll work it out. Let's take care of your leg."

"You don't have to—"

"When your leg hurts too bad, you're cranky and you can't do as much work."

"And you need me to work the ranch."

"Yes." She stood, knowing it was an unkind thing to say and using it to get back at him for this—this unsettling development. She hurried into the kitchen with a swish of skirts and returned with the bowl and towels.

As though he deserved the reminder of his purpose there, he got up and followed her into the bedroom. She turned her back while he removed his pants and reclined beneath the sheet. "Where did you sleep last night?" he asked.

She turned back and placed the oilcloth beneath his thigh, mentally distancing herself from this man who now shared her life...her home. "On the floor."

"In here?"

"Yes."

"I don't want you to sleep on the floor."

"I don't want *you* to sleep on the floor."

"Can't we share the bed?"

She paused, keeping her gaze on the towel in her hands, and pulled the shawl a measure tighter around her shoulders. Her heart skipped a beat, and she didn't understand why. She'd thought out this arrangement, mentally prepared herself for each situation and development.

"I mean just share the bed. Not…anything else."

She believed he meant that. And if he desired to make more of their sleeping arrangement, she had already determined she could do that, too. It would happen sooner or later anyway, wouldn't it? "I guess we can. This is hot."

"Go ahead."

She placed the steaming towel on his mutilated flesh and he released his breath in a hiss. She didn't derive any pleasure from knowing the remedy hurt him. After repeating the treatment several times, she opened the bottle of liniment and rubbed it into his scarred skin, hoping the oil and the massage would help to ease and stretch the taut new skin.

The lower half of his long leg, his knee and his shin, were muscled and covered with dark hair. His foot was nicely proportioned and his toes long, curly hair sprinkled there, too. She wondered if Tye had that dark dusting over all his limbs as well as his chest. Joe had been fair-haired.

She was thinking about him as a man…as a husband. The thoughts shocked her, but she couldn't help herself. "Tye?"

"Hmm?"

"Lottie. She's—she was—a prostitute?" She couldn't look at him.

"Yes."

"Rosa, too?"

"She was. She's getting married."

"You...you *knew* these women?"

"I knew Lottie."

"In the biblical sense."

"It was a long time ago."

"But you said there was nothing serious between the two of you. Just friends. Don't you think *that* is serious?" She had a difficult time imagining doing something so embarrassing with someone you weren't "close" to.

It took a long time for his reply. "You're right," he said finally. "That is something serious. At least it should be."

Suddenly, inexplicably, she hated the idea of him with those other women. "You don't go there anymore?"

"No!"

"I don't think it would be good if you went to see one of those women."

"I'm not going to see anyone. I told you, Lottie was a long time ago."

"Well, husbands shouldn't do that. They should...be with their wives."

"I agree."

"And you're a husband now. If you want to do that, you shouldn't go to town."

"You mean I should come to you. My wife."

Heat flared in her entire upper body, and she knew

he could see her embarrassment even in the light from
the lantern. Was that what she'd been getting at? No.
She simply didn't want him humiliating her in an unnecessary manner. "Yes."

"And what if *you* should want to…do that?" he
asked, and she imagined she heard a smile in his
voice.

Why, she'd never initiated such a thing with her
own husband! Surely he didn't think she'd be the one
to ask him! "I am not having this conversation with
you, I am simply saying you mustn't shame me by
going to town for that. I already have to deal with
what people think of us getting married, and now I'll
have to deal with this child. I won't cope with that,
too."

"I won't go."

"All right."

"But I think you should be the one to tell me when
you want to. I'm a man, I can be ready anytime.
You're the one who needs to adjust to the whole
thing. You know, get comfortable and choose when
the time is right. You were married, you know what
I'm talking about."

What on earth *was* he talking about? She turned to
view his face.

He was studying her with a hot look that started
butterflies fluttering in her stomach. And he was serious. The situation struck her full force. He was lying
in her bed, the bed she'd shared with Joe, but he
seemed to take up so much more room. She'd touched
him, no matter how innocently, and she'd had un-
seemly thoughts of his body. Images of him with

those other women had disturbed her. She'd shocked herself. "I'd better go wash my hands."

She gathered her supplies and left the room, only to wash her hands, splash cool water on her face, then stand in the kitchen with her heart beating crazily in her throat. Finally, she gathered her wits, blew out the lantern in the other room, checked the fire and returned to the dim bedroom.

He'd finished undressing and lay against the pillow, one arm over his head, exposing a thatch of dark hair beneath. His chest, above the sheet, was covered with thick black curls, just as she'd wondered. He lay with his eyes closed, so she studied him, her knees weak, her heart racing as though she were preparing to jump off a cliff.

This new husband was so much older than Joe had been—so much more of a man. But then Joe would be older, too, if he were still alive. That had been years ago. Intimacy with Joe had been...*comfortable.* Thinking of Tye in that way was anything but comfortable.

He opened his eyes and caught her staring. "I won't look while you undress," he said.

Meg turned away and fumbled in a drawer for her nightgown. Locating it, she blew out the lantern before removing her dress and underclothing.

"You didn't have your corset on under that dress, did you?" he said, his voice a husky suggestion in the darkness.

"How did you know that?"

"Just did."

"You were thinking about my undergarments?"

"Yeah."

She'd never known anyone so embarrassingly frank.

"Don't tell me you didn't think about me. Especially when you got me out of my pants and into your bed. Something crossed your mind."

Meg gasped and pulled her nightgown on quickly, buttoning it up to her throat.

"Get in."

She stood there trembling, though the room was warm and her body temperature even warmer.

"Told you we were just going to sleep together," he said. "Nothing else."

She calmed herself with a deep breath and eased onto the mattress, careful not to inch too close or make a move to tilt him toward her. He did take up more room than Joe ever had. She lay flat on her back, the sheet tucked snugly beneath her armpits, and stared at the darkened ceiling, afraid of herself, afraid of the way her head and her body reacted to this man.

"Until you're ready," he added.

Oh, Lord. She would never sleep again.

Tye had fueled the stove and heated water, and now carried a pitcher back to the bowl on the bureau. Meg mustn't have slept well, and he saw no reason to wake her now. She lay on her side with one hand curled daintily beneath her cheek, the other on his pillow.

The sheet had pulled loose from the end of the bed, exposing a delicate foot and a length of silky calf. Tye's belly ached with the desire to place his face against her morning skin and inhale her. Taste her. *His wife.* He'd start at her foot and make his way up her leg....

Don't you think that *is serious?* she'd asked. He'd never looked at intimate relations from her perspective before, so he'd never considered just how serious they could be. He'd never thought of sex as right or wrong, serious or not. In his experience it had been merely a fact of life. Sometimes pleasant, sometimes manipulative, sometimes a service, sex had never taken on the serious aspects he could see it having with someone like Meg.

Yes. With Meg, it would be serious.

He forced himself to face the mirror and lather his whiskers, tamping down the unruly thoughts that would have him in a state of arousal all day. He smiled, remembering her gentle and flustered request that he not visit a whore.

As if there were a whore in the entire state with more appeal than Meg. As if there were a woman in the world with more appeal. He'd admired her from the first time he'd seen her.

She'd been nine—ten, maybe—and sitting on the school lawn with the other girls. They'd been braiding one another's hair, and Jacky Mabley's sister—he couldn't remember her name...Joanie? Janie?—sat behind Meg, separating Meg's tawny tresses. Sunlight had glinted like golden fire in her hair, and Tye had wanted to tell Jacky's sister not to spoil that spectacular display by hiding Meg's hair in braids. But he hadn't, of course. He hadn't even spoken. He'd just walked around them as if he were going somewhere, and stopped to take a longer look at Meg. She'd smiled at him, her new adult teeth pearly white.

He'd looked away and run into the schoolroom to study his times tables. None of the kids played with him, and Mr. Brickey let him come in early from lunch so he didn't have to endure the humiliation of their childish cruelty.

Meg had always had a smile for him. Even when they grew older, when the other girls and their mothers refused to look him in the eye, Meg had met his eyes and smiled.

He guessed he'd always loved her.

Tye stared hard at his reflection, shocked that there were words to go with what he'd felt. She'd always been untouchable. A town girl. Joe's girl. Joe's wife. He'd never allowed himself to analyze his feelings; that would have been disastrous. Futile.

But now. Now. She was…his wife.

Tye made the last stroke across his jaw, slowly wiped away the lather with his damp towel and turned.

She studied him, those tawny eyes shot with golden sparks like the morning sun.

"Morning," he said.

She drew her seductive foot up beneath the sheet. "Morning."

"I'll bring you some water."

"I slept so late."

"Not really. I woke up early." He dumped the water outside and returned with a fresh pitcher for her.

She was sitting, holding the sheet to her breast. Her

hair tumbled around her shoulders in becoming dis-
array and tempted a man's fingers. "Thank you."

He curled his fingertips into his palms. "You do a
lot of thoughtful things for me."

"I do? Like what?"

"Like bringing me water, pouring my coffee, nursing my leg."

"Those are just ordinary things."

"Are they?"

She studied him, her eyes pretty with sleep.

"I wouldn't know." He'd never had a wife. Never
had a father to know how married people behaved
around each another. "Did your mother do all those
things for your father?"

"Yes."

"Did you do them for Joe?"

"Yes."

He realized she was trying not to stare at his bare
chest, and he pulled another clean chambray shirt
from the drawer she'd stocked and donned it, rolling
the sleeves back. "Joe's?"

"Yes. I thought you needed more work clothes.
That way I don't have to wash them so often."

"Sounds sensible. I'm off to milk," he said.

She nodded.

He headed for the barn, the image of her in the
morning forever in his mind…and in his heart. Meg.
Joe's wife.

A buggy pulled by a single horse headed up the
road. As the vehicle drew closer, Tye recognized
Niles Kestler. The man pulled the buggy around to
the front door. Tye followed.

"Hatcher," he said, pulling to a stop.

"Kestler. What brings you out?"

"I wanted a word with you."

"Come on around to the kitchen and have a cup of coffee. Nobody uses the front."

Niles frowned but prodded the horse, and Tye followed the buggy to the other side of the house. Niles got down, brushing dust from the sleeves of his jacket and his impeccably creased trouser legs.

"Come on in." Tye stood back and allowed the slender man to pass by. "I'll let Meg know you're here."

Niles removed his derby and nodded.

Tye stepped into the bedroom and Meg glanced up in surprise. One hand went to the already perfect hair she'd just pulled into a knot. She fastened the top button of her pink-striped shirtwaist.

"Niles Kestler's here."

"I thought I heard a wagon. Whatever does he want?"

"Don't know yet. He's in the kitchen."

"I'll be right out. I started the coffee."

Tye returned to the other room. Major bumped against the screen door until he jostled his nose in and appeared with a stick of wood.

"Good boy." Tye used the stick to prop the door open as he'd seen Meg do. "Get more."

The dog tore off.

Meg entered, smoothing the skirt of her faded work dress self-consciously. "Niles! What a surprise." She glanced at the stove where the pot had begun to boil.

"I was just getting breakfast started. Will you join us?"

"No thank you. I've eaten."

"The coffee will be ready in a minute. Have a seat."

She appeared more flustered than usual. Normally, she was at ease in her kitchen, but their visitor's presence seemed to throw her off.

Niles seated himself on one of the benches, placing his hat on the table.

Hastily, Meg picked it up and hung it on a hook.

Major returned with more wood. Tye patted his head and gave him a lump of sugar. The dog plopped down by the stove.

"I've had an offer for the ranch," Niles said, ignoring their morning routine and coming directly to the point. The words were directed at Tye.

Tye took his time seating himself.

"The Circle T is not for sale," Meg said tightly.

"I'm speaking with Mr. Hatcher," Niles pointed out.

Meg's body stiffened visibly, and her face grew pink. The tight set of her mouth revealed her anger.

"Meg hasn't seen reason on this from the beginning," Niles said to him. "I'm hoping you will. I've found someone willing to offer more per acre than Joe paid for the property. You won't get another offer like this."

Tye met Meg's flashing eyes, their tawny color darkened to the hue of fiery whiskey.

"Meg already told you," he said, turning back to Niles. "The ranch isn't for sale."

"Five more days and you won't have a choice," Niles replied. "Take the offer while you can still get something for Joe's land. If you let the bank take it back, you'll get nothing and you won't even have a way to support your wife."

Rage simmered in Tye's veins, rage and helplessness and a burning humiliation he'd felt enough of to last forever. He had sufficient savings to make the note good this once. But if he spent it, what would he use to start his packing plant?

But selling was out of the question. Even if he didn't have plans of his own for the land, he'd given Meg his word.

"We're not selling."

Niles stood. "I thought a man like you wouldn't have his head in the clouds. You already understand how dismal the hopes of keeping this land are."

"A man like me has learned not to let stuffed shirts have the say in matters that don't concern them," he replied easily.

"This concerns me," Niles argued. "You're going to see just how much this concerns me when I bring the foreclosure notice."

Tye stood, facing him. "Make sure you use a nice soft piece of paper to write it on because you'll either eat it or I'll stuff it up—"

"Tye! Niles, the coffee is ready."

"No thank you." The man went for his derby. "My business is finished here. You can't help people who don't want to be helped." He stopped. "You deserve this man, Meg." He settled the hat on his head and exited the door.

Tye didn't move to follow him.

The sounds of the horse and buggy leaving floated in to them.

"Thank you, Tye," Meg said softly.

"For what?"

"For not agreeing to sell."

He raised his head and studied her. "I gave you my word."

She nodded. "Yes, you did."

"Five days," he said, ignoring the appreciation in her voice. She wouldn't be so grateful after those days were gone unless he used the money he'd saved. And right now he saw no way around it. Using his money would earn him three months to come up with something else before the next note was due.

And now that he'd faced down Niles Kestler, Tye had even more at stake. He set his jaw stubbornly. "A man like him" had learned to meet his knocks head-on.

He went to the bedroom and returned with one of his rifles.

"What's that for?"

"Aldo rode in and said a cat got one of our calves last night. We're going after him."

"I'll pack you a lunch in case you have to go far."

He turned away from the look in her eyes and headed out the door. He didn't deserve her gratitude. His bravado toward Niles had been pure bluster; he hadn't a clue what he was going to do. But he had only five days to do it in.

Five lousy days.

Chapter Seven

After Tye and Aldo tracked the mountain lion and Tye shot him, Aldo went back to the herds and Purdy helped Tye cut more pines for the fences. Tye worked from dawn to dusk for three days, sawing, cutting, thinking—planning how he'd raise enough money to pay the next banknote. He had enough in the bank for one payment only.

Late at night he worked on the cat's hide, scraping and cleaning and softening the leather, thinking… thinking.

The tiring work made it easier to sleep at night. He fell asleep exhausted rather than lying awake, smelling the woman beside him, hearing her soft breathing, the rustle of her bedclothes, and aching. *Aching.*

Meg had saved supper for them each night, and this night, after Purdy had eaten and gone to the barn, Tye picked up his plate and carried it to the pan of sudsy water. "I'm going into town to pay the note in the morning," he announced.

She took the plate from him and scrubbed it. "No need."

"What?"

"No need to make the trip. I did it today."

"You...?" He stared at her. "Where did you get the money?"

She rinsed the plate and wiped it dry without looking up. "I sold something."

He looked around, strode to the end of the room and took note of her mother's china cabinet and the other furnishings still in place. "What?"

"Something I didn't need."

"What?" he asked again, more insistently.

"A ring."

Her words made it around the fog in his head and he filtered through them. Immediately, he focused on her hand. She still wore the silver ring he'd placed on her finger. But the unease didn't leave his chest. "Joe's ring?"

"No."

No? Her restraint irritated the hell out of him. "What ring, then, *dammit?*"

She glanced up at him warily. "My father's wedding ring."

Having said that, she moved away to place the plate in a cupboard. Tye ran a hand through his hair in annoyance. "You sold your father's wedding ring, but not Joe's."

His thinking at this point was irrational, he realized, but her action stabbed him with humiliation and... something else he couldn't define.

"That ring is small, Tye, not worth much, really. I'll sell it if I need to, but if I don't, I thought it should be saved for Edwina or Wilsie, or perhaps one of

Gwynn's children. An heirloom, sort of, since I have
no children to give it to. My father's ring was large
and heavy—I got enough for the banknote and the
seed.''

Tye's supper felt like a stone in his belly. A claw-
ing regret climbed its way through his chest. Shame
was a familiar companion, but one he detested with
all his being, and one he didn't care to share with
anyone else. ''Who'd you sell it to?''

''O'Roarden, the only pawnbroker in Aspen
Grove.''

''He probably didn't even give you what it was
worth.''

She said nothing to that, just stood with her back
to him, her head lowered. Of course she hadn't gotten
what it was worth. How could a person place a real-
istic value on a keepsake? It had no doubt been in-
valuable to her.

''I'm sorry,'' he said softly, regretting his anger,
regretting he'd been unable to do a thing as simple
as make the loan payment before she'd had to sacrifice another part of her heritage. His inadequacy had
never been so hurtful to another person before. He
could bear it himself, but for her to suffer it shamed
him beyond endurance. ''I'm sorry you had to do
that.''

She turned slowly and he recognized tears when
she looked at him. ''It's okay, Tye. I'd do it again. I
still have the ranch.''

The ranch. Joe's ranch. She'd give up anything,
wouldn't she? Do any unpleasant and ugly thing to

keep her precious Joe's ranch. Even marry *him*. "Yes. You still have the ranch."

He turned and escaped out into the darkness to smoke. And think.

He was tired but not sleepy. Not now. He sat on a stump a distance from the house and watched the lights go out, all but the one in the front room. She left it burning low so he'd find his way to bed.

Chill mountain air seeped through his clothing while regret eased through his knotted pride, pushing his own feelings aside and forcing him to look at hers. She'd lost too much. Her husband. Her dreams. She was a brave, strong woman, a determined woman. She'd proven she would make any sacrifice to keep this place. Any sacrifice, even sharing the ranch with him. *Even sharing a bed with him.*

This was a joint effort, and he had yet to pull his own weight. He was angry that she'd come up with a solution before he had, and humiliated that she had the means instead of him.

She shouldn't have to lose everything dear to her. He wouldn't allow any more sacrifices on her part. And he'd get her father's ring back for her—somehow. If she'd received enough for the payment *and* the seed, he probably didn't have enough in the bank, but he could earn the rest. Jed Wheeler hadn't wanted to let him go, claimed he could get anyone to clean up, but a piano player improved the atmosphere and made people spend more money.

In the past Tye had disciplined himself to get by without much food. Sleep had to be the same. He crushed his cigarette butt beneath his heel and headed for the barn to saddle a horse.

Meg hadn't realized Tye would be so angry over the ring. She'd done what she had to do. She hadn't seen a choice.

She drifted into a light sleep. He returned hours later and climbed into bed, his hair smelling like smoke. Where had he been all that time? The saloon?

He must have fallen asleep immediately, for his breathing grew deep and even, and he relaxed his long body and draped one leg over hers. The physical contact kept her from returning to sleep. Not because it was unpleasant—but because it wasn't. She'd missed someone to lie with, someone to hold her, someone to dispel the loneliness.

Joe had been a solid, comforting presence beside her at night, and she'd longed for that. Sometimes he had turned to her, touched her through her cotton gown, kissed her tenderly, reverently, and joined their bodies. Now those times seemed like only a sweet dream.

She'd told Tye he could do that. He had every right as her husband. And he'd told her...he'd said she would have to tell him when *she* was ready, because a man was "*always* ready." What had that meant?

She wished he would consummate their marriage though, so the waiting would end. The thought, and his hair-roughened leg against hers, created unsettling feelings she didn't know what to make of. If he turned to her, she'd relish his warmth, his weight, his possession.

Why?

He wasn't Joe.

Perhaps it was just unnatural for a man not to—not to *turn to* his wife like that.

Perhaps he'd… No. He'd told her he would not turn to one of those women in town.

Toward dawn she fell asleep thinking she hadn't taken care of his leg that night.

Meg awoke cranky the following morning. On her way past the idle fireplace, she paused before it and studied the thick fur rug that had been placed there.

"Thought it looked like a good spot," Tye said from behind her. "All right?"

Tired, head hurting, she nodded.

She scorched the first griddle of hotcakes and had to toss them out. Even Major turned up his nose at the charred disks in the yard, and she mumbled under her breath as she stirred more batter.

Gus and Purdy ate as quickly as they always did and hurried off to do chores. Tye poured himself another cup of coffee at the stove and stood looking out the screen door. "I'm going to work on the fence for the south pasture today," he said. "I'll be in at noon."

Meg scrubbed at the blackened griddle.

"Are you all right?"

His voice, so close, startled her. She stopped her furious scouring and nodded. He stood directly behind her, his breath fanning her neck. Remembering his leg touching hers and the wanton thoughts that followed, she fought down the flutter in her chest. Tears prickled behind her eyelids, and she knew they were irrational.

"Anything you want me to take care of before I go?"

She took a calming breath. "No."

"All right, then." His hand and corded forearm appeared in her vision, placing his empty mug on the drain board. His boot heels scraped the floor as he moved away. "Thanks for breakfast."

The screen door banged shut. Major barked.

Meg let the tears fall unheeded, wondering when she'd grown so weak.

The men didn't say much during the noon meal and were seemingly glad to leave the house. By supper she'd pulled herself together and managed a decent meal and some light conversation.

Tye left the house as soon as darkness fell.

She sat with her rocker pulled before the fire and listened to the snap and hiss of the burning wood. Was this to be her life, then? A husband who worked hard and played harder? He'd promised he wouldn't shame her with a slattern; he hadn't promised not to visit the saloons.

Again, he came to bed long after midnight, the night chill emanating from his body.

"Where were you?" she asked into the darkness.

He hesitated only a moment before replying, "The Pair-A-Dice."

The scent of smoke and the yeasty smell of beer drifted to her. "Were you drinking?"

"I had a couple."

"Was that necessary?"

"I thought it was."

"Are you a drunk, Tye Hatcher?"

"No, ma'am."

She turned on her side away from him. She wouldn't chance him cozying up to her this night. She needed her rest.

Saturday night he stayed out longer than usual but was up and ready for church without her asking. A new tension had developed between them, brought on by his nightly trips to town and her lack of knowledge over what to do or say to correct the situation.

Once again, Meg endured stares and whispers and deliberate snubs as they attended the worship service and made their way out of the tiny church.

Reverend Baker greeted them warmly. "I'm looking forward to dinner again," he said, shaking Tye's hand and smiling at Meg. Tye had invited him this time.

"Why don't you ride out to the ranch with us," Tye offered. "I'll bring you home later this afternoon."

"That sounds right nice," he said. "Won't have to rent a buggy that way."

Tye led Meg down the church steps, his hand at the small of her back. He adjusted his hat on his head, the brim angled down over his eyes.

Edwina, decked in a starched black dress and bonnet, stood with a gaggle of her friends in the shade of a young oak tree. Her adherence to her mourning garb shouldn't have made Meg feel uncomfortable for wearing her apricot ombre with the pleated bust and yoke that her mother had sent her last winter, but the way they stared, she felt as if she'd worn only her old red flannel petticoat.

"I understand Tye Hatcher is spending his nights in the saloons," one of them said.

Tye's fingers tensed at her waist.

"*Joe* never sullied himself in those vulgar surroundings," another replied, deliberately loud enough for them to overhear. "Of course, Joe's parents brought him up right."

Meg's steps faltered.

Tye took her arm securely and led her to their wagon.

She glanced up.

A muscle twitched in his jaw. Concealing a grimace, he bent one knee and made a step of his fingers. His hat hid his face.

Meg placed her hand on his shoulder and her sole in his palms and accepted his assistance onto the wagon. She was at a loss for what to say to him. He'd placed himself in this particular circumstance.

"Tye—"

"The reverend should be coming soon." He peered toward the church, squinting beneath the brim of his hat. "Most of the flock has waddled off."

"Tye." She said it softly this time, almost a reprimand for his outrageous comment.

"Here he comes."

"I'll sit in the bed so he can ride up here with you." With a swish of skirts, she climbed over the back of the seat and settled herself in the wagon bed.

Reverend Baker hauled himself up, and they were on their way.

At the ranch, the men found something to do while she donned the only silk apron she still owned and ran a palm over it fondly. Her mother had always worn a silk apron over her good clothing on Sundays. Meg set the table with the linen and china and laid out the dinner she'd left cooking that morning.

Gus and Purdy joined them, and Reverend Baker said grace. The minister took turns eating with nearly every family in Aspen Grove. If he hadn't heard gossip about her and Tye before now, he would soon enough. It would amaze Meg if the citizens condoned the man eating with them. Surely they would have something to say about that!

Should she mention to Tye that she'd been hasty in insisting he attend services with her? He'd made it part of his weekly routine now, and she didn't want him to think she'd changed her mind or that she was ashamed of his company.

She hadn't believed the people she'd known all her life could be so narrow-minded about her marriage. She'd seen their treatment of Tye, heard the talk, but she'd never figured they would turn against *her*. Why, she was one of them!

At least she had been.

He had warned her. And she'd chosen to give them the benefit of the doubt, chosen to believe they'd come around. Perhaps they just needed more time. It hadn't been long, after all. Then again, how could she expect the townspeople to approve of Tye, when even she had her doubts now? She was growing angry with him for betraying her trust by riding off to the saloon every night.

"You're a fine cook, Meg," the reverend said, finishing his peach cobbler and reaching for his coffee cup with the scalloped edges. "Thank you."

"Thank you for the compliment, Reverend. It was my pleasure."

"Shall we retire for a little man talk?" he suggested, giving Tye a wink.

Tye stood. "Excuse us."

"Certainly." She watched them pluck their hats from the hooks beside the door and leave the house.

"I'll do the dishes," Gus offered, flicking his hand at her as though she were a pesky fly.

She glanced at her mother's china.

"I'll be careful," he said. "Ain't broke nothin' yet, have I?"

He hadn't. She changed into her day dress and Joe's knickerbockers and saddled a horse. She'd ride out and check on the cattle. A ride always made her feel better.

Hunt and Aldo had gone to spend the afternoon with their folks, so she wouldn't run into them. She rode along the stream, cut south and spotted Tye's new fencing. It stretched for a good quarter mile as far as she could see. She couldn't fault his work. The posts looked solid, and he'd chosen straight, strong trees as poles.

How he'd managed so much was beyond her.

She'd made a good choice in asking him to marry her. Hadn't she?

Meg rode on, locating grazing cattle, and finding

pleasure with the growth and apparent health of the calves. She turned back in time to put together a light meal before milking.

The old men joined her. "Your mister hasn't come back from returnin' the preacher to town," Gus said.

Meg acknowledged the information with an irritated nod. Tye had an early start on the evening if he intended to spend it in a saloon. Were the saloons open on Sunday nights? The sound of the wagon approaching caught her attention, and Meg hated the sense of relief she experienced at Tye's early return. She figured it would take him a while to put the horses up, so his voice outside the back door surprised her.

The screen door opened and she glanced up.

She couldn't have been more astonished.

With one arm, he held a tiny girl, her white-stockinged legs dangling against his holster. She wore a ruffled blue dress and a matching bonnet. Beneath the bonnet, dark hair escaped in ebony ringlets. Her violet eyes were huge and round and glistening with tears.

Tye eased the door shut behind him with his free arm and stepped farther into the room, taking off his hat and snagging it on one of the hooks. The child had one hand on his shirtfront, and the closer he drew to Meg and the two men, the tighter she gripped the white cotton in her fist.

"This is the nice lady I told you about," Tye said, placing his hand over the child's on his chest, hers disappearing beneath it.

Meg drew her stare from his huge hand to his face, then let it skitter to the girl.

She stared at Meg, her lower lip trembling. She had pale ivory skin, almost translucent in its delicate beauty, and against its whiteness her lips were shiny and pink like spring berries. She was the most beautiful child Meg had ever seen.

"Her name's Meg," he said, and for a minute she had forgotten he was talking to the child about her. "Meg, this is Eve."

Eve. The child he'd promised to care for. *Forever.*

She met Tye's gaze again, reading urgency and questioning desperation in their depths. Why had he brought her now? Why this night? Why without notice or forethought or...

Had Lottie died?

"Hello, Eve," Meg said gently. And then, remembering they had an audience, she turned. "This is Gus. And Purdy."

"Hey, there, little missy," Gus said with a nod, and an unexpected smile split his grizzled face.

Eve didn't say anything, but her expressive gaze moved from the two old men back to Meg, intuitively picking up on her discomfort. She ducked her head against Tye's shoulder, hiding her face.

Meg was so startled by this unannounced arrival and the sight of the diminutive creature in Tye's embrace, her head barely held a coherent thought. She wanted to ask him a dozen questions, but the child was of an age to understand their conversation. "Are you hungry, Eve?"

The child burrowed her face into Tye's neck. He

carried her to one of the benches and sat, placing her beside him. She didn't release his shirt, and he kept his arm securely around her. "Can we take your hat off?" he asked.

"It's a bonnet." Her voice, muffled against his shirt, seemed as tiny and delicate as she.

"So it is," Tye said, and tugged the ribbons loose and removed it. The top of her hair had been caught up and fastened, and the rest cascaded across her shoulders in shiny, sausagelike curls.

The five of them ate in silence, Eve eating only what Tye managed to slip between her lips. She chewed with her nose in his ribs, and Meg actually found some humor at the sight and grinned.

"I have some cookies," she said, removing plates from the table. "I don't suppose anyone has any room left, though."

"I do," Eve said, facing the table for the first time. Her hesitant gaze darted from Meg to Gus and Purdy and back. She actually sat up a little straighter.

"I 'spect I have some room, too," Gus said.

Meg set a plate of cookies on the table and placed a glass of milk in front of Eve.

"Thank you, ma'am." Tye took a cookie from the plate and laid it on the table in front of the little girl. If she wanted it, she'd have to let go and pick it up.

She turned forward, snatched up the cookie and took a bite, keeping her watchful attention on the adults around the table. Tye kept his arm behind her back for her to lean against, a security she seemed to crave and a gesture Meg wouldn't have expected him to know the child needed. She looked at him in a new light.

Eve finished her cookie, drank half of the milk and leaned against Tye.

Gus cleared the table, then he and Purdy headed for the barn.

"Where's the dog?" Eve asked.

Meg had been folding her apron and she paused only briefly, going on as if she hadn't heard.

"He's outside somewhere," Tye replied.

"Does he come in the house?"

"He carries in wood for the stove, and Meg lets him stay in the kitchen."

"Can I see him?"

Meg met Tye's gaze. "I'll call him," she said. "He's probably chasing squirrels."

She stepped out back and called Major's name a few times. She rang the bell next—that usually brought him running. Finally, he came loping across the darkening yard, leaves stuck to his fur.

Meg knelt and pulled them off, then opened the screen door. "Here he is."

Major wagged his tail, sniffed the air and approached Eve. Wide-eyed, she curled into Tye's side again. "He's too big!"

"He's a big one, all right." Tye swiveled on the bench, pulling Eve onto his lap and placing a hand under Major's chin. "He wants to smell you. That's how he says hello."

With her tiny hands drawn up under her chin, Eve warily watched the dog sniff her skirt and her stockings. "Hello, doggy," she said finally, her falsetto voice warbling.

"His name's Major."

"Watch," Meg said, coming around to sit a safe distance away on the same bench. She took a cookie from the plate and broke it in two, garnering the dog's undivided attention. "Sit, Major."

The dog promptly plopped on his haunches, his enormous tail sweeping the floor behind him. His tongue lolled expectantly as he stared at the cookie Meg held.

"Not yet," Meg said firmly, and reached to place the cookie on his snout. "Not yet," she repeated. The dog sat amazingly still, balancing the sweet on his nose. "Okay!" Meg said.

With a flurry of his enormous jowls, Major ducked his head so that the cookie bounced from his nose, and he caught it in his mouth, swallowing it in one gulp.

Eve let out a surprised giggle and brought her palms together in excitement.

Major stared at Meg expectantly. "Good boy," she said, and fed him the other half of the cookie.

Still laughing, Eve touched Tye's face with one flattened palm. "Did you see?"

He grinned. "I saw."

"Do it again, Meg, do it again!" she cried.

Amid Eve's delighted giggles, Meg repeated the trick until Tye claimed, "We have to stop. Major will get sick from all those cookies." And then in an aside to Meg, he asked, "How long did it take to teach him that?"

"Major is Joe's dog," she said softly. "Joe taught him."

Something flashed behind his eyes. Tye looked at the dog as though he'd somehow spoiled the happy mood he'd hoped to create. "I'd better start the chores."

"I'll do it. You two stay here." She got up.

"Thank you," he said, and she knew it wasn't the milking he was referring to. It was for helping to put Eve at ease.

"You're welcome." She hurried to the barn. Gus had already started the milking.

"I put the horses up," he said.

Meg had forgotten all about the team; Tye must have, too. "Thanks, Gus."

"There's a bag and a trunk in the back o' the wagon."

"I'll get the bag. Tye can get the trunk later. Can you get the pails?"

He nodded and carried the milk to the house. Meg handled the bags, covered the pails and wished Gus good-night, thinking all the while about this latest development, feeling eager for the chance to speak with Tye.

She couldn't get the picture of him with that little girl out of her head. Over and over, she remembered Eve's hand grazing his cheek, demanding his attention with a touch he could overcome with the flick of a wrist. But the child had won his immediate compliance by her mere helplessness. No. Because of it.

Meg poured water over beans to soak for the next

day's meal before blowing out the lantern in the kitchen and discovering Tye around the corner.

He sat on the floor, Eve sleeping in his arms, her fingers once again gripping his shirtfront like a lifeline. Major sprawled beside them. Tye glanced up, a look of confusion on his face. "What do I do with her?"

Meg looked her over. She was still fully clothed. "Is she staying?"

He nodded.

"Maybe there's a nightgown in the bag I carried in."

"Sorry. I forgot about her things. And the horses—"

"Gus took care of the team. You can get the trunk later. I guess we'd better get her out of those clothes and figure out where she's going to sleep."

"How about the pallet I made in the attic? I can bring those blankets down. I'd suggest she sleep in the bed with you and I sleep out here, but…"

Meg nodded. "But I don't think she likes me."

"She will. It's just that everything's strange to her, and she's scared."

"Tye, did—"

"We'll talk after we get her settled," he said, and leaned to place Eve on the braided rug. He straightened, flexing his leg, and reached for the rope to pull down the attic stairs. Working together, Tye and Meg made up a padded bed safely away from the fire he'd started earlier, and Tye gently placed Eve on the thick nest.

Meg unbuttoned Eve's shoes and slipped them off,

rolling her stockings off next. Tye went for the bag Meg had left in the kitchen and set it nearby.

She worked the dress and petticoats from the sleeping child.

Tye turned his back.

She slanted a glance at his broad shoulders. "What are you doing?"

"Giving her some privacy."

"She's asleep, Tye. Besides, she's…she's…how old is she?"

"Five and a half. Her birthday's behind Thanksgiving."

Meg blinked at that one, but said, "Turn around here and help me."

"No, I—"

"Come on now, she's like a noodle."

Reluctantly, he turned.

"Why, you're embarrassed," she said with a grin.

But he helped Meg stuff limp arms into sleeves. And in minutes they had Eve in a white cotton-and-eyelet nightgown and covered with a crisp sheet that smelled of outdoors. Major curled up beside her and eased down with a canine sigh.

Meg exchanged a look with Tye.

"Maybe the dog will keep her company. You know, a warm body if she gets restless," he suggested.

She did know. She'd slept with the scruffy animal a few times herself during the long, lonely nights of Joe's absence. "He can stay."

"I'm going out for a minute." Tye let himself out the front door.

She moved into the bedroom to get her own clothing changed. Turning down the lamp and reaching for the window shade, she noticed the orange glow of Tye's cigarette at the edge of the yard. She pulled down the shade, dressed in her nightclothes and climbed into bed.

He entered the room minutes later, closing the door purposefully. He removed his gun belt, rolled it around the revolver and stored it under the bed. Meg shut her eyes. She listened as he stripped off his clothing, piece by piece, emitting a stifled groan.

She sat up. "I didn't take care of your leg."

He sat on the edge of the bed, his bare spine and shoulders to her, pulling the bunched trousers from his foot. "Nobody took care of my leg before I came here, and I did okay."

"But the hot packs make it feel better."

"Yes," he said softly, "they do."

She realized then that she was talking to his naked back and that he wore only his white cotton drawers. He stood up and moved to the face bowl, meeting her glance in the mirror.

Meg turned the other way.

"Now who's embarrassed?" he asked with a chuckle.

"Shall I go for some hot water and the liniment?"

Water splashed. "No." He returned and sat on the bottom corner of the bed. "Look at me."

Her heart fluttered foolishly. Looking at him was more disturbing than it should have been. Her common sense railed against it.

"Please?" he added mildly. "We need to talk."

Chapter Eight

Meg turned those vulnerable hazel eyes on him.

He would have spared her this if he could have. But it was done. He'd given his word, and now he had a child depending on him. "Lottie died today. There was a message for Reverend Baker when we got to his place. I went over to Rosa's and helped her make arrangements."

"I'm sorry, Tye. I know she was your friend."

"I hadn't seen her for years until recently," he said, not expecting or needing her sympathy. "Of course I'm sorry she went like that, and I'm sorry Eve lost her mother. But don't be sorry for me. Eve's the one who needs the comforting."

Every once in a while her gaze returned to his bare skin, but she'd force it to his eyes or to the quilt. "So, Eve is here for good."

"Yes."

"When is the funeral?"

"Tomorrow. Didn't have anyone to notify, so soon as the casket's built, the reverend's ready."

"Will you take Eve?"

The question had crossed his mind, but he hadn't had much chance to think about it. "Do you think she should go?"

"I guess so. We took Forrest and Lilly to Joe's funeral. Otherwise, wouldn't she wonder what happened…to the body and all?"

"I guess so. I don't know what to do with a kid." He ran a hand through his hair distractedly.

"I don't reckon anyone does, Tye. You just sort of have to learn it as you go along. And as long as you're trying to do what's best for them, you can't go too far wrong."

Their eyes met again in the lantern light.

"I don't mean for this to be a concern between us," he said gently, meaning Eve, though she was much more than a concern. She was a responsibility, a person to share the rest of their lives with, a helpless human who needed comfort and love.

"I know that," she said, speaking as fairly as she always did. He'd been the one taking advantage. Knowing she didn't think less of Tye because of his parentage, he'd expected she wouldn't think less of Eve for hers. He'd taken that for granted.

So far Meg was doing all the giving and he was doing all the taking, and that shamed him. But he had nothing to give except hard work, and as yet that hadn't paid off in any visible manner.

Lord, she was beautiful! She'd let down her hair and brushed it until it gleamed. The honey-colored tresses cascaded across her pale shoulders. What on earth did he have to give her that was worthy of her?

The ring. He would get her father's ring for her.

And the ranch; he'd do everything in his power to make it the best it could be. For her. Because she loved it so, and because it meant so much to her.

"I'll come with you, Tye."

"What?" He'd lost the thread of their conversation.

"To the funeral tomorrow," she clarified.

He felt as if a stone were lodged in his chest, and he had to work to breathe around it. "Are you sure you want to do that?"

"I'm sure. It'll be better if we're both there."

She was right. If he went alone, tongues would wag doubly fast. He nodded.

"Now, you'll let me see to your leg." She stood and moved to leave the room. "The water is still hot, it will only take a min—"

Tye caught her wrist and stopped her from leaving.

She stared down at his hand and her pulse fluttered in her throat. He felt the gentle throb in her wrist, too, and loosened his hold. The scent of violets encamped in his senses, and when she raised her luminous eyes to his face, his heart threatened to leap from his body. "Thank you," he said simply.

"Let me get the water and towels," she said.

He freed her hand. For a long moment she didn't move. Finally, with a swish of linen, she opened the door and left.

Tye removed his cotton drawers with a groan and covered himself with the sheet. Her nursing had become pure torture. He purposefully counted patchwork stars on the rumpled quilt.

She returned and he still sat on the side of the bed.

He helped her place the oilcloth beneath his leg but didn't recline, as was his usual position while she treated his leg. She used tongs to wring the first towel, then, gingerly, her fingers. He stared at the outline of her breasts beneath her soft linen gown and noted each gentle movement with tormentingly rapt attention. The image of covering them with his hands nearly made him groan aloud again.

She raised her face. "Ready?"

He tore his gaze to hers and nodded, welcoming the distraction.

Gently, she laid the steaming towel on his scarred thigh. He rode the sensation of pain until too quickly it dulled, and her hair became his focus. He wanted to reach out and touch the silky tresses, wanted to know if they felt every bit as glorious and warm as they appeared in the golden light. As he'd cleaned and brushed the mountain lion's fur, he'd been reminded of Meg, of tawny beauty and softness that disguised underlying strength.

His fingers tingled with the wanting.

She replaced the cooling cloth with another hot one, and he barely even noticed. Her hands were red from the heat, and he had the sudden urge to hold them between his, kiss them, press them to his own hot flesh.

"I'm sorry," she said.

He focused on her eyes. "What?"

"That hurt you."

He must have made a sound. He shook his head. "No."

Finally, she blotted his thigh dry and reached for the liniment bottle. "No," he said. "Not tonight."

"But, Tye, it—"

"No," he said firmly.

She drew her hand back. "Did I do something—"

"You've done everything right. Everything. It's…it's intolerable for me."

"What is, Tye? The pain?"

"No, not the pain. You! This! Us!" He gestured with a sweep of one hand, encompassing her in her thin linen gown and him in nothing, and the fingers of that hand ended up thrust into his hair against his scalp, frustration and thwarted desire eating him alive.

With a curse, he tugged the protective sheet from beneath his leg and tossed it aside. He pulled the covers over himself. "Get into bed."

Meg obediently set her supplies aside, blew out the lamp and crawled into bed. The erotic scent of her hair drifted to him like a siren call.

Tye thought of Eve out in the other room. He thought of the funeral they would attend the following day. He thought of the cows he had to milk in the morning and those he'd have to round up and brand in another week, and into the night he concentrated on anything but his wife beside him.

And finally he slept. And dreamed of her.

She smelled as wonderful as he remembered. Her hair was as velvety thick and soft as he'd only before imagined. One slender arm across his torso brought her plush breasts against his chest. With only the thin layer of linen separating their skin, heat radiated between their bodies. Her hard nipples brushed his side, rubbed the back of his wrist. He turned his hand and greedily cupped a fleshy mound. She laid her head on his shoulder, her hair a taunting caress against his face and neck.

He groaned. He was as stiff and ready as he had been for weeks. She pushed her breast into his palm and made an eager mewling sound in the back of her throat.

Her breath ruffled the hair on his chest, hardened his nipples. He rolled on his side toward her.

Beneath the bedclothes, he fumbled in the darkness, found her rounded backside and pulled her against him hard, pushing against her at the same time.

She wrapped her arm around his neck and her warm breath grazed his ear.

Quite naturally, he slid his hands beneath the hem of her gown and raised it, his fingers sliding along warm, satin skin, molding against her defined hip-bone, dipping in at her waist, drifting higher and drawing a shiver from her as he found her naked breast and rolled her nipple between his fingers.

Meg pressed her face against his neck, and he leaned above her. He ran his hand back down, dipped a finger in and around her navel, discovered a silken thatch of curls and tested the dewy folds beneath.

She curled her fingers into his hair and pressed her lips against his neck with a smothered cry. He shifted his weight onto her.

Their bodies seemed made for each other, hers eager, warm and pliant, his seeking, parting her thighs, easing into her with careful restraint.

Nothing had ever felt so wonderful, so fulfilling and tantalizing at the same time. Nothing he'd ever done had been this important, this all-consuming and alive.

Her knees hugged him snugly, her body sheathing him tightly, her arms locked around his neck.

This was a dream come true. He took time to run his palms against her skin, to enjoy the feminine curves and textures and to elicit her sighs of pleasure.

The mildness of their first joining quickly disappeared.

Her entire body tensed against him.

Her teeth dug into his neck.

Tye had never concentrated as hard on anything as he did on recognizing the signals her body sent and intensifying her pleasure. "Like this?"

"Yes." Her hands moved to his hips and her fingers pressed into his flesh, restraining him.

"Slower?"

"Yes."

Tye gritted his teeth and thought about the cows.

Her breath caught and held.

"Now?"

"Yes."

He held her as tightly as possible without crushing her, kissed her damp temple, inhaled the rapturous fragrance of her hair and spent himself inside her.

Her gentle tremors encased him. Beneath him Meg's body went limp, but her fingers had come back to stroke his hair. The rigid muscles in his thigh jumped, and he eased himself to a more comfortable position for them both.

Her skin was warm and damp and very real against his. His heart thudded at a clear, precise rate. The scents of violets and musk mingled unmistakably. He wasn't sure at which point he'd become aware that he was awake and not dreaming. It didn't really matter. It had been better than any dream he'd ever had.

He smiled against her fragrant hair.

She adjusted her gown and rolled to her side. He followed, wrapping himself behind her spoon-fashion, noting her delectably round and firm backside, unable to imagine a better place to snuggle. With her scent in his head and her body tucked against his, he drifted back to sleep.

Meg awoke at sunup, the heat of Tye's long form pressed along her back. Her eyes hadn't even opened before she remembered what had transpired during the night.

A warmth bloomed in her chest, and her face and neck grew hot at the shocking memory. More so at her shocking behavior and reactions. Trying not to disturb him or jostle the bed, she untangled herself, straightened her gown and padded out to warm some water. Her body ached in embarrassing places. She needed a bath.

The fire was started and the water beginning to warm when Tye entered the kitchen behind her. She didn't turn around.

"Morning," he said softly.

"Morning."

He came up behind her and she tensed without thinking. He didn't touch her. "Are you all right?"

"I'm fine."

An uncomfortable minute passed. "I'll go milk."

She nodded, relieved. He grabbed his jacket and the door opened and closed. Quickly, Meg poured water and carried the pitcher past the sleeping child to her room. She closed herself in, removed her wrinkled nightgown and bathed, using the basin and the towels.

Her body didn't seem like her own. She smelled different. She felt different. She felt…disloyal. But that was crazy. Joe was dead.

She had loved Joe, and she'd never thought to ever take another man to her bed or to her body.

Her traitorous body. She donned her clothing swiftly, as though covering herself could hide or change what had happened.

She'd been lonely for a long time.

Besides that, she had settled herself to the idea from the start. She'd even given Tye permission. And last night…last night, with her shocking responses, she'd even given him *encouragement.*

Well, now it was done. They could end the tension of waiting and get on with their lives, their purpose. It had been sensible.

She told herself that when the men came in for breakfast and she still couldn't meet Tye's eyes. In the corner of her vision, he ate his eggs and drank his coffee.

A cry sounded from the other room, and Tye shot off the bench and around the corner.

No risk, no obligation to buy...now or ever!

HOW TO PLAY

"PINBALL WIZ"
and be eligible to receive
THREE FREE GIFTS!

1. With a coin, carefully scratch the silver circles on the opposite page. Then, including the numbers on the front of this card, count up your total pinball score and check the claim chart to see what we have for you. **2 FREE** books and a **FREE** gift!

2. Send back this card and you'll receive brand-new Harlequin Historical™ novels. These books have a cover price of $4.99 each in the U.S. and $5.99 each in Canada, but they are yours to keep absolutely **FREE**!

3. There's no catch. You're under no obligation to buy anything. We charge you nothing for your first shipment. And you don't have to make a minimum number of purchases — not even one!

4. The fact is, thousands of readers enjoy receiving books by mail from the Harlequin Reader Service®. They like the convenience of home delivery and they like getting the best new novels before they're available in stores...and they love our discount prices!

5. We hope that after receiving your free books you'll want to remain a subscriber. But the choice is yours — to continue or cancel, anytime at all! So why not take us up on our invitation, with no risk of any kind. You'll be glad you did!

FREE
MYSTERY GIFT!

We can't tell you what it is...but we're sure you'll like it! A free gift just for accepting our **NO-RISK** offer!

PLAY

"PINBALL WIZ"
2 FREE BOOKS &
A FREE GIFT!

CLAIM CHART

Score 50 or more	**WORTH 2 FREE BOOKS** PLUS A MYSTERY GIFT
Score 40 to 49	**WORTH 2 FREE BOOKS**
Score 30 to 39	**WORTH 1 FREE BOOK**
Score 29 or under	**TRY AGAIN**

YES! I have scratched off the silver circles. Please send me all the gifts for which I qualify. I understand that I am under no obligation to purchase any books, as explained on the back of this card.

349 HDL CPPK   246 HDL CPN6

Name:
_____
(PLEASE PRINT)

Address: _____ Apt.#: _____

City: _____ State/Prov.: _____ Postal Zip/ Code: _____

DETACH AND MAIL CARD TODAY!

Offer limited to one per household and not valid to current Harlequin Historical™ subscribers. All orders subject to approval.

PRINTED IN U.S.A.
© 1998 HARLEQUIN ENTERPRISES LTD. ® and TM are trademarks owned by Harlequin Enterprises Limited.

The Harlequin Reader Service® — Here's how it works:

Accepting your 2 free books and mystery gift places you under no obligation to buy anything. You may keep the books and gift and return the shipping statement marked "cancel." If you do not cancel, about a month later we'll send you 6 additional novels and bill you just $3.94 each in the U.S., or $4.19 each in Canada, plus 25¢ delivery per book and applicable taxes if any.* That's the complete price — and compared to the cover price of $4.99 in the U.S. and $5.99 in Canada — it's quite a bargain! You may cancel at any time, but if you choose to continue, every month we'll send you 6 more books, which you may either purchase at the discount price or return to us and cancel your subscription.

*Terms and prices subject to change without notice. Sales tax applicable in N.Y. Canadian residents will be charged applicable provincial taxes and GST.

If offer card is missing write to: Harlequin Reader Service, 3010 Walden Ave., P.O. Box 1867, Buffalo, NY 14240-1867

BUSINESS REPLY MAIL
FIRST-CLASS MAIL   PERMIT NO. 717   BUFFALO, NY

POSTAGE WILL BE PAID BY ADDRESSEE

HARLEQUIN READER SERVICE
3010 WALDEN AVE
PO BOX 1867
BUFFALO NY 14240-9952

NO POSTAGE
NECESSARY
IF MAILED
IN THE
UNITED STATES

Meg followed more slowly, discovering him standing and holding the sobbing child, her face buried in the crook of his neck.

"I want my mama!" Eve wailed.

"I know you do," he said gently, awkwardly patting her back. "I know."

Meg allowed herself to look into his dark eyes, and she read only concern…and the powerlessness she'd seen before. "Eve," she said. "You and I have to get prettied up for the service today. Would you like me to tie ribbons in your hair?"

"I want my mama," she said again.

She had to speak around the lump in her throat. "I think we'll get you washed up, and then you can try a couple of fresh eggs. Do you like hot cocoa?"

She rubbed her eyes with her fisted knuckles and nodded.

"Good. We'll be fine, Tye."

They locked gazes. He was going to have to trust her with this child. He couldn't look after Eve and do the work he needed to do, too. Meg knew it wasn't that he didn't trust her. He hesitated only because Eve didn't trust her yet. He didn't want Eve frightened because he wasn't there. The child seemed to draw comfort from him.

Meg identified well with that feeling.

"I'm leaving you with Meg to eat and get ready," he said, and bent to place her on her bare feet on the floor.

With eyes as round as saucers and her lower lip trembling, Eve watched him turn and go back toward the kitchen. Seconds later, the door opened and closed. Those violet eyes latched warily onto Meg's face.

"Well, kiddo, we may as well get used to one another," Meg said.

Eve didn't speak a word the whole time Meg fed her and dressed her and brushed and tamed her gleaming black hair. She said nothing until Tye returned to change, and then she asked where the dog had gone.

It seemed odd doing all these personal things for a small person she'd only just met, but the thought that there was no one else and that Eve had no choice but to trust her softened Meg's heart toward the child even more. Tye had told Meg that Eve would go to an orphanage if she didn't come here. She could have been fostered out to anyone. Anyone.

But she hadn't been. By some divine providence she'd been entrusted to Tye and Meg. That duty was weighty and sobering, but Meg knew now she wouldn't shirk or resent it.

Everybody needed to feel safe. And she vowed Eve would feel safe with them.

Tye entered the kitchen and poured himself a cup of coffee. Meg observed him standing near the stove, Joe's shirt stretched across his broad shoulders, one hand resting at his hip, and a responding thrill shot through her chest. The memory of what they'd done in the secretive cloak of night shocked and excited her at the same time, and she fought to control her reactions lest he turn and catch her and know what she'd been thinking.

The sun hadn't come out that morning. She went

in search of a coat for Eve, finding a long woolen sweater and buttoning her into it while Tye changed into what she'd come to think of as his wedding suit.

She and Tye donned hats and jackets and the three of them rode on the wagon into town. Reverend Baker, Rosa Casals, Jed Wheeler and a few saloon patrons were the only ones joining them at the brief graveside service.

They stood on the rocky patch of ground on the outskirts of Aspen Grove where crude markers jutted from the earth in no particular pattern. Someone had built a wooden fence years ago, and a church committee fought time and weather each spring by repairing and whitewashing it.

Meg had never before attended a funeral that didn't take place in the church and conclude here. She glanced around at the few mourners, listened to the reverend read from his Bible and couldn't bear to see the service end without a song or a conventional gesture of some sort.

Reverend Baker glanced around, too. Tye stared at the casket they'd lowered into the fresh opening in the ground and tirelessly held the orphaned Eve.

Meg's heart fluttered, but she opened her mouth and started singing, ''Amazing grace, how sweet the sound...''

To her complete and delighted surprise Tye joined her, his voice a clear, true baritone that carried across the windy hillside. Rosa and the reverend joined them, and after three verses, they stood in silence for several minutes.

Jed and the other men broke off and headed back toward Main Street.

Rosa hugged Eve and Tye. "I'll be packing and leaving," she said to him. "Royce Parks is coming for me day after tomorrow."

"Well, good luck," he said with a nod. "I hope you're happy with him."

"Five children will keep me busy," she said with a rueful smile. "I probably won't have too much time to worry over being happy." She ran a hand over Eve's hair. "You take good care of her, now."

"We will," he promised.

Rosa turned, took Meg's gloved hand and gave her a warm smile that revealed a crooked tooth. "Enjoy this new family," she said with a squeeze. "And don't settle for anything less than all you want out of life."

"Thank you," Meg said. "Best wishes on your marriage."

With pursed lips, Rosa nodded. She turned and walked away. Eventually the reverend followed.

Tye nodded to Meg and they climbed onto the wagon seat and headed for the ranch. The sun broke through the clouds as they reached their land, and Eve had fallen asleep against Meg's side.

Tye carried her in, placed her on the bed and changed into his work clothes.

"I didn't know you could sing," Meg said as he crossed the kitchen.

Tye studied the way the bow of Meg's apron flattered her nicely rounded backside and remembered the silken feel of her bottom. "Don't know many

church songs,'' he replied. "You picked one I knew.''
He stepped behind her, and she edged away as though
she were uncomfortable with the closeness.

She picked up a pan. "What's your favorite pie?''

He studied the silky-looking tendrils that hung
against the back of her neck, wanting to press his lips
there. "Don't have a favorite,'' he said finally.

He stood right behind her, his lips near her ear.

From his vantage point, he noticed the pink blush
creep up her ivory cheek. Was she embarrassed about
what they'd done? She obviously wasn't comfortable
with him. Did he still seem like a stranger to her?

"I haven't even kissed you,'' he said, realizing it
at the same time he spoke it. He hadn't courted her,
hadn't eased her into a physical relationship, and now
he regretted his lack of romantic preparation.

Her skin grew redder than ever. She deliberately
shied away from his nearness, but still she said nothing.

Perhaps it had suited her just fine, after all. He'd
known whores who wouldn't kiss the customers. Was
kissing too intimate for her? Were her kisses something she'd saved for Joe?

"Kisses are for lovers—is that what you're thinking?'' he asked, not hiding the resentment in his tone.

Meg's heart ricocheted inside her breast and embarrassment clawed at her skin. She hadn't been
thinking anything. She didn't know what to think!

"What are *we*?'' he asked.

She didn't know what they were. She wasn't sure
of anything anymore, least not herself or her feelings.

His boots thudded across the floor toward the hooks. The door opened and closed, and he was gone.

Meg released the breath she'd been holding and pressed her hand to her thudding heart. She closed her eyes and a tear rolled down her cheek.

Silently, so as not to wake Eve, she entered her room and opened the horsehide trunk at the foot of the bed. She touched Joe's hairbrush, his razor and mug and picked up the bundle of letters, reminding herself, castigating herself.

She'd done what had needed doing. She'd done what Joe would have had her do. She'd clung to his dream with all her being and held his memory and his land dear.

Why, then, did she look twice at the hairs caught in the bristles of his brush, trying to remember their exact color? Why did the image of shiny dark hair and strong, callused hands come to the forefront of her thoughts?

Meg held the letters to her breast, tried to recapture their importance and sentiment, but heard only Tye's questioning words: *Kisses are for lovers.... What are we?*

Chapter Nine

The sky overhead had turned dark and the gray underbellies of fat rain clouds hung over the landscape. Tye strode to the barn, not eager to spend time cooped up with the men yet not willing to force his company on Meg. He uncoiled and recoiled the length of new rope he'd been dragging behind his horse for weeks in hopes of loosening it up. The hemp was finally getting soft and pliable, and, satisfied, he looped it over a nail and pulled down his saddle.

Perching on a nail keg in the open barn door, he worked oil into the leather, noting the first pelting drops of rain that spattered in the dust outside. That day he'd awakened more relaxed and feeling better than he had in a long time. The memory of Meg's eager body and their unexpectedly satisfying union left him half-aroused and more than happy with himself.

But her embarrassment and avoidance had dimmed his pleasure. What was going on now? Was she sorry? She'd been the one to suggest he satisfy his needs with her, and he never would have if he hadn't known she'd been as eager and as ready as he was.

And the more he thought back over it, the more he was sure he hadn't pressured her. He didn't know which of them had actually initiated the act; it had been a gradual yet mutual joining; she had been a willing participant. He wasn't dull enough to think he'd done anything against her wishes.

But maybe that assessment was unfair. Maybe she'd been half-asleep and not really using all her faculties for a decision.

No doubt Joe had known the proper way to make love to a lady. He'd probably never been driven by his baser instincts. Meg knew Tye had been with other women. Perhaps that dirtied him in her esteem, too.

Or maybe she hadn't liked it.

Tye recalled her moist welcome, her eager movements, the way she clutched at him, clung to him. No, she'd liked it.

The oily rag stilled on the leather. He stared at the worn saddle. She'd liked it. His weakness for her had him aroused just remembering.

Another thought stole in to eat away at his short-lived pleasure. Maybe in the darkness of night she could pretend he was Joe. And in the daylight she had to see him for who he was.

The thought hit him like a kick in the chest. It knotted his stomach and sickened him.

He stood, grabbing up the can of oil and hurling it against a wooden beam with all his might. With a disappointing thud, the can hit the wood and fell to the hard-packed dirt.

Tye kicked his saddle and pain shot up his leg.

He limped in a circle and cursed inventively until Purdy appeared from the back room. "Somethin' ailin' ya?"

Tye waved him off, leaned against the doorjamb and lit a smoke. He inhaled deeply and held it in his lungs until they burned, then drew another punishing breath and finally exhaled.

Major appeared from the depths of the barn and sniffed around Tye's ankles. Tye glanced down at Joe's dog. He looked around the inside of Joe's barn, then peered through the sheets of rain at Joe's house.

Quickly finishing with his saddle, he returned the supplies to their shelves and saddled a horse. He wasn't getting anything done here; he might as well ride into town. That's where everyone would be until the rain either let up or got so bad they had to go ride the river for stuck cows.

He donned his hat and slicker and mounted the horse, riding slowly past the house. He peered at the light in the window, noted the smoke coming from the chimney and, as if a ghost were on his tail, spurred the mare into a run for Aspen Grove.

Meg couldn't say she was surprised that Tye didn't come for supper. He hadn't remained home evenings before Eve had arrived, but she'd hoped that the child being here would make him feel obligated to stay. Obviously, it made no difference.

"Where's Tye?" Eve sat near the fire, her ever present rag doll in her lap.

Meg looked up from the dress she was mending. "He went into town."

"When will he come back?"

"Probably not till late. After you've gone to sleep." *After I've gone to sleep.*

The child's lower lip quivered at that reply, and Meg chastised herself for her thoughtlessness. She stuck her needle in the fabric and laid the skirt aside. "What shall we do to pass the time this rainy night?"

Eve shrugged.

"What did you and your mother do in the evenings?"

"Mama worked at night."

"Oh." Meg bit her lip. She was really earning favor this way. "Well, I work in the daytime, so you and I will have time together in the evenings."

"What about Tye? Will he be here?"

Meg wished she had an answer. She wished she knew what lured him to town every night. "I don't know. Sometimes. What would you like to do? Shall I read to you?"

Eve moved to sit on the footstool and adjusted her skirts primly. "Okay."

Meg opened a drawer of her grandmother's china cabinet and pulled out *McGuffy's Eclectic Reader,* which had been hers as a child, as well as a couple of books Lilly had left behind. Running her fingers over the cover of the Charles Perrault collection of fairy tales, she found she missed Gwynn and Harley's visits. Her in-laws had never stayed long, finding the house and amenities lacking, but at least the family had been a diversion for an afternoon or evening.

"Whose book is it?" Eve asked innocently.

"It's my niece Lilly's."

"What's a niece?"

"A niece? Well, if you have a brother or sister, their little girl is your niece."

"You have a brother or a sister?"

"I have several. And several nieces, too." Before she had to explain that Lilly was her niece by marriage, she opened the book and read.

Eve listened politely, occasionally stroking her doll's dress. Halfway through "Puss In Boots," Meg stopped. "Are you enjoying the story?"

Eve nodded sleepily.

"Shall we save the rest for tomorrow night?"

"All right."

Meg poured Eve a glass of milk and herself a cup of coffee. They ate the few cookies that were left.

"Can Major come in tonight?" Eve asked.

"To sleep with you?"

She nodded.

"I guess it doesn't hurt anything for him to sleep in here." They made a trip to the outhouse and Major found them on their way back. Meg dressed Eve in her nightgown and took her time brushing her thick dark hair into shining waves and braiding it. Finally, she tucked her into the pallet.

"If Tye comes, tell him I was a good girl," Eve said.

"He knows you're a good girl."

"Okay, but make sure he knows."

"Why, Eve?"

The tiny girl shrugged. "'Cause Mama said I must be good for Tye."

Meg took one of the dark curls that escaped near Eve's ear in her fingers. "I'll tell him."

Eve gave her a halfhearted smile and rolled to her side, the doll beneath her chin.

Meg stroked her hair tenderly, wishing she was more of a comfort to the child. Maybe she'd needed to talk about the funeral that day. Meg didn't know what to say to her. Tye should have been here for her. She was his obligation, after all.

How thoughtless of him to go off and abandon Eve when she needed him here with her. He'd been concerned enough about the girl to accept responsibility for her, and now that she was here, where had that concern flown?

Meg worked herself into a full-blown huff, then wondered if she was really mad about him leaving Eve or if she was mad about him leaving her.

Both, she realized. For reasons she didn't wish to examine, she felt abandoned, too. Well, Tye was her husband. She had every right to expect him to behave like one.

Eve had fallen asleep, so Meg checked the fire and took herself off to bed.

She'd been dozing when sometime later she awoke to the sound of Tye's clothes rustling and his weight dipping the mattress.

He smelled of rain and faintly of smoke, but she didn't detect liquor.

She couldn't say why she rested easier when he

was beside her. It was as though her house were in order when he came home, and so, anger forgotten, she allowed herself to drift back into sleep. She'd barely closed her eyes when his hand threaded into her hair and his fingers stroked her cheek.

Instinctively, she brought her hand up to his and nuzzled his palm. Warmth spread through her insides at his gentle caress, and her heart started its crazy pounding. Guilt and ecstasy warred, and sensory pleasure and aggressive need won out. She rolled against him and pressed herself along the length of his strong body.

He gripped her scalp hard and pulled her face up to his, unerringly finding her mouth in the darkness and covering it with his. For a first kiss, it wasn't hesitant or exploratory. It was demanding and eager. This urgency between them was foreign and somehow shameful, but Meg held her misgivings at bay by kissing him back and losing herself in the sensual gratification.

He didn't taste like liquor; he tasted like Tye and faintly like mint. His lips were firm and insistent, and she welcomed the kiss while denying in some distant recess of her mind that she shouldn't.

He kissed her long and breathlessly, pausing to taste her lips, her chin, her cheek. He kissed her with slow and tender persuasiveness, blocking caution from her mind and resistance from her body, and she remembered his words, *Kisses are for lovers.*

His tongue coaxed her lips apart and he kissed her deeply and soundly and with delectable thoroughness. Meg had never been aroused like this. She squirmed against him. He wedged a knee between her thighs, a poor substitute for her desire, but she made an appreciative sound.

He tugged at her nipples through her cotton gown until she wanted to cry her frustration.

And then his hands began their marvelous journey beneath her gown, along her electrified skin, setting her nerve endings ablaze.

Meg clutched at his shoulders and drew him against her, over her, into her. Nothing existed but the two of them and this wild, unchecked quest for release. The aching fullness brought an immediate and unexpected wash of pleasure, and she sobbed it against his mouth.

"Say my name," he said insistently, framing her jaw with one strong hand.

Meg fought for a coherent thought. "Tye," she whispered.

"Again."

"Tye." This time the word came out as a hoarse utterance.

"Again."

She said it once more and he thrust against her forcefully, muscles straining, as though he sought to grind himself into her very being. The metal headboard thudded unrestrainedly against the wall and Meg gripped the sheets for a measure of stability.

He groaned.

She whispered his name.

He slid to her side and gathered her tightly against him.

And Meg cried. A purging release of emotion and

pleasure, and something far deeper than their physical bonding.

"I didn't hurt you?" he asked, his tone conveying distress at the thought.

"No."

He kissed her temple and smoothed her hair, and beneath her palm his racing heart slowed its pace. Outside the rain pounded steadily.

A twinge of guilt pierced her when she thought of the letters in the trunk at the foot of the bed, so she pushed the thought from her mind and concentrated on the softness of the mattress beneath her, the warmth and strength of Tye's arms around her, the enticing smell of his skin and his solid body along hers.

Here was someone to hold her. Someone to share the nights. She wouldn't feel guilty for that.

The following day Purdy remained at the house with Eve while Gus, Tye and Meg rode out to search for cows, a task more suited to spring. Carefully, they inspected the marshes for animals that had wandered too far from the bank and become immobilized in the mud.

Meg called out and the men joined her, finding only the head and horns of a steer visible above the water. Tye's gray had proven himself the horse with the ability to pull on a rope without getting skittish, so Tye waded out and slipped a loop over the steer's horns.

He waded back, mounted, wound the end of the rope around his saddle horn loose enough so that he could drop it quickly, then urged his horse backward.

The cow's struggles aided the gray, and the pulling tore the animal loose and dragged him up on the bank.

Tye dropped his rope immediately.

The steer gained his feet and charged. Prepared, Tye galloped out of the way and observed as the animal shook his head, then found some brush and worked off the rope.

Meg rode out to recover it and carried the muddy rope back to Tye.

He took it from her, their gloved hands bumping. "Good job, cowboy."

God, he loved her smile. Even with her hair hidden beneath a dripping hat and wearing a slicker that could fit two of her, she was the prettiest thing he'd ever seen. He didn't tell her so. He'd learned she was uncomfortable with any expression of their attraction or any words of an intimate nature. Her reasoning was still a puzzle, but his fear that she had to force herself to imagine him as her past husband had been ungrounded.

She might not pretend he was Joe, but she no doubt wished it were Joe here with her instead of him. She'd loved her first husband. The fact wounded him anew each time he let himself think of it.

Tye headed them along the river in search of calves or weaker stock. Meg rode alongside him. "Eve asked about you last night."

"What did she ask?"

"She wanted to know where you were and if you were going to be with us in the evenings."

"What did you tell her?"

"I didn't know what to tell her, Tye. I tried to assure her you'd be there sometimes."

He didn't say anything. From beneath his hat brim, he just studied the landscape with a watchful eye.

"She's a good little girl, Tye, but I think she needs you to spend some time with her right now. You're the one she trusts. You're her only comfort in her suddenly lost world. She probably needs to talk about her mother."

"I'll do what I can."

No explanation. No excuses. No promises. Irritated, Meg looked away.

They'd gathered a few calves and headed them back toward the herds by the time she spoke again. "What are we going to do about Eve during roundup?"

"What do you mean?"

"I mean, I've never had a child to look out for before. I work the cattle just like everyone else. We're too shorthanded for anyone to stay at the house with her."

"Who stays to do chores?"

"Purdy. Riding is harder for him."

Tye nodded. "Eve can come to camp with us. She'll stay with the chuck wagon. Gus handles that, right?"

"He and one of the fellas from the Bar Sixteen."

"That way we'll be with her every night. There's a meeting day after tomorrow at the Bar Sixteen to plan how we'll work the territory. Everybody's short-handed. We'll camp at the usual sites. It might take us a lot longer at each one than it used to because of so few reps."

"It'll be a far cry better than the roundups during the war," she said. "Most of us barely kept enough cattle alive until spring to have any to sell. And half of them aren't branded. We'll have to trust one another to sort them out fairly this year."

"You held it together, though." His words were as serious as his expression. "I can't imagine how, but you did it."

"I had to keep looking to the future," she said. He'd reined in near an outcropping of rust-colored rocks, and she stopped beside him. "Every day and every night I prayed for the war to end, and for..."

"For Joe to come home?"

Tears blurred her vision. "Yes. And my self-pity was so small, considering what he was probably going through, what all of you were going through."

"You couldn't have spent much time feeling sorry for yourself. You had too much work to do."

She shrugged. "Some."

"You wouldn't have been human if you hadn't felt a little sorry for yourself."

"Did you?"

"Sure. Cried in my beans every time my toes got so cold I couldn't feel them anymore. Once my regiment got lost, and after marching in circles for two days, we stumbled into a whole camp of Rebs. After the smoke cleared and the remainder of us hightailed it for cover... Well, let's just say that was one of my more self-pitying days."

Meg studied his profile against the late afternoon

sun. Tye was always frank. And he always managed to make her feel better about herself...about nearly everything...except Joe.

At first she'd been so appreciative of his insight into the probability of the army actually having shipped the correct body. She'd experienced a certain kinship because he'd been a soldier like her Joe.

But now...now so many confusing elements played into her already chaotic feelings that he was more a chafing reminder than a comfort.

He reminded her that Joe was gone.

He reminded her of all that she'd lost.

And he reminded her that she was a woman.

A woman who'd loved her husband. She'd wanted to be Joe's wife since she'd been a young girl. She'd dreamed of it, planned for it, waited for the day. And she'd married him and pledged her love and fidelity.

Meg tried to recall how those vows about "until death do us part" went. She certainly hadn't stopped loving Joe after his death. What had that part meant?

"So does that sound okay with you?"

She refocused. "What's that?"

"Eve coming to camp with us."

"I guess we don't have a choice, do we?" Any choice had been Tye's when he'd accepted responsibility for the child.

As if reading her thoughts, he said, "Do you resent her? Or the extra work?"

Meg looked inside herself and replied honestly. "No, Tye. I don't resent her. I'm grateful for her company."

He adjusted his hat, an unnecessary act but obviously a gesture to cover his reaction to that comment. Nudging his horse with his heels, he picked up their pace.

Tye spent that very evening in town. But this time he didn't wake her when he came to bed.

A long and tiring week passed until the rain stopped and the sun came out and roundup began. Hunt and Aldo rode out with the other reps to locate and sort strays. Gus and Lem Higgins set up camp. The two old men entertained Eve while they cooked and doctored ranch hands and kept fires going.

After chasing cattle, smelling scorched hides and watching dehorning, Meg didn't eat much that first evening. The men bathed in the river, then Tye followed her to the bank and stood guard with his back turned while she washed in the frigid water.

The rest of the men played poker, but Tye read from *Alice in Wonderland* by the fire. Ever since Meg had spoken to him, he'd made a particular effort to spend time with the child. A few times he'd even brushed her hair until she grew sleepy-eyed.

Meg watched him now, reading to Eve, patiently stopping to answer her never-ending questions. Against her will, her thoughts strayed to all the nights the past week that he'd come to bed and not touched her.

She should have been happy because she didn't have to experience the sanity-eating guilt that had followed both highly charged encounters.

She had only her experiences with Joe to compare with what had happened between her and Tye, and the comparison shamed her. She'd been happy with Joe. She'd loved him. Theirs had been a respectful, appropriate relationship.

Tye, on the other hand, made her crazy.

She hadn't married him for love. The physical details of their marriage were supposed to be perfunctory and matter-of-fact, not disturbing and memorable—definitely not unforgettable. The fact that she was even thinking about it now was all wrong. What on earth was the matter with her?

Tye settled Eve into her bedroll, spoke with Gus, then saddled a fresh horse and rode off.

Meg dragged her aching body into her own roll, clamped her eyes shut and cursed herself. Why did she get so angry over what he did in town at night?

He wasn't visiting the sporting women, of that she was fairly sure. He'd have to be more than a mere mortal to keep up the pace he did during the day and entertain ladies in the evening.

This camp would keep them apart at night now, and she should be grateful for the time to regroup. She had to force her thoughts on to other subjects, and she hated herself for that growing weakness.

She awoke once during the night, glanced toward Eve and discovered Tye awake on Eve's other side. Their eyes met in the waning firelight, his dark and vigilant.

"Go back to sleep," he said softly. "You have a couple of hours left."

She closed her eyes and obeyed.

Several evenings later, the reps from the Double Oarlock, along with Mitch Heden, shared their campfire and their meal. Meg scooped a ladle of stew over Tye's biscuits.

"Thank you, ma'am," he said, and moved to sit with the others.

Meg served the next hand, prepared herself a plate and sat on one of the few stools Gus had brought along.

Mitch spoke to Tye, and they laughed.

She hadn't seen him laugh often. The corners of his eyes crinkled, and his teeth shone white in the stubble that covered his face since they'd been camped.

He sat perched on his bedroll, his right leg extended as it usually was. He'd unbuttoned his leather jacket and left his hat somewhere. The firelight danced on his hair.

Here among these men, he seemed no different than any of them. If the reps or the ranchers on this roundup considered Tye beneath them, they hadn't shown it. Mitch spoke to him the way he did to any rancher.

Tye glanced up and met her gaze.

She smiled and broke off a piece of her biscuit.

Ma'am, he'd called her again. They'd shared the intimacies of the marriage bed in the dark, but he never called her by name. As she remembered his forceful insistence that she say his, and the obvious pleasure it gave him, a glow that she had no business conjuring up tonight or any night ignited inside her.

She tamped the feelings down, unwilling to give them credence, afraid to give them a name. She had a level head and a goal in her sights. Tye was her partner. Feeling more than friendship or even fondness and appreciation wasn't in the plan.

Meg finished her meal and helped Lem wash the tin plates and cups in a bucket. Gus left for the Circle T to check on Purdy and the house. Mitch and his men called their thanks and rode back to their herd.

Eve had moved to stand beside Tye. He snagged her around the waist and pulled her onto his lap, where she sat, content to stroke the dress of the doll she seldom laid down.

"Are you leaving tonight?" she asked, and Meg strained to hear his reply.

"I was thinkin' on it," he said.

"Where do you go?"

"I have things to take care of in town. Grown up things."

"Maybe I can come with you."

He studied her face. "I don't think so. You need to stay here and go to sleep."

"I'm not tired."

Meg observed Tye's gentle expression. Eve gave him one of those pleading, violet-eyed looks. He shifted her to his other leg. "I don't have to go until later."

The child bounced delightedly and patted his cheek, her smile brighter than the stars overhead.

Meg poured herself and Tye fresh cups of coffee and joined them near the fire. Her body ached everywhere, and she eased herself down with a groan. Immediately her thoughts went to Tye's leg. He hadn't seemed to limp too badly for all the strain he'd been giving it. "How's your leg?"

"Holding out. I've used the liniment every night."

"I noticed the bottle was missing."

"Did you need it?"

"Wouldn't mind some on my shoulders."

"I'll do it for you before you turn in."

She agreed with a nod.

"Tye's not going to take care of things till later," Eve said.

Meg smiled and nodded.

She and Tye locked gazes. Meg chastised herself for the direction her thoughts took just meeting his eyes.

"Why can't Major come to camp with us?" the child asked.

"Major stays to guard the house and barn," Meg explained. Joe hadn't had enough time before the war to teach the dog about cows. And Meg tended to spoil the animal rather than train him.

"When do I get to ride a horse?"

Poor kid was probably bored within the confines of the campsite. Gus tried to entertain her, but he had work to do, too.

"You can ride with me for a while in the morning," Tye said.

Her eyes widened. "On *your* horse?"

"Yep."

She grinned. "What's his name?"

Tye glanced at Meg. The horse he preferred was from her herd. After riding several, he'd chosen the gray for her surefootedness and temperament.

Meg shrugged. "Doesn't have a name that I know of. She's not one we foaled. Guess Tye'll have to name her."

"How about Gray?" Eve asked.

"She's not really gray," Tye said. "That's kind of a trick on your eyes. Her skin is black and her hair is salt-and-pepper. She'll get lighter as she gets older."

"What, then?" Eve asked.

He considered for a moment. "Sweetfeet," he said with a grin.

"Sweetfeet?" Eve giggled her amusement, and Meg joined their laughter.

Tye told them about an army horse he'd ridden during the war who used to bite his shoulder when he let his guard down.

Despite her denial that she was tired, Eve snuggled against him and her eyelids drooped. Before long, she slept.

Tye tucked her into her bedroll and returned with the liniment. "Loosen the top of your shirt," he said.

Meg glanced to find Lem already rolled up and snoring beneath the wagon. Gus had planned to stay the night at the ranch, and Hunt and Aldo had gone to play cards with the Bar Sixteen hands.

Not embarrassed enough to miss out on relief for her aching muscles, she unbuttoned her flannel shirt and let it sag around her arms.

Tye slid the straps of her chemise from her shoulders, and shivers skittered up her neck and along her spine at his touch. Seconds later, his hard, callused fingers worked the liniment into her flesh.

She closed her eyes and gave herself over to his strong hands and the penetrating warmth. Meg smiled at her thoughts.

"What's so funny?" His voice beside her ear surprised her. She hadn't realized he'd been leaning forward to see her face.

"If I'd known all it took to have you stick around for the evening was a pitiful, pansy-eyed look, I'd have had Eve work on you a lot sooner."

His hands stilled.

She turned to see he wasn't smiling. She placed her hand over his. "Tye?"

"I don't go because I want to," he said gruffly.

"Then why do you go?" she asked. "Nobody makes you."

He pulled his hands away, and she turned as he corked the bottle.

"Tye?"

He set the bottle aside and stood, reaching for his leather jacket where it lay near his bedroll.

"Please don't leave tonight."

His movements stilled. He straightened without picking up the coat. Slowly, he turned to face her.

She hadn't pulled up the shirt, and his gaze dusted her shoulders, her hair, her face. His compliance was evident in the tender way he studied her even before he nodded. "All right."

She took a few steps closer, shocking herself with her boldness. "Kiss me."

Chapter Ten

Tye's expression changed from tender to hesitant. He glanced toward the wagon, but he moved forward, took hold of her upper arms and lowered his head to hers. .

Meg sensed the underlying caution in his hands and lips. He kissed her gently, deliberately, ending the kiss and meeting her eyes.

"Now say my name," she said.

At that echo of his own passionate demand, which they both remembered vividly, his dark eyes blazed. "Why?"

"Because I want to hear you say it. You've called me 'ma'am' from the day we met at the mercantile."

"Meg," he said tightly. "Meg Hatcher."

Meg Hatcher. She'd never heard the two names spoken together before, never even thought them. But they had been spoken now, making the name real. The use of Tye's last name seemed disloyal somehow. She pulled away and adjusted her shirt before he could see the pain in her eyes, before she could add any more foolishness to her impulsive behavior.

Had she thought to test him? Had she hoped to prove something to one of them? She had. She'd convinced herself of her failing common sense. "Go," she said. "Go on to town and do whatever it is you do."

"I said I'd stay tonight."

"I don't want you to. I want you to go."

"That wasn't what you wanted to hear, was it? You didn't want to be reminded of who you're married to."

"No—yes, I mean...I don't know."

"Sweet Meg has a dirty little secret, doesn't she?"

Hesitantly, she turned back. "What do you mean?"

His dark eyes had become hard, his expression unreadable. The change frightened her. He leaned forward and ran his thumb across her lips. "You like it when I touch you. You ache when I kiss you. You're burnin' for Tye Hatcher, not your precious Joe, and you're ashamed of it."

Her cheeks flamed. Her ears roared. She wanted to cover them and turn her face away, but she didn't. She couldn't. She couldn't move or think. Her lips burned where he'd touched her.

"What would those Telford biddies think if they knew how eager you were in the dark? If they knew how you groaned my name and let me put my hands all over you? If they knew how hot and wet you were for me?"

Stunned, Meg fought to comprehend what was happening. He couldn't be saying these things to her. He couldn't be humiliating her and deliberately hurting her like this. She brought her shaking hands up, brushing his hand aside with her wrist and covering her burning face.

"You thought you were testing me just then, but you weren't," he continued. "You were testing yourself. And you failed. You're ashamed of what you feel."

She heard him walk away. She heard his horse greet him and the creak of leather. Minutes later, hoofbeats sounded into the night.

Meg lowered her hands slowly. The fire still flickered and snapped. Eve still slept soundly several yards away. The sky was still up there, wide and black and full of stars and mysteries.

But who had she become? She didn't know. A few tears of anger and self-pity rolled down her cheeks and she brushed them away with an open palm.

Why had he said those things? How had he known? How had this whole mess happened?

She flung herself on her bedroll and stared at twinkling stars that seemed to accuse her. Damn Joe for dying on her and leaving her to this!

Damn Tye Hatcher for confusing her and jumbling everything up! Of all the stinking, conceited, rotten things to say to her. What did he expect from her?

She hoped he stayed in town all night. She hoped he moved to town. She hoped his surefooted horse threw him into a ravine and broke his other leg.

Near dawn she repented for that last wicked thought. And after Tye had entered the camp, taken care of his horse and crawled into his bedroll, she thanked God for knowing when not to listen.

*   *   *

She hadn't denied it.

Tye joined two of the reps in moving their herd to the Double Oarlock's camp. The sun had come out full and hot, and he rode the edge of the herd with sweat trickling beneath his shirt.

He should have gone to her this morning, apologized for raising his voice and saying those crude things and upsetting her. That's what a gentleman would do. It was what Joe would have done. But they both knew Tye wasn't a gentleman. And no one expected better from a good-for-nothing bastard.

Besides, he had a little pride left.

He cut off a yearling trying to break away and headed him back into the bunch.

So it was in the open between them. Meg had needed him and she'd married him. She treated him well. She'd never spoken down to him or let on as if he were beneath her. And she liked his lovemaking in the secretive cloak of night.

But she was ashamed of him.

Maybe it had been easier to pretend Joe's family and her friends snubbing her didn't bother her as long as there'd only been the ranch as a factor between them. But now there was more.

She enjoyed the physical side of marriage with him. As long as she could pretend nothing had happened or that she hadn't been affected, she had been able to cope. But he'd brought her shameful desires out in the open and her careful pretenses had been shattered.

He'd thought Meg was different. Or he'd hoped.

He'd chosen to come back here. He'd faced his heritage straight on. He had only himself to blame.

But he was here now, and he'd made a pact with Meg. She'd entrusted him with her ranch, and he'd given his word. Besides, there was Eve to consider. Tye would have to work this out for himself in his own time. He didn't know if he could live with Meg and not make love to her. Besides, he wanted children. So did she.

Neither did he know if he could make love to her and pretend. Pretend it meant nothing. Pretend it didn't happen. Pretend she wanted him for who he was and not just as a replacement or an occasional release.

He might be a lot of things, but he was not a fake. And he damned well wasn't Joe.

A few of Mitch's men took over driving the cattle through a gate into a corral, and Tye headed Sweetfeet toward the stream for a well-deserved drink. Pulling his kerchief off, he soaked the fabric and wiped his face and neck while the horse drank.

Maybe he'd deluded himself—for just a week or two—that something would really come of this marriage. But her flaming embarrassment and her lack of denial had straightened his head out quickly enough.

He was Tye Hatcher. He'd always been Tye Hatcher and he would always be Tye Hatcher. He wasn't Joe and never would be. Marrying a respectable woman in dire financial straits wouldn't change who he was or the way people saw him. Just as fighting side by side with their good sons and brothers hadn't changed the way they saw him.

It had only changed the way he'd seen himself.

He still had to prove himself.

He staked the gray in the shade near a patch of grass and joined the men branding.

"Did you see me this morning, Meg? Did you see how high up I was?" Eve demonstrated her question on tiptoe with a hand raised into the air above her head.

"I saw you. You're a good rider."

"Tye says he will let me ride all the way to town with him after the cows are all caught."

"That will be great fun, won't it?" Meg had assumed the task of washing clothes and repairing the men's foxed breeches since she *was* the only female on the range and Gus's eyesight wouldn't allow him to even find the needle anymore.

On a line stretched from a wind-bent cedar to the chuck wagon, clean, damp clothing flapped in the warm breeze. Meg concentrated on reinforcing the seat and inseam of the pair of Tye's pants she held.

"Can you read me some more of Alice?" Eve asked.

"I can't until later," Meg replied. "I have to get these chores done before supper."

Eve looked at the doll in her lap, and the brim of her bonnet hid her face.

Meg glanced up from her work. "You all right? You know I have work to do."

"I know. Tye has work to do, too. An' Gus."

For Eve's sake, Meg regretted this particularly busy season.

"I wish Major coulda come."

"He's keeping Purdy company. Maybe by next year Tye will have him used to the cows."

"Why do we have these dumb cows, anyway?"

"They're worth a lot of money. The more we keep healthy and the more that are born, the more money we can make."

"Oh." She got up and moved closer to Meg. "I got a money."

"You do?"

"Uh-huh. It's silver. I keep it in my special box that was my mama's. You want I should show it to you?"

Meg had seen the box when she'd unpacked Eve's things, and she'd noticed the child holding it a time or two. "All right."

Eve scampered to the carpetbag holding her belongings and returned with her prized possession. It looked like a simple cigar box to Meg. The child opened the container importantly, revealing the red felt lining that had been glued inside. The faint scent of cedar wafted to her. Eve proudly displayed the contents for Meg to view.

"See?" She held up a silver dollar.

"Goodness! You're a rich girl."

"Yep. And this here's my hair from when I was a baby." She unfolded a paper, revealing a silky dark curl.

Meg admired it appropriately.

"And this here is a thimble." She placed the tarnished thimble on one tiny finger and showed it to Meg.

"We could shine that up when we get back to the house," Meg offered.

"It would be shiny like yours?"

Meg showed her the sewing implement on her middle finger. "This one was my grandmother's, and it shines."

"Okay." Eve dropped it back in the box atop a few bits of ribbon and several train ticket stubs. Carefully lifting out a wrinkled handkerchief with tatted edges, she opened it for Meg to see what lay inside. Meg studied the ladies' neck chain. The polished gold pendant was round, set with rhinestones in the shape of a crescent moon—an unusual piece of jewelry.

"It's very pretty." Meg watched her refold the handkerchief and replace it. Such a pitiful few items for a child to remember a mother by. "You can wear it when you're bigger."

Eve nodded, a downhearted expression portraying her loss and misery. "Mama told me Tye was gonna be my family."

A knot formed in Meg's chest. "Yes," she whispered, thinking of the house full of parents and siblings in which she'd grown up. A sudden pang of shame pierced her. She'd been so pleased to get away from them and out on her own. She had never appreciated her blessings. "We're happy to be your family," she assured the child.

"How come you don't have your own boys and girls?"

Meg blinked, taken aback by the question. "I, um…" She couldn't explain to a five-year-old that she'd had little opportunity to have children before

Joe had gone off to war and been killed. "God just hasn't given me any babies yet."

Eve's sparkling dark eyes widened. "God gives you babies?"

It was as good an explanation as any. And true. "Yes."

Eve closed the lid of her box and a half smile turned up her rosy lips. "Golly."

Meg watched her return the box to her bag and resume her place with the doll. She toyed with the yarn hair and whispered something Meg couldn't hear.

Meg picked up her mending, wishing she could share her amusement with Tye. The easiness they'd once shared had disappeared, and Meg accepted the blame. She'd let her physical and emotional desires get in the way of their agreement. She hated herself for it, but she didn't know how to turn them off. If she'd known how, none of the unpleasantness between them would have happened.

He made her want him, pure and simple. And those feelings befuddled her.

He wanted to talk about things she didn't want to discuss. He made her feel things she didn't want to feel. He'd misinterpreted it all, but she didn't know how to straighten that out. Or if she wanted to straighten it out.

This misunderstanding was the buffer she needed to keep things safe. As long as he was angry at her and thinking she was ashamed of him, she didn't have to deal with her feelings. And right now she was too confused to deal with anything but the tasks at hand.

Meg finished her mending and took the clothes from the line so she could help Gus with the next meal.

By the time roundup ended, Tye was as grateful as everyone else for life to get back to normal. With their return to the house came the problem of their forced intimacy at night, and so, though it made her angry, his staying in town until late was a blessing. He returned home so exhausted that he fell into immediate slumber and slept like a rock.

A town social was planned for the first Saturday night after roundup to celebrate Founder's Day. For the ranchers, their wives and families and the reps, this was a much anticipated yearly event.

This year especially, the first year of normalcy after the war's end, Tye overheard dozens of conversations in which the festivity was mentioned with expectancy.

The event also coincided with something toward which Tye'd been working. As of that week, he had enough money saved to buy back Meg's ring. Declining Jed's appeals to stay on at the Pair-A-Dice, he took his final pay and made a beeline for the pawnbroker's on Friday.

Tye waited his turn while a perfumed woman in a jaunty hat perused the watches and rings and O'Roarden quoted her prices. Finally, she made a purchase and left.

O'Roarden took his time lighting a cigar, shifted it to the corner of his mouth and spoke around it. "What'll you have?"

"My wife's ring. I spoke with you and you told me how much she owed to get it back."

"Yeah." The man opened a ledger, flipped a few pages and quoted Tye the price.

Tye placed the bills on the counter.

"You got the receipt?"

"The receipt?"

"Can't sell it to ya without the receipt."

Tye met the man's eyes directly, wondering if this rule was for everyone or just for him. "I'll be back."

He stuffed the money in his pocket and stormed out the door. He'd wanted it to be a surprise. All this time he hadn't shared his plan with Meg; he didn't want to spoil it now. The only way he could get the ring without her knowing was to find the receipt. That shouldn't be too difficult; it was a small house. But he'd wanted to give it to her the following night, and that didn't leave him any time.

Returning to the ranch, he found Gus sitting in the dooryard peeling potatoes. Eve was playing with Major a few feet away.

"Watch, Tye!" she called. She threw a stick and the dog bounded after it.

Tye smiled and watched indulgently for several minutes.

"Where's Meg?" he asked.

Gus dug eyes from a potato with the end of his knife. "Rode out to check on those new calves."

"I'll be right back, Eve. When I come back, would you like to ride into town with me?"

She stopped in her tussle to get the slobbery stick away from Major. "Yes! Can I ride a horse?"

"You can help me hitch the team, how's that?"

"Aw-right!"

Tye entered the house and opened a few cupboards, finding nothing but dishes and foodstuffs. In the other room, he glanced through Meg's china cabinet, even peeking inside the sugar bowl. He made his way into the dim bedroom, feeling like a thief but still wanting to surprise Meg with the ring.

The tin on her bureau held ribbons and buttons and hairpins. He opened the top drawer, and the scent of violets drifted to his nose. He peeked beneath chemises and lace collars. The remainder of the drawers held only clothing.

Perhaps she kept it in her reticule, but he'd never seen where she kept the bag. He turned, noting the trunk at the foot of the bed, and raised the lid. Several items sat in a shallow tray-type liner. An open box held a few slips of paper, and he lifted it out, quickly finding the receipt signed by Ben O'Roarden. Tye smiled and slipped it into his shirt pocket.

As he reached to replace the box, the other contents of the trunk caught his attention. A man's hairbrush, razor and shaving mug. A stack of letters tied with a faded ribbon. A grievous feeling ate at him.

He picked them up, turning the top one so he could read the lettering. He flipped through the pile. It was plain they'd all been written by Joe.

Beneath the letters was a white dress shirt, neatly starched and pressed, and a black string tie. Coiled in the corner sat a tooled leather belt. Tye's heart constricted painfully and his breath caught in his chest.

Joe's things.

He didn't care. He shouldn't care. She had her right
to her memories. Tye hadn't meant to invade her privacy, but now that he'd seen these things, shame
filled him. Tye dropped the letters on the clothing and
replaced the box. He lifted the liner out, cautious of
what he'd see beneath, but found only a crocheted
blanket and a stack of what looked like tablecloths.

He replaced the tray and closed the trunk quietly,
hating the bereft feelings that swamped him. Unerringly, his gaze moved to the spot where the pair of
black boots had stood when he'd first seen this room.
They were gone and, he realized, had been for some
time, but he hadn't given the empty spot notice until
now.

Increasing heaviness weighed on his chest. He
could have lived quite well without seeing all her
keepsakes, the things of Joe's she clung to.

It didn't matter, though. Giving the trunk a last
look and studying the bed for a moment, he left the
room. Joe was alive in her heart; that's where the
threat to Tye's chance of ever winning Meg existed.
He may have possessed Meg's body, but Joe still held
her heart.

He grabbed Eve's bonnet and left the house.

Tye patted the inside pocket of his coat, the ring
resting snugly in its flannel drawstring bag. In buying
the heirloom back, he'd done his part to pay the banknote. He could consider the pawned ring a loan of
sorts, and now he had paid Meg back. He would love
to see Niles Kestler eat his words about delivering the
foreclosure notice, but having the note paid and

knowing they had two more months of security left was satisfaction enough.

"Let's go find something for *you* now." Tye held Eve's hand securely, and she walked alongside him on the boardwalk. "I have a few coins left."

"Licorice?" she asked, her impish smile delighting him.

"If you like."

"Oh, I like licorice."

Ahead a bell tinkled. Trussed in an ebony dress and sporting a wing-brimmed black hat with a curling black feather, Edwina Telford emerged from the mercantile. Her fair-haired daughter-in-law appeared just behind her.

Edwina drew up, watching Tye and Eve approach. She took on an expression of combined puzzlement and disapproval. "What*ever* are you doing with that child, Mr. Hatcher?"

"I'm takin' her for a licorice whip, Mrs. Telford. And how are you this fine day?"

"Where are the child's parents?"

"Well now, I guess that would be Meg and me, since Eve lives with us. I'm right here and Meg is probably at the ranch fixing our supper. You'll have to excuse us so we can do our shopping and get back. I hate to miss Meg's cooking."

He strode past where she stood, an affronted expression straining her features and puffing her chest.

"Want we should save you a piece?" Eve asked Edwina on the way past.

The woman gathered her skirts and huffed away.

Her daughter-in-law gave an apologetic little smile and followed.

"Don't she like licorice, Tye?"

Tye patted Eve's hand. "I think she just got up on the wrong side of the bed this morning."

"Oh." Eve tried to look back over her shoulder, but Tye led her into the store.

Emery Parks gave Tye his usual blistering glare, then, since there were no other customers, moved to the counter where Tye waited. He noticed Eve and his eyebrows climbed his forehead. He obviously recognized her from former visits with her mother, or perhaps she'd been in with Rosa.

"Hello, Mr. Parks," came Eve's polite greeting from Tye's side.

Emery ignored her and eyeballed Tye. "What do you want?"

Tye leaned down to Eve. "Stand right here for just a second, sweetie," he whispered.

She nodded demurely.

He then lowered his face as close to Emery Parks's as possible without climbing over the counter and standing on his shirtfront. "A touch of courtesy for the child would be a good place to start."

The man's eyes widened.

"Eve said hello, Mr. Parks." Tye's low voice held a barely veiled threat. "I'd answer her if I were you."

Emery's mottled skin and the tips of his ears turned bright pink. His pale blue eyes showed his concern for what Tye might do. He cleared his throat.

Tye straightened and took Eve's hand once again.

"H-hello," Emery said to her.

Tye accepted that greeting with a curt nod. "We'll take six licorice whips, please."

The mercantile owner wrapped their candy in a scrap of paper and accepted the pennies Tye handed him.

"Thank you," Eve said.

Emery's gaze skittered to Tye but immediately returned to the child. "You're welcome."

"I'd also like a couple of work shirts," Tye added.

Emery led him to a counter where he made a selection and paid.

"Nice doin' business with ya," Tye said, touching the brim of his hat. They strolled from the store, and Tye rationed them each a piece of the savory candy.

"You like licorice, too, Tye?"

"It's my favorite."

She chewed her treat and rewarded him with a radiant smile.

All the way home, she slept. His arm ached from holding her for so long, but he didn't care. Her pleasure in the trip had been worth the small discomfort.

He stood from the wagon seat and slid carefully to the ground. Purdy met him, offering to rub down and water the team. Tye thanked him and carried Eve to the house.

Meg and Gus were putting the finishing touches on the evening meal when Tye entered the kitchen, Eve draped in his arms. Meg acknowledged him with a smile and scooped hot whipped potatoes into a crockery bowl. "Didn't know if you were going to make it in time for supper."

"I'm learning not to miss your suppers."

His words brought Meg's head around. He held the child with a smile, but he'd been serious. He'd filled out since he'd been there; his chest and arms were fuller. And he'd been eating larger portions.

Wiping her hands on her apron and stepping closer, she noted the black ring around Eve's lips. "Spoiled her meal, did you?"

He grinned and the sight caught at her heart. "It was worth it. She loves licorice."

"I see that." She reached high and took his hat from his head. It was warm from the sun and smelled like his hair. She remembered his accusing words about her feverish attraction for him and busied herself hanging his hat.

Tye cast her a questioning look.

Eve roused in his arms, and Meg gave her a smile. "Hi. I missed you."

"Oh, Meg! We took the wagon to town and we shopped. Tye bought me licorice."

"What an adventure. Looks like the trip wore you out."

"Only a litto. What do I smell?"

"Gus's fried chicken."

Eve licked her stained lips. "Yummy."

"Let's go clean you up."

Tye placed Eve on her feet, and she followed Meg to the sink. He washed after they were finished, and within minutes Purdy and the Eaton brothers arrived.

They all sat and ate together, the meal delicious, the atmosphere comfortable. Once they'd finished and Gus took over the cleanup, Tye stepped close and whispered, "Let's go outside. I need to talk to you."

Chapter Eleven

She followed him hesitantly, feigning indifference. She didn't want him analyzing her feelings or her actions again. Major found his new friend, and giggling, Eve chased him around a tree stump.

"Edwina and your sister-in-law—"

"Gwynn?"

He nodded. "Saw us in town today. And I think Emery Parks recognized Eve."

The topic of his concern relaxed her. "She isn't a secret, Tye. Everyone is going to know sooner or later."

"I know." He watched the child playing with the dog. "I thought you might want to be prepared. For tomorrow night."

Meg didn't want to believe that people would be judgmental about Eve, but she already knew better from the way they'd reacted to her marriage to Tye.

"Remember when you told me you didn't care what anyone said about you marrying me?" he asked.

Still watching Eve, she nodded.

''You said you didn't need the town's approval to do what you think is right.''

''I remember.''

''It wasn't as easy as you thought it would be. And this won't be, either.''

She turned to face him. ''If anyone says anything hurtful in front of her, they'll have to deal with me.''

He seemed pleased by her words. ''I...''

''What?''

''It just makes me so mad to think of anybody treating her—treating her the way I know they can.''

''Like they've treated you.''

''Yes.''

And he thought she was ashamed of him. There was no way to explain the truth without revealing more than she could cope with. She'd seen how cruel people had been to Tye. She didn't want the same for Eve. ''Tye, can we adopt her? Legally?''

''You'd want to?''

''Yes, of course.''

His concerned expression softened. ''Lottie had the attorney draw up some papers before she died, making me Eve's guardian. All we'd have to do is see the judge.''

''Let's do it, then.''

He grinned.

She wasn't used to his smile, and a funny feeling slid through her chest.

''Thank you, Meg.''

Her heart skipped a beat at his use of her name. She was falling apart again. She forced her gaze away from his dark eyes and studied Eve.

She thought he would say something more then, but he didn't. He joined Eve in finding a suitable stick and throwing it as far as he could for Major to retrieve. They played the game until Tye told Eve he had something to do.

He disappeared for half an hour, then showed up driving the wagon full of lumber toward the house. Eve and Meg followed him around to the front, where he parked the wagon and climbed down to open the tailgate. He stacked lumber at the corner of the house.

"What are you doing?" Meg asked, watching in curiosity.

"He's buildin' a porch," Eve piped up. "We bought the boards today."

Meg couldn't have been more surprised. "A porch?" she asked, staring.

"A porch," Tye confirmed, and continued to move wood from the wagon.

By the time he had it all unloaded and the horses back to the corral, the sun had waned and a chill gripped the evening air.

Tye built a fire in the fireplace, and Eve brought her stack of books. "Will you read to me, Tye?"

"What would you like to hear tonight?"

"We haven't read this one yet. It has pictures."

Tye accepted the small leather volume. "*Songs of Innocence.* William Blake." He opened it and scanned a page. "It's poetry."

Eve climbed into his lap and settled herself comfortably, obviously secure in his affections.

"*Alice in Wonderland* and that one there belongs

to Meg's niece, but these other ones was Meg's when she was a little girl.''

''You read this when you were little?'' he asked, glancing at Meg.

''My father read it to me until I was at least eight,'' she said with a shy shrug.

''Tell me about your father. I remember his building on Rose Street. And I remember seeing him bringing you and your sisters to school. He had a beard.''

Meg nodded, her eyes suddenly misting at the recollection of her father. ''In the winter. Mama always made him shave it off, come spring. I don't know why.''

Tye's deep blue eyes were full of sincere interest. A half smile softened his always sad expression. ''And he read to you?''

''He read to all of us. He ordered us books from the East as soon as he learned of English translations. We had a whole shelf of books in our house.''

''That was your daddy, Meg?'' Eve asked, her attention captured. ''Did he live with you?''

''Yes. We all lived together in town. The Pratts own the house now. It has a window seat along the east windows in the dining room, and another up in the bedroom my sisters and I shared. Father used to read to us in the parlor every evening. And on Sunday he took one of us for a buggy ride. I remember how I looked forward to the Sundays when it was my turn to go.''

''Why only one of you?'' Eve asked.

''Well, I guess with so many children, he wanted to take a little special time with each one.''

"Did you sit on his lap when he read?" Eve asked.

"When I was small, I did." Both Tye and Eve listened with wistful expressions, their hair the same dark sheen against the blazing fire. Neither had known a father's love or attention the way she had.

Several minutes passed in companionable silence before Tye opened the book and began reading. His deep, velvety voice caressed the words and phrases and brought them to life.

Eve snuggled against him, engrossed. She was only five. Tye would make up for her years without a father, Meg was certain. But no one could ever make up those years for him or fill the place of a parent in his heart.

If only people knew the Tye she knew. If only they saw the inherent goodness and the love he had to share, they wouldn't think less of him for something he couldn't help. What made people so judgmental and cruel?

After their story time, Meg got Eve ready for bed and tucked her into her cozy pile of blankets. "Give me kisses, Tye," she demanded.

He knelt and covered her cheeks with kisses. She giggled and hugged him around the neck. Meg watched their play with a pang of envy.

"Where's Major?" Eve asked.

Meg opened the door, but she didn't have to whistle. The dog bounded in and crossed the room to lick Eve's face.

"He just licked off all my kisses," Tye teased.

"No, he didn't. He's giving me more." She

wrapped an arm around the animal's neck and he settled down beside her.

Within a few minutes child and dog slept. Eve liked the dog better than she did her, Meg thought.

She straightened out her sewing basket and made a list of items she needed from the mercantile. She glanced over to where Tye sat in the overstuffed chair. He'd closed his eyes and rested with his head against the chair back and palms on his thighs.

"Aren't you going into town?" she asked.

"Nope."

Meg got out her few remaining pieces of stationery and her bottle of ink, and prepared to write a letter to her mother. Her gaze was drawn back to Tye. "Is there any particular reason you've decided to stay home tonight?"

He didn't reply.

"Tye?"

He'd fallen asleep. She smiled to herself. Nobody could keep going at the pace he had for the past month. It was a wonder he hadn't fallen asleep and toppled from his horse during the day.

She had neglected writing her mother before roundup, not wanting to explain her hasty marriage, but now she wanted to tell her mother about Tye and Eve. Mother would remember Tye. What would she think? What would she say when she wrote back? During the war and after Joe's reported death, Mother had repeatedly invited Meg to come stay with her and her husband, Charles, in Denver. Meg's mother had loved her first husband, had raised her family in Aspen Grove, but after Meg's father had died and her brothers and sisters were married and gone, she had been happy to remarry and move to a less provincial locale.

Perhaps she'd understand Meg's desire to keep the ranch. Or perhaps she'd consider Meg foolish for not coming to the city to mend her heart and eventually find a new husband.

Meg labored to keep the tone of her letter light, to keep her confusing emotions a secret. She signed and folded the letter, then blew out the lantern.

"Tye?" She touched his shoulder.

"Hmm?" He peered at her through slitted lids.

"It's late. You should lie down."

He rubbed a hand down his face and got up, moving into the bedroom. By the time Meg checked Eve and the fire, he lay beneath the quilt, snoring lightly.

She washed quietly, changed clothing and slipped into bed. Her letter had made it all sound so simple, as simple as she'd planned it. From the words she'd written, her mother would never guess the turmoil that dogged her thinking night and day. From the beginning she'd believed Joe would have wanted her to go through with this plan. But would she have wanted it the other way around?

What if Joe had immediately remarried? What if he'd invited some other woman to their bed and she'd set him on fire?

Meg squeezed her eyes shut and turned to her side, curling up as far away from Tye as she could without falling off the edge of the mattress. Joe's letters were filled with his sincere pledges of undying love and faithfulness. He wouldn't have allowed her memory to vanish or have taken another woman to his bed and his heart so easily.

With increasing self-reproach, she tried to remember his face, the color of his hair in the firelight. His smell.

The faint scent of tobacco drifted on the night air, a scent that combined with the sun-dried linens and the smoke from the candle she'd extinguished to drive home the fact that everything was different now.

This might be the same house and the same room and even the same bed, but nothing was the same.

Joe's death had changed her world.

And Tye had set it on fire.

Meg hadn't worn her yellow linen dress for more than a year. She had aired and pressed it and, after finding matching hair ribbons and her cream-colored silk shawl with fringe, she stood before her mirror, fussing with her upswept hair.

"You look beautiful, Meg."

She smiled at Eve. "So do you. You'll be the prettiest girl there."

"Really?"

"Really. I've never seen hair as beautiful as yours."

"Mama said my hair is shiny as a raven's wing. I never saw a raven, so I don't know if it's so."

"It's so. I'll show you a raven."

"Are you two lovely ladies ready?"

Tye stood in the doorway, tall and handsome in his white shirt, bolo tie and elk-hide vest, his boots pol-

ished to a shine. At his hip he wore the ever present
.45 and holster.

"We're ready," Eve piped, and ran to wrap her
arms around his legs. "Carry me, Tye!"

He picked her up effortlessly and smoothed her
skirt. "Don't want to wrinkle this pretty dress."

"What about your shirt?" She touched his collar.

"Nobody's gonna look under my vest."

"Maybe you'll take it off."

"If I do, people will just have to see wrinkles."

Eve grinned. "C'mon, Meg."

"Right behind you. I have a couple more pies to
pack." She followed them moments later.

"There are blankets in the back for the ride home,
in case it's cool," Tye said, assisting her up to the
seat.

Gus and Purdy waited in the wagon bed.

"Whoo-ee, look at the missy!" Gus called. "Hurry
up, Tye! The Double Oarlock hands will get all the
prairie oysters ahead of us!"

"I'm sure there'll be plenty." Tye clucked to the
team with a grin.

"What's prairie oysters?" Eve asked from her
perch between Meg and Tye.

Meg studied a spot on the horizon with diligence.

"That's the Founder's Day specialty," Tye replied.
"Each ranch takes turns cooking their own secret rec-
ipe."

Apparently satisfied, Eve moved on to another
question. Meg listened to their exchange all the way
to town. Tye was inexhaustible in his explanations
and stories. Meg learned more about him every time

she was close enough to overhear his conversations with Eve.

Since it was the only building large enough to accommodate all the ranchers and townspeople, as well as protect them from the weather, the livery had been scrubbed and cleaned and the animals corralled out back.

Long tables had been set with refreshments: barrels of beer, pans of baked goods, jars of pickled eggs and trays of potatoes baked in their jackets, as well as the traditional roundup specialty.

Gus and Purdy headed for the food.

"Hatch, we need a hand with a couple of barrels," Jed Wheeler called to Tye.

"I'll be right back," Tye said.

A platform for the musicians had been constructed of planks, and several men tuned fiddles. One of the wives from the Lazy B always played the harmonica, and Meg spotted her among the other women.

A commotion sounded outside and a half-dozen men unloaded a piano from the back of a wagon and lifted it onto the platform. Several heads turned toward Fiona Hill, who smiled nervously, and Meg stifled a chuckle at the thought of the woman's clumsy renditions of hymns being pounded out for the celebration.

Before long the music began. Eager to celebrate, the ranchers, wives, reps and merchants ignored the off-key selections and mingled on the dance floor. Eve stood at Meg's side, watching the activities with fascination.

Catching Meg's eye, Reverend Baker made his way toward her. "Good evening, Meg."

"Good evening, Reverend."

"How's little Eve doing these days?"

"She's doing quite well, actually," she said over the choppy music. "She positively dotes on Tye, and the feeling is mutual. I've grown quite fond of her myself. Tye and I have decided to adopt her."

"That's wonderful news. I know she'll be a blessing and a comfort to you, as well as the other way around."

"I believe you're right."

"I'm always glad to see roundup over and church attendance pick up again."

"We've missed the last couple of services. We'll be there again tomorrow."

"I'll look forward to that." He bent forward to give Eve a pat on the head. She smiled up at him, then turned her attention back to the dancers. The reverend moved into the party.

Meg took Eve's hand and wandered through the milling people toward the tables of food. "Are you hungry, sweetheart?"

Eve shook her head.

"Maybe you'll change your mind when you see what's there."

Eve's eyes widened at the impressive display of dishes. She chose a chicken leg, a slice of bread and a dessert, and Meg carried her plate in search of a place for her to eat.

Gus motioned to them from where he was seated

on a row of hay bales across the back wall. "The missy can eat with us," he offered.

Meg settled her with her food and, promising to bring her a drink, headed back to the tables.

Laughter rippled through the gathering. Meg spotted Fiona moving away from the piano with a grin. A handful of men urged Tye to take a seat on the bench before the keyboard.

He obliged, coordinated briefly with the other musicians, then led into a smooth, lighthearted waltz.

A murmur ran though the crowd, and delighted dancers paired off on the sawdust-covered floor.

Tye knew piece after piece, popular tunes as well as old favorites, and played song after song, many with words he sang for the listeners' pleasure.

No one asked Meg to dance. She wasn't surprised, really: her standing in the community had taken a serious punch in the past month. The only one who'd said more than two words to her had been the preacher, and he didn't dance. It had been a long time since she'd danced with Joe. She swayed to the music, remembering those days and the admiring glances of all the other young women.

Finally, Tye left his station at the piano, and the musicians continued without him. He made his way through the crowd to where Meg stood.

She looked up. "I'd heard you used to play at the saloon, but I didn't know you were so good."

"Yeah, well, I don't know if I'm 'good.' Maybe just 'better.'"

She grinned at his reference to Fiona's exuberant attempts.

"Want to dance?"

She glanced around, a little surprised, a little embarrassed. On the other side of the dance area she spotted Niles Kestler frowning at them. "Yes. I'd love to."

Tye was a good dancer. He led smoothly, one hand at her waist, the other holding her right hand, his steps not at all ungraceful, even though he favored one leg. Meg learned the unusual gait, the comfortable pace he set, and allowed herself to relax and enjoy the dance and the music. It had been a long time....

Several songs later, Tye led her to the side. "Where's Eve?"

"She's back with Gus and Purdy."

"Let's go outside for a few minutes. I have something for you."

"All right."

Emery and Claudelle Parks whispered something to each another as Tye led Meg toward the door. Meg chose to ignore their rude gossiping and stares.

The evening air was clear and cool, a rain-scented breeze drifting down from the mountains. Tye took her arm and led her across the side street and up onto the boardwalk until they reached the front of the next building, where an oil lamp burned. There he stopped and stood awkwardly for a moment.

"What is it?" she asked.

"Well, I want to— I have something for you."

"What?"

He reached inside his vest and pulled out a tiny flannel bag with a drawstring. Taking her hand, he placed the bag in her palm.

Meg felt the small object inside through the fabric. With the fingers of her other hand, she traced the circular shape. Puzzled, she glanced up into his dark eyes.

Loosening the drawstring, she pried the bag open and turned it upside down. A large gold ring fell into her palm. Meg held it closer to the coal oil lamp. Could it be?

"Is this—" She picked it up and held it between her thumb and forefinger. "This is my father's ring."

Tye nodded.

"How did you get this?"

"I earned the money to buy it back."

"How?"

"Working."

Working. He'd earned the money for this ring by working. Her mind raced across the concept. Working all those nights he'd ridden into town? All the nights she'd mentally accused him of numerous dishonorable acts. "Working at night?"

He nodded.

Meg closed her eyes against the rush of stinging shame. She'd thought the most horrible things of him. She'd imagined him doing anything but working. She'd thought he'd been drinking…visiting loose women. She'd thought the worst. "Doing what, Tye?"

"Playing at the Pair-A-Dice, like before."

"All those nights you were gone you were playing the piano to earn the money for this?"

A frown creased his handsome brow. "Aren't you glad to have it back?"

Unable to keep his gaze any longer, she placed the ring back in the bag and drew it tightly shut, clutching it in her fist. "I'm glad to have it back, Tye," she said softly. "But I'm ashamed of myself."

"You don't have anything to be ashamed of," he assured her. "You're the kindest, most good-hearted person I've ever known, Meg."

"No. No, I'm not." That last came out in a broken voice.

He engulfed her fist in his. "Yes. You are."

His warmth suffused her fingers and spread up her arm until it radiated through her entire body. She looked up hesitantly. "Thank you."

So simple. Such insignificant words for an enormous act of kindness.

"You're welcome," he said.

Gently, he cupped her cheek with his other hand. In the golden light, their eyes met. Meg felt like crying. She blinked furiously.

Tye laced his fingers into her hair behind her ear, stroked his thumb over her cheekbone. Meg's breath caught in her throat.

"Are those happy tears?"

Anticipating his kiss with a flutter in her breast, she whispered, "Yes."

"Good."

Music and laughter floated from the livery next door. A moth batted against the dome of the coal oil lamp.

She wanted him to hold her then, to forgive her for her doubt and her mistrust. For some demented reason she didn't understand, she craved his assurance and his acceptance.

"I'm thirsty," he said, drawing his hand from her cheek. "We'd better get back inside."

The loss of his heat and his touch left her feeling bereft. How foolish of her to want him to kiss her out here like this where anyone could happen by and see. She gathered her wits and followed him back to the livery.

"There you are," Reverence Baker said, spotting Tye. "I was just looking for a bit of gentlemanly conversation."

"Out-of-doors, Reverend?" Tye asked.

"Why, yes, don't mind if we do."

Tye cast her an apologetic glance, and she watched them exit through the back door. She checked on Eve and discovered Lilly Telford sitting beside her on a hay bale.

"Well, hello, Lilly. It's nice to see you."

"Hello, Aunt Meg—I mean, Meg. I'm not 'apose to call you aunt anymore."

"Oh." The information stung like salt in an open cut, but irritation quickly followed the pain. How cruel of the Telfords to turn the children against her. "Have you missed your *Alice in Wonderland* book? Eve has enjoyed it very much."

"Oh, no. Mama got me a new one. It has pictures."

"I'll bet they're pretty."

"They are. 'Cept the Cheshire cat is kind of scary. I had a bad dream after I looked at the pictures of him."

Meg started to reply, but Harley's voice interrupted. "Lilly. Come back and stay near your brother."

"But, Papa, I found a new friend. This here's—"

"Lilly, return to the other side of the room right now and stay with your brother."

With a fallen expression, Lilly stood. "Bye, Eve. I gotta sit with my dumb brother."

"Bye, Lilly," Eve said, and watched the other little girl scamper away.

Harley took Meg's elbow and pulled her a few feet away. "You have a lot of audacity bringing that prostitute's child to this respectable occasion." One eyebrow lifted in reproach. "What have you fallen into, anyway? Everyone's talking about Hatcher and that kid."

Righteous anger burned inside Meg. "Eve has just as much right to be here as anyone else."

"What are *you* doing with her?"

"Tye made a promise to Eve's mother. He was obligated to keep it."

"What kind of man makes promises to a whore?" Harley hissed against her ear.

"An honorable man, Harley."

"Think about what you're doing and saying, Meg. Just think about it. No self-respecting man is obligated to a woman like that. Or to a child like that— unless the child is his."

"No, Harley, no. You don't understand."

"Oh, I understand just fine, Meg. You're the one who doesn't understand. Or care about your standing in this town."

"You don't know anything about Tye."

"I know everything I need to know. And what I know tells me you've made a big mistake." He released her elbow and moved off through the throng.

Meg struggled with the anger and embarrassment warring inside her. It was bad enough Harley spoke about Tye without even knowing the man, but how dare he say things against Eve—an innocent child!

"Meg, I'm thirsty," Eve called.

Meg met Gus's stare. The old-timer shook his head in disgust.

"I'll get you a drink," Meg replied. "I'll be right back."

Edwina met her halfway to the drink tables.

"Hello, Mother Telford," Meg said, putting on a stiff smile.

"I'm no longer your mother since you chose to align yourself with that disreputable Hatcher *miscreant*."

Meg fortified herself for another attack.

To her surprise, tears welled in Edwina's eyes. "You could have lived with us, Meg. You could have saved your good name—and our Joe's."

"Edwina, please, dear," Meg said with a catch in her throat at the older woman's obvious hurt and dismay. "We've gone over and over this. You know how I feel about keeping the ranch."

"What does keeping the ranch have to do with that child? You continue to bring scandal to our good name."

"I'm sorry you feel that way," she said, controlling her voice and choosing her words carefully. "I never intended to hurt you. All I ever wanted was to keep the Circle T, you know that. Tye has kept more than his share of our arrangement. He works harder than any two men. He's honest. He's dependable. And he takes his obligations and his promises seriously.

"And even more important than all those things, Edwina, he cares about others. He's been hurt by small-minded people—" she glanced about to see who was watching "—like *you*—his whole life, but he hasn't let that turn him into a mean, insensitive person. Far from it. He intends to see that Eve has a good life. And I'm going to help him do it. We're adopting her."

"You'll regret this," Edwina said. "My poor Joe would turn over in his grave if he could see how you're behaving. I'm sorry he ever married you in the first place."

Meg bit her lip. Her anger was no armor for the woman's wounding words. Would Joe see Meg's side of this or would he agree with his family? There was no way she'd ever know that.

She stared Joe's mother in the eye, swallowing the hurt that threatened to rise up and pour out in a rush of anguished tears.

Finally, Edwina spun in a flurry of black taffeta and rustling crinolines and stomped away.

Meg glanced at the surrounding eavesdroppers. Holding her chin high, she poured two cups of punch and carried them back, handing one to Eve.

"I made a new friend, Meg. Did you see her? She's your niece you told me 'bout."

"I saw her, honey."

From the corner of her eye, Meg noticed a short figure in a calico dress move toward her. Fortifying herself for another attack, she turned and, to her great surprise, recognized Mitch Heden's wife, Annie. She wore an almost sympathetic expression and gave Meg a friendly smile.

"Hi, Meg."

"Annie."

The other woman reached for her hand and Meg took hers, noting the less-than-smooth skin of a rancher's wife. She was sure her own palms felt the same, and it was an odd comfort.

"Mitch told me you had a good winter, didn't lose many head."

"Not at all."

They spoke briefly about roundup and then Annie added, "Mitch is happy for Hatch that he has a chance to work a place of his own. He's worked for us over the years, and we've come to know him better than most. He needed a chance like this."

Her obvious compassion moved Meg immeasurably. "I needed him, too."

"Congratulations on your marriage. The boys were down sick or I would've come to the wedding."

That news was a balm to Meg's bruised and aching feelings. She squeezed Annie's hand hard. "Thank you. You don't know how much it means to me for you to say that."

"I think I do."

Tye skirted the gathering and came across to them. "Miz Heden," he said.

"Hatch. You're looking fit."

"Meg's as fine a cook as you are."

"Flatterer," she said with a smile, then released Meg's hand. "You two ride over some Sunday."

"We'll do that," Tye replied.

Annie turned and headed away. Her kindness touched Meg, but it couldn't make up for the hurt the Telfords had inflicted. Meg's evening had been ruined, and she wondered why she'd thought it would be any different.

Tye looked Meg over. "Is something wrong?"

She shook her head but said, "Maybe we should go now."

"If you're sure."

"I'm sure."

Tye turned to Gus. "How about you?"

"I was ready an hour ago."

"Where's Purdy?"

"Card game over yonder."

Meg led Eve out while Tye found Purdy. Behind her she heard a few of the men call good-nights to Tye.

"You all right?" Tye asked, helping her onto the seat.

"I'm fine."

"Did something happen back there?"

She shook her head. Inside her chest, a sick ache consumed her. One minute she wanted to cry and hug Tye, erase all the insults he'd suffered and show him love and acceptance. The next minute she had the sweeping urge to strike out at him, hit him and punish him for making her doubt herself, for making her doubt her love for Joe. She couldn't blame him for her humiliation and the Telfords' treatment; she'd marched into this marriage with her eyes wide-open and Tye's fair warnings ringing in her ears.

Eve fell asleep against Gus's side in the wagon bed. Tye carried her in, then hurried back out to put up the horses and check the stock in the barn and the corral.

Meg changed Eve into her nightdress and tucked her into her pallet with her doll. She paused to brush her dark hair away from her forehead, thinking how much the tresses resembled the color and texture of Tye's.

Harley's accusing voice came to her again. *No self-respecting man is obligated to a woman like that. Or to a child like that—unless the child is his.*

Unless the child was his....

Chapter Twelve

Doubt rose up like a great ugly beast in her breast. Had Tye fathered this child? As much as he hated his own illegitimacy, if that were true, wouldn't he have married the child's mother and given Eve a name? Yes, without a doubt, he would have.

Meg had already done Tye enough injustice by believing the worst of him regarding his nights in town. She'd made a fool of herself over that, while he'd proven himself as honorable as always.

She must give him the benefit of the doubt in this situation. If Eve were his child, he would have told Meg.

She tucked the covers under Eve's chin and went into her room to change her own clothing. She took the ring from her dress pocket and dropped it from its flannel pouch into her palm. Lamplight glittered from the gold band.

She stared at it until the gold blurred, remembering the heart-wrenching questions Tye had asked about her father. Remembering, too, her father.

He would have liked Tye, would have respected him.

She closed her fingers over the ring. Several minutes later, she returned it to its former place of honor in her bureau drawer. *Thank you, Tye.*

Rapping lightly, Tye pushed open the partially closed door. Meg stood before her bureau, her fingertips resting on the front of the top drawer. Her hair flowed in waves over her shoulders and glistened like warm honey in the lamplight. She looked over at him, a meditative look on her lovely face.

"You need more time?"

She shook her head and moved to the bed. "No."

Tye carried in a kettle of warm water and poured it into the basin. He removed his gun and holster, rolled the belt around it and placed it beneath the bed. Unbuttoning his shirt, he shrugged out of it and washed his face and hands and arms. He turned once and found her propped on her pillow, watching him.

"I smelled smoky," he said.

"I don't mind."

"No?"

She shook her head. "It'll still be in your hair when you come to bed. I'm used to it. How's your leg?"

"The leg's good."

"You haven't been limping much."

"No. It's stronger."

"Sure doesn't harm your dancing."

Her compliment warmed him. "No?"

"No." She snuggled down beneath the star-patterned quilt. "It had been a long time since I'd danced."

"Since Joe was here," he said at the reminder.

"Yes. Since then."

"What did you do with his boots?"

"His boots?" She frowned a moment. "Oh. I gave them to Hunt."

"Why'd you do that?"

"I don't know. They were good boots. Hunt's feet looked about the same size.... Something wrong with what I did?"

"Not at all. It surprised me, is all."

"You don't think of me as generous?"

"I see you as very generous. But I *know* you're sentimental."

"Is that bad?"

He sat on the edge of the bed. "No."

She climbed from the bed and rounded the end in a moment's time, kneeling before him in a puddle of white cotton and taking his boot heel in hand.

Her willingness to serve him seemed wrong. "Meg, you don't have to do that."

"I want to."

He studied her lovely tawny eyes and pulled his foot from his boot with her help. Meg set it aside and reached for the other. "I got them off by myself every night when you were sleeping," he said.

She grasped the other boot. "Sometimes I was sleeping."

The boot came off and she placed it with the other. Did that mean she'd been lying awake waiting for him? Quickly, Tye got up and reached for the cloth he'd washed with. "Here."

She stood, a quizzical expression lining her forehead.

Holding one wrist at a time, Tye cleansed her palms and the insides of her fingers with the cooled cloth. ''I just came from the barn.''

She allowed his touch, watching him perform the task without looking up. He studied her delicate hands, remembering the feel of them on his skin. He had an overwhelming urge to pull them to his face, to kiss her palms, to draw her fingertips into his mouth and taste her. Dancing with her tonight had been one of the greatest pleasures of his life.

Sweet, sweet Meg. So many times in the past he'd studied her without her knowing. So many times he'd admired her feminine grace and golden beauty. So many times he'd seen her with Joe and experienced a keen pull of envy. Joe had won her heart. Joe had initiated her to lovemaking. For the millionth time, Tye cursed fate for his own unworthy position. He'd spend a lifetime regretting not being a man who deserved a woman like Meg.

She'd danced with him tonight. The event was almost as incredible as the fact that she'd married him, had given him her body. If only she could be as proud of him as he was of her.

But she had danced with Tye Hatcher in front of the citizens of Aspen Grove. He wanted to take her in his arms and waltz her around the room for good measure.

Tye didn't realize his washing had become a caress until she pulled the cloth from him and draped it over the side of the bowl.

He unfastened his pants and slid them down while she hurried back to her side of the bed. She turned down the lamp's wick, plunging the room into darkness. Tye stretched out beneath the covers.

In the blackness he relived those moments with her in his arms.

"Tye?"

"Yes."

"I want to apologize."

"For what?"

She was quiet for only a second. "For my dishonesty."

He sighed, thinking he didn't want to hear this. "I can't imagine you not being honest."

"I thought the very worst of you all those nights you were gone."

"I figured that."

"But you let me think it."

"I've never told anyone what to think of me. Wouldn't do much good."

"But you could have explained."

"I'm not much for explainin'."

The silence stretched longer this time. "You're right," she said finally. "A person doesn't have to defend himself when he knows he's not in the wrong. Actions speak louder than words, don't they?"

He turned his head at the vulnerability in her voice. "Someone say something hurtful to you tonight?"

"It doesn't matter."

"Matters to me, Meg," he said softly. "These people used to be your friends and your family. It's because of me you've lost that."

"No. It's because of *them* that I've lost that."

"I'm sorry," he said lamely. "I'd make it up to you if I could."

She turned toward him, and his heart skipped. "Thank you for my ring, Tye."

In the dark, she brushed the back of the hand he'd draped across his chest, then placed her hand over his. Her touch moved upward, accidentally brushing his nipple, finding his face and outlining his lips with her fingertips. *Tell her you love her.*

He rose on his elbow and leaned over her, relishing her hand against his face. She pressed her plush, warm body against his eagerly, the thin sheet separating them. He kissed her, and she curled her fingers into the hair at his neck, meeting his lips with hers, responding in the way that drove him mad and made him forget she didn't love him back.

Tye broke the kiss, captured her hand and brought it back to his chest, where he held it firmly in his, his heart pounding beneath. "You don't owe me anything."

"You insult me if you think I can be bought," she replied, her voice husky.

It would be so easy to run his hands over her, to grow mindless in his passion and take her. He wanted her with all his heart. He loved her, his sweet and beautiful Meg. But his thoughts traveled to the trunk at the foot of the bed and her precious treasures that lay within. She may have given Joe's boots away, but she still had shirts and ties and letters…his hairbrush and shaving gear. She still clung to his things…still held fast to her love for him.

He placed his thumb over her lips, sealing them.

This was still Joe's bed. Still Joe's wife. The knowledge pierced his heart as sharply as the rejuvenating nerve endings pained his leg. Each time the knowledge hit with a force that made him want to cry out.

There had been no one in Tye's heart before Meg. It belonged to her wholly and without reservation. The thought of her enduring love for Joe quelled his ardor as effectively as a dunk in an icy lake.

He released her and lay back against his pillow.

"Tye?" Her hand came searching.

He grasped it and held it fast against his chest. "Go to sleep," he said softly. "It's late."

Her silence could have meant anything. Disappointment. Embarrassment. *Relief.*

Earning the money for the ring hadn't actually improved his position in her eyes. She was merely grateful. He didn't want her to sacrifice herself because she felt obligated to him. He still had to show her he was as good as any man. The only way he knew to do that was to show his merit.

She relaxed her hand and he stroked her fingers, willing her to sleep to reduce his temptation. Why did everything of importance have to hinge on money and respectability? Even horses were worth more when they were of good breeding.

If he had papers on those horses he planned to stud, he could get a lot more, he thought, forcing his thoughts elsewhere. A few of the Circle T mares had come into season; he should be hearing from other ranchers soon.

Beside him, Meg's breathing grew deep and regular. He rested his thoughts and his body and sought sleep.

Meg had never dreaded church in her entire life. This morning she thought up a dozen reasons to stay home, though she never voiced one of them. She'd made such a point of insisting Tye go with her, never considering how much easier it was for him to stay home than to face the silent ridicule of the townspeople, that she couldn't show herself a coward now.

He'd attended at her side, and he'd endured the looks and the cold shoulders just as he always had. She guessed she could hold her head up and face them if he could. After breakfast, she donned her deep red calico dress, pinned a brooch at her throat and took her silk bonnet from its box.

She dressed Eve in a lightweight worsted skirt and a ruffled, pink-checked gingham blouse she'd sewn for her. She dabbed a spot of dirt from her only good white gloves and pulled them on.

"Am I pretty, Tye?" Eve asked in her delightfully guileless manner.

He lifted her onto the wagon seat with the indulgent smile Meg was growing to covet. "You two will be the prettiest ladies at church."

Eve seated herself and proceeded to adjust her skirts importantly. "If my mama was there, she would be the prettiest. Isn't that so, Tye? You said my mama was the prettiest."

Tye glanced sideways at Meg as he helped her up onto the seat. "That's so, Eve."

"Do you take after your mama, Eve?" Meg asked, wondering.

"What's take after, Meg?"

Tye climbed up and urged the horses forward.

"I mean, do you look like her? Was her hair black and shiny like yours?"

"She had red hair. And lots of freckles. She didn't like 'em much, but they didn't cover up too good. I didn't think she needed to cover 'em up, did you, Tye?"

"Nope."

"She was beautiful, wasn't she, Tye? And she smelled good, too. Well, before she got sick, I mean."

Meg pulled the child to her side for a hug.

"But don't feel bad, Meg. Tye told me you was second-pretty to my mama."

Heat rose uncomfortably up Meg's neck and face. Slowly, she turned her gaze to Tye.

He wore an apologetic expression, and his dark eyes seemed to beg her understanding. His mouth opened, but he closed it again without saying anything.

Meg couldn't help the smile that inched the corners of her lips upward. "Well, I guess second to such a beautiful woman is still awfully good," she said teasingly. "At least Tye didn't say I couldn't hold a candle to your mama."

He rolled his eyes.

"What would that mean?" Eve asked.

"Nothing, darling. I'm just teasing Tye."

The child's chatter as they neared Aspen Grove helped to alleviate Meg's nerves. The run-ins with

Harley and his mother the night before had bothered her more than she wanted to admit.

They arrived early, and Meg appreciated not having to enter the building after all the others were seated and staring. She wondered if Tye had planned it that way. Near the stairs, he helped them down, then pulled the wagon away.

Meg and Eve entered the church.

Gwynn met them in the tiny foyer. "Meg," she said, and stepped forward to embrace her.

Meg hugged her back, then, taking both her gloved hands, glanced around in surprise. "Where are the others?"

"There's a women's luncheon this afternoon to celebrate Celia Kestler's new baby. Harley had a table to deliver and Mother Telford took over a cake. Forrest and Lilly are with them. I told Harley I had to help prepare Communion. I pray God will forgive that lie. I really hoped to see you before they got back."

"What did Celia have?"

"A boy."

Meg had never felt so left out. She glanced around, wishing the Hedens came to church more often. Annie was the only one who'd greeted her pleasantly in public since she'd married Tye. "How nice."

Tye entered the cool, dim church and stopped at Meg's side. "Mrs. Telford," he said politely.

"Mr. Hatcher." Gwynn blushed, and she and Meg released their joined hands.

"Did you know God gives babies to ladies?" Eve piped up from Meg's side. "My mama told me I didn't need to know where babies come from, but Meg told me.''

Gwynn's cheeks flushed even more.

"When God gives Meg a baby, I'll prob'ly get to play with it all the time, just like my very own doll baby.''

Meg felt the heat creeping up her own face. She hadn't said anything at all to Eve about the possibility of her having a baby. She hadn't actually considered it. She didn't dare look at Tye.

"Let's go sit down.'' Tye stepped in to rescue her, took Eve's hand and led her to their pew.

"Is everything all right with you?'' Gwynn asked, genuine concern in her eyes.

Meg nodded and took the hand her former sister-in-law extended. "We're doing just fine.''

"With all the talk, I guess…well, I didn't know what to think.''

"He was working nights at the Pair-A-Dice to earn some extra money,'' Meg whispered, the truth once again bringing tears to her eyes. "He's a good man, Gwynn. Not at all deserving of the talk and the treatment he gets from these people.''

"I was so afraid for you, afraid of what you'd gotten yourself into, risking everything to hang on to that ranch like you did.''

"Well, it worked,'' Meg assured her. "Niles offered him more per acre than Joe paid for the land and he refused to take it.''

Gwynn squeezed her hand. "You look different whenever I see you now. More relaxed, I guess. As long as you're happy, I'm glad for you.''

Two older women entered the church and stared as they passed.

"Thank you for talking to me," Meg said.

"Take care of yourself." Gwynn released her hand and moved away.

Meg gathered her composure and joined Eve and Tye.

He studied her with a concerned lift of one ebony eyebrow.

Meg gave him a watery smile. Eve's comment about the baby blocked anything else from her thoughts, and she had to look away. Had Tye considered that possibility? He'd told her he wanted children. He hadn't touched her for weeks, however, and if last night's lack of interest was any indication, even God couldn't give her a baby.

Reverend Baker entered then and placed his Bible on the wooden pulpit. Embarrassed over her lustful thoughts, Meg pushed them from her head.

From the back of the church, Fiona Hill hurried forward, her arm in a white sling fastened around her neck. She spoke to the preacher, and he patted her shoulder and said something in return.

The two of them conversed with their heads together for a minute before Reverend Baker raised his eyes and scanned the few early parishioners. When his gaze lit upon Tye, a smile creased his face. He said something to Fiona and hurried toward their pew.

"Tye," he said, shaking the hand offered. "I wonder if you'd be so good as to help us out this morning."

"I—er—I'll do what I can," Tye said.

"I'm afraid Miss Hill has taken a spill and hurt her wrist. She won't be able to play this morning. Will you take her place at the organ and lead the hymns?"

Tye's face recorded absolute shock. His mouth opened and shut twice before he discovered his voice. "I've never played an organ, Reverend. And I only know a few of the songs I've heard sung here the past month."

"Then those are the songs we'll sing. Playing an organ is just like playing the piano. Fiona can show you the footwork."

Tye shot Meg a glance. She merely shrugged. "Do it if you want to, Tye, but you don't have to."

Tye looked back at the preacher and something passed between them, something potent and private. Tye wiped his palms on his thighs and stood.

He towered over Reverend Baker and Fiona as the trio stood conversing, Tye with his head lowered in concentration, Fiona gesturing with her good hand. They stepped to the organ and continued to speak. Finally, Tye nodded; Fiona smiled and took a seat.

Meg realized the church had filled and was buzzing with early morning greetings and speculation over the man now seated at the organ. She glanced around, finding heads straining to see and several stares directed at her.

She smiled and waited expectantly like the rest.

Reverend Baker welcomed them and opened with a prayer. He nodded at Tye, and the strains of "A Mighty Fortress Is Our God" filled the building. Full chords and fluid runs were a sharp contrast to the choppy version of the hymn they usually heard. Even Fiona smiled and heartily sang along.

"Holy, Holy, Holy" came next, followed by "For the Beauty of the Earth" and "Amazing Grace." Reverend Baker nodded at Tye again, and Tye ended the songs. Eve, who'd been sitting on the edge of the pew, swinging her feet in time to the music, stood and clapped wildly. "That was real good playin', Tye!"

From her position in the third pew on the left, Edwina craned her neck to observe. Meg silenced the child by taking her hand and pulling her firmly back to her side.

Tye returned to their seat, and Eve pulled away from Meg to reach for him. He took her tiny hand, and when she scrambled to sit on his lap, he adjusted her skirts and kissed the top of her head.

After the sermon, Tye once again took his position at the organ and played something that sounded suspiciously like "My Bonnie Lies Over the Ocean" as the congregation filed out the door into the waiting sunshine. Excited voices rose and a smile flashed here and there. The improved service seemed to have left everyone in a pleasant mood.

Waiting calmly at the end of her pew for him to finish and join her, Meg endured more than the usual number of stares. A man and wife she remembered seeing at the Founder's Day dance the night before nodded at her on their way past. "What a lovely service," the woman said to her husband. "Mr. Hatcher's playing adds so much."

Her husband mumbled something in agreement.

Tye ended the piece he was playing and joined Meg and Eve, following them to the door.

"Wonderful job, Tye," the reverend said, pumping his hand. "Thank you for obeying the call to serve the Lord with your talent today. See you next week, son."

Tye accepted the man's gratitude and settled his hat down over his forehead as they exited.

"Where did you pick up that particular talent anyway, Tye?" Meg asked, curious.

"In a saloon," he said with a grin. "Friend of my mother's taught me when I was a kid."

"Taught you to read music, too?"

"Nah. One of the schoolteachers did that. Evenings."

"Which one?"

"Mr. Carmichael."

"Tall and skinny?"

Tye nodded.

"What a generous thing to do." She glanced over. "Or did your mother pay for lessons?"

After lifting Meg and Eve to the wagon seat, he sat and picked up the reins. "Sort of," he replied.

His meaning became clear, and Meg's cheeks blistered. She *had* asked. "I'm sorry," she mumbled.

"Why? We don't have to pretend, do we, Meg? You and I? I certainly don't hide anything from you."

His life had been public knowledge for as long as she could remember. Rather than hide his upbringing or run from it, Tye faced the truth head-on. She admired him all the more for his direct honesty. "No.

We don't have to pretend,'' she replied. ''I do appreciate your truthfulness...in all things.''

Funny how Tye had the most to hide, yet he was the most honest with her...and with himself. And she, respectable Meg, hid from the things she didn't want to face. And what she didn't want to face was that Joe's memory was slipping farther and farther into the background, and that Tye had begun to consume all her thoughts, as well as her secret longings and desires.

And she didn't know what to do about it. Maybe her only choice was being honest with him.

A verbal admission was beyond her capability. There were no words to describe her feelings. Nothing coherent even formed in her mind when she recalled their physical exchanges—it was all tactile, all deep-buried emotions and magnetic senses. She'd never taken anything more than a passive role in lovemaking, had never spoken of such immodest things to a soul, had never given the act more than its proper insignificant place in her thoughts.

But it had no proper place where Tye was concerned. And it frightened her. She lay beside him that night, wanting him to touch her, aching for the unmentionable pleasure and mind-drugging release, and chastising herself for those coarse desires.

Honesty. The word haunted her. Tye believed she was ashamed of him. And she'd allowed that rather than face herself and her frightening desires. He hadn't touched her since that day—the day he'd brought her desire for him into the open.

Honesty. She owed him the truth.

Meg's heart pounded with the inexpressible anguish of her denial. "Are you asleep?"

He rustled the sheet, turning. "No."

"There's something I have to tell you."

"All right."

"I wasn't honest with you."

His response took a moment. "About what?"

"That day we argued…sort of argued. You said all those things about—about my—wanting you."

"I'm sorry," he said softly. "I should have said I was sorry."

"No. No, you were right." Oh, Lord, her skin flushed hot and prickly in her embarrassment. "About that part, I mean, but not about the other part. That's the part I wasn't honest about."

"I'm confused," he said.

"You said that I was ashamed for the Telfords to know—to think that—that we—"

"I shouldn't have said that, Meg. It was crude."

"Wait. I have to finish."

He waited in silence.

"You said I was ashamed that I let you do that."

"Aren't you?"

She tried to form words. "Not for the reasons you think." She hurried to explain. "It's not you, Tye. It's not you. I'm not ashamed of you. It hurts me that you can even say that or think it. We've always been friends, and it never mattered to me what others thought."

"I believed that once," he said into the darkness.

"Well, it's true. It's still true. I was proud of you

today, playing the organ for Reverend Baker. I'm proud of you earning the money for my ring. I was proud of you during roundup—you worked hard and long and did a good job for the Circle T. I'm not ashamed of you, Tye.''

She wasn't ashamed of him.

Her words filtered into Tye's mind and he allowed them to sift through years of contrary belief. She'd said she was proud of him. A knot welled up in his throat. Meg had said she was proud of him. He felt as if he were six years old and his mother had patted him on the head.

She wasn't ashamed of him.

He struggled for composure.

''I'm confused by the way you make me feel, is all,'' she said, her sweet voice warbling. ''I'm ashamed of me. Of my behavior. But I'm not ashamed of you. Never you.''

He sorted through that admission. Recognition dawned on him slowly. He'd never slept with anyone other than a whore in his whole life, and he had no comparison for Meg's feelings or behavior. ''What is it exactly that you're ashamed of doing if it's not making love with me?''

A frustrated sigh escaped her. ''Oh, this is so hard. And so embarrassing.''

''Meg, I know you liked what we did. I know you enjoyed it.''

''Yes,'' she said softly.

''Is it that you don't think you should feel good with me because I'm not Joe?''

''Honesty,'' she whispered.

"What?"

"That was part of it. At first."

That was probably normal. She'd felt disloyal to Joe's memory.

"But…it was more because…because it was never like that with Joe."

Anguish weighed like a rock on his chest. Perhaps her honesty was better forgotten if it pierced his heart this way. No doubt Joe, the renowned saint, behaved in a more gentlemanly manner in bed. Tye hadn't been trained in the finer points of making love to a lady. *Don't say any more. Don't kick me while I'm down.*

"I'm sorry," was all he could manage.

"I loved him, I truly did."

I know you did. I know you do.

"But…"

He didn't want to hear it.

"When you and I are together, it's more. It's frightening. I think about it afterward. I think about doing it again."

He let those words ease into his mind. Enlightenment dawned. He leaned up on one elbow and stared as though he could see her in the darkness. He almost wept at her endearing self-doubt and naiveté. He reached and found her silky soft cheek in the dark. "I'll be damned."

"Tye!" The bed dipped and Meg heard him pad across the floor. The sound of a flint striking echoed, and a moment later the halo of the lamp revealed his nakedness.

Chapter Thirteen

She turned her face away.

He moved again and lit the lantern she'd left on her bureau. His shadow flickered across the room as he returned to the bed.

"What are you doing?" she asked, blinking as her eyes adjusted and doing her best to avoid staring at his lean, muscled body.

"I want to see you." He leaned above her and she closed her eyes. He kissed her and she melted into the sensations. With his gentle lips, he coaxed a response. Meg loved it when he kissed her this way. He took his time, lingering over her mouth with slow and deliberate care. He ran his tongue over her lower lip and she met it with her own, wrapping her arm around his neck and falling into a vortex of rushing, inflaming pleasure.

He stopped long enough to unbutton the row of buttons at her neck. "What are you doing?"

"I told you. I want to see you."

Meg fought down stinging embarrassment and allowed him to ease her nightgown up and over her

head. Wanting to cover herself, she kept her eyes
tightly closed and brought a hand to her face.

"Look at me, Meg."

She opened her eyes and met his through her fingers.

"Have you never made love with the lamps on?
Or in the daylight?"

She'd lived with Joe for more than a year before
he'd had to leave. In all that time he'd never seen her
naked. He'd never asked. She'd never considered it.
But now...now here was Tye wanting to look at
her...and *asking*. "No."

Minutes ticked by. Tye ran a hand along her arm,
up over her shoulder and, nudging her hand away,
bracketed her face with his palm. She looked into his
deep blue eyes and plainly saw the wonder and the
need. "You're so beautiful, Meg. It's a shame to hide
your beauty in the darkness—as long as you're sure
you're not ashamed of doing this with me."

Was she ashamed of experiencing this all-
consuming, frantic need and pleasure with him? He
started to move away, but she clutched his shoulder
and held him fast.

He lowered his mouth to hers and kissed her willing lips again. His kiss, always so tender, always so
simultaneously stirring and fulfilling, eroded her
qualms.

She laid her hand tenderly along his granite-cut
jaw.

He trailed kisses along her chin, her throat, her
shoulder, gooseflesh rising along her skin. His hot,
moist lips found and kissed the tip of one breast and

the skin beaded, leaving Meg anticipating more. He didn't disappoint her, pulling her nipple into his mouth and creating new and white-hot fire in her limbs, in her belly and lower.

No, she wasn't ashamed of this incredible new awareness. It was simply foreign to her experience and her thinking.

"You're so beautiful." His voice, hoarse and low, vibrated through his chest and against her ribs. "So smooth and so soft everywhere, Meg." He ran his palm over her hip and her belly, slid his fingers into her curls, and shamelessly, she opened herself to his glorious touch. "Do you like this?"

She felt beautiful when he touched her, kissed her, looked at her. "Yes."

"I just wanted to hear you say it."

A ripple coursed through her.

He suckled her other breast. "I always want to make it good for you," he said.

She opened her eyes and found his earnest expression focused on her face. "It's good, Tye."

"The way it was the last time. I want to make it that good for you."

She absorbed his words, his meaning, another kind of shame ebbing through her veins. He knew? He knew of those unspeakable sensations she'd never even placed coherent thoughts with? Meg wanted to turn away, more to hide this carnal need than her face and body. She raised a trembling hand to her eyes as if she could mask her mortification.

"No, look at me. Keep your eyes open." Tye took her hand and drew it to his lips. He kissed each finger, took the tip of one between his lips and gently sucked the pad against his tongue.

Heady sensations rocked Meg's senses, and her already melting body liquefied. Her fluttering breath caught in her throat.

"What is it that makes you want to hide from me?" he asked.

She shook her head. There were no words. There'd never even been conscious thought before.

"Do you know what it is I want for you?"

"I—I'm not sure. I don't think so."

"Meg, you don't have to be ashamed or embarrassed. It's as natural as breathing or eating."

Meg's skin burned hotter. "Is that true?"

"It's true." He drew one finger deliberately up the inside of her thigh and back down, a slow, torturous route, and leaned to press a kiss to the inside of her knee.

Meg buried the instinctive reflex to draw her knees together and felt every inch of her skin quiver. She'd never known this mad crush of need, had never wanted anything as badly as she wanted these frightening new sensations Tye had brought to life. His skin glowed golden in the lamplight, his blue eyes filled with passion.

The muscles of his strong shoulders and neck were defined by the shadows the lamp created. She ran her hands over his skin, relishing his strength and maleness. If she was as beautiful to him as he was to her, she understood his desire to see her.

The dark furring across his chest snared her attention, and she raked her fingers through the silky mass.

With his clever fingers and seeking tongue, Tye urged her to the very edge of rapture.

An urgent sound escaped her, and she raised her hips.

He moved upward, his breath puckering her nipple. "You're ready for me, Meg."

"Yes."

"Now?" he asked.

"Yes."

His hard limbs moved over her, his hair-roughened skin sliding against hers, and she pulled him to her with a greed and a quivering urgency she didn't stop to think about so that his less-than-gentle entry was her own fault. That very roughness was the catalyst that sent her over the edge.

"This is it, Meg," he said, not only knowing what was happening to her but aiding the cataclysmic feeling with prolonged and forceful thrusts. "This is it."

She cried out and dug her fingers into his back, riding the rippling wave of ecstasy.

Tye slowed his movements then, kissed her face and her neck and the crest of each dewy breast. She opened her eyes and discovered his caressing smile.

He kissed the corner of her mouth and she turned into the kiss instinctively, wrapping her arms and legs around him.

He gave himself the pleasure of long, slow, steady strokes that varied in intensity and tempo. He ended the kiss, lifting himself to look at her face. He ran his thumb over her lower lip, slid the tip into her mouth against her teeth and rubbed gently until she opened her mouth and touched her tongue to his salty skin.

His eyes darkened. Strangely enough, Meg wasn't embarrassed by his earthy appetite or his frank and open pleasure in her body and her mouth, nor by this uninhibited, soul-rocking union. His face, his neck and shoulders were rigid with the fervor of his purpose, and she tested the muscle and sinew beneath his skin, finding his body toned and solid.

His strength was a delicious contrast against her softness. Meg bit the pad of his thumb and ran her tongue over it, eliciting his groan.

He pulled his hand away, gripped her hips hard and spent himself inside her, against her, around her, her name a litany on each gusted breath.

He lay with his head on her breast, his palm flattened on her belly, their hearts slowing, their damp skin cooling.

"That was it," he said softly. "That was what I wanted for you."

Meg knew exactly what he meant now, but she said nothing.

"Meg?" When she remained silent, Tye raised his head. Her dark honey gaze turned to his. Tendrils of damp hair clung to her temples. He threaded the hair away from her skin. She seemed so embarrassed by his words, he would have thought her innocent if he hadn't known better. "It embarrasses you to talk about this?"

Her gaze moved to his shoulder, and she nodded.

"But you were married. This happened with Joe, right?"

She brushed his damp shoulder with her fingertips. "Sometimes."

"Sometimes?"

"A—a few times."

He studied her flushed face with intensity now.

"It…just happens," she said defensively. "It's not something I can control."

Tye absorbed those words. Those startling and innocent words. "When it happened…with Joe…did he know about it? Did he try to make it happen?"

She shook her head. "I don't think he knew. I'm sure he didn't."

"It *is* something you can control, Meg, my heart. By telling me what you like and when to wait for you."

"You mean it's okay?"

"It's more than okay. I don't think we should ever stop until it's been okay for you." His beautiful lips curved up into a smile. "I've already learned some of the things you like and I plan to discover as many more as I can."

"This isn't shameful, is it, Tye? What we've done? I mean, doing this isn't just for making babies?"

"I think the good Lord assured man's continuance by creating baby-making so pleasurable. If He didn't want us to enjoy it, He would have thought of something else, or He wouldn't have said we'd be one flesh."

She laughed. Tye turned his nose against her breast and inhaled. He reached for a fistful of her hair and pulled the skein against his nose and mouth. Earthy and honest, she thought, threading her own fingers into his hair and understanding his tactile pleasure with enlightenment.

Of all the things he'd done for her, this newfound sense of freedom was perhaps the best. She didn't have to be ashamed of anything with Tye.

A tiny niggle of guilt tried to wedge its way into her consciousness. Joe would have wanted her to be happy. But would he have wanted Tye to reach her on a level that he never had?

Meg tamped down that doubt. He would have wanted her to be happy. And Tye made her happy.

Tye got up and extinguished the lamps.

For a fleeting second, she wondered where her nightgown had flown. But then Tye eased behind her, adjusted his body so that he cradled her from behind, her head pillowed on his arm, and Meg closed her eyes in sleepy contentment she'd never before known.

She woke during the night, his heat and his hardness a titillating distraction from sleep.

"Are you awake, Tye?"

He kissed the back of her neck. "Do you know no one calls me Tye except you?"

"Eve does."

"Because she mimics you."

"Don't you like it?"

His hand slid up her belly and cupped her breast. "I love it."

"I have to tell you, I wondered if you'd ever call me anything but ma'am."

He pressed openmouthed kisses along her shoulder and sent shivers along her arms and to her breasts. "My mama taught me to be respectful."

"Who taught you all these other enjoyable things?"

"A gentleman never tells."

"I told you about me and Joe." The inflection in her voice betrayed the seriousness of her question.

He drew lazy circles around her nipple. "My mother was a whore, Meg. Those were the women I grew up around. None of the girls at school would give me the time of day."

"And Lottie? Was she someone special?"

"We were friends. When no one else cares if you live or die, any friend is special."

"But you didn't marry her. Was that because of her...occupation?"

"Because I didn't love her."

"And she didn't have a ranch."

His hand stilled.

"I didn't mean it like that, Tye. I just meant there's more than one reason to get married. You don't have to love the person."

No, but you should at least have the *hope* that someday they *will* love you, he thought.

She surprised him by turning to face him, guiding his hands back to her breasts, then placing her hand on his shoulder. "You know what I like now, Tye. How about what you like? Can you tell me?"

She discovered their likes were mutual.

"Eve said you promised her a 'picwic,'" Meg said the following noon when Tye came in for lunch.

They exchanged a look that held secrets, a look of awakening and wonder only lovers share, and Tye warmed all the way to his toes. He'd never known the joy he'd experienced with Meg. If only—he caught himself and replied, "A what?"

"A 'picwic.' I figured out what she meant when she said you told her we'd take food and drinks and eat out-of-doors."

"Yes." He grinned, hanging his hat and taking a seat. "I guess I did promise her that."

"Why don't we do it this Saturday?"

Tye thought over the mental list of things he had to do, then cast them aside. Nothing was more important than his new family. "All right. Saturday."

Gus and Eve entered the kitchen, and Gus helped Eve onto the bench beside Tye.

A rancher had sent word that his mares were ready to cover, and Tye planned to take over the stallion that afternoon. "Meg," he said, buttering a slice of bread. "Joe had those liver chestnuts sent to the ranch while he was down south, didn't he?"

She spooned gravy over his plate of biscuits. "A couple of men delivered them."

"They didn't happen to give you any papers, did they?"

"Not that I remember. That was almost two years ago. Why?"

"There's something unusual about those animals. They appear to have some Arabian blood, but I'm not sure. They're fifteen hands high, but their heads are neat and their ears small, more ponylike."

"They're hardy animals," Gus said. "Healthy, and don't seem to mind weather. Admired 'em ever since they got here."

"They'd make great mounts if they were gelded,"

Tye commented, "but I have a feeling they're worth more as breeders. Joe never said anything about them?"

"I never saw Joe after he sent those horses home," she replied. "And he never mentioned them in his letters."

Tye sipped his coffee, absorbed in his thoughts.

"Maybe there's something I missed among his papers and things that were sent to me," she thought aloud.

"Will you look?"

"Now?"

"I'd really like to know."

She wiped her hands on her apron and left the room. Several minutes later, she returned with a pouch of papers. "Maybe there's something in here."

An odd sensation dipped in his belly at more evidence of how she'd preserved all of Joe's possessions. The letters and grooming items in her trunk came to mind.

Tye dismissed the painful thoughts, pulled a stack of records from the leather pouch and leafed through them. A few official-looking documents caught his eye and he examined them closely. "Hot damn!"

"Tye!" Meg admonished.

Tye ignored her and laughed aloud, waving his discovery for the others to see. "Yorkshire Flame," he read from the first paper. "A Welsh cob, listed in section D in the studbook. We've got us a papered stud." He looked up again. "I've read about this breed—they're mountain horses."

"What does this mean?" she asked. "They're really worth something?"

Tye flipped through the pages. "All three of them. Papers are officially signed by someone named Brescia. Looks like..."

"What?"

"Looks like Joe won 'em in a poker game."

"No," Meg said, her voice disbelieving. She'd never known Joe to gamble.

"Here's the man's signature." Tye held it out for her to see.

She took the paper and read it herself.

"Smart of ya to cover our mares with him," Gus commented with a raised eyebrow.

"You did?" Meg asked, looking up excitedly.

"They look like they'd have stamina as saddle horses," Tye said with a shrug. "Had to make some kind of choice."

"So now what?"

"Now when I take old Yorkshire Flame a-courtin', I show his papers, and we can get a handsome price for his services."

"Did Joe know how much they'd be worth?" Meg asked.

"'Course he did. This man wouldn't have put up valuable horses unless the stakes were high."

Meg stacked plates.

Tye went for his hat. "I'll be gone the rest of the day." *I'll miss you,* he wanted to say, but Gus was still picking up dishes, and the words seemed too familiar.

"We'll be waiting," she said, as though she too

felt the desire to touch or say something more before they parted. His gaze drifted across her hair. Surely his feelings for her were blatant in his every look. He couldn't look at her without a gut-wrenching twist of unrequited love wrapping him in knots. What a pathetic idiot he'd become.

"Carry me outside to wave goodbye," Eve said, enviously free to show her need for affection.

Tye picked her up, hugged her and gave Meg a final nod. Turning, he left the house, relieved that Meg had saved Joe's papers but disturbed that, even in death, Joe was still providing for Meg better than he could.

He'd been quiet ever since he'd brought her the stud money, enough to pay another three-month banknote. The rancher he'd done business with told another, and by Saturday, they'd had to deposit the cash in the bank.

Meg thought he should have been dancing for joy. She herself sang and daydreamed as she did her chores. But it wasn't only the money. The money had been the icing on the cake after their relationship had blossomed into intimacy.

She'd never known how exhilarating and wonderful it felt to cast one's inhibitions into the wind and enjoy another person wholeheartedly. Each morning she paused before the mirror and saw the change Gwynn had mentioned. She did look different. And she certainly felt different. She was so exhilarated some mornings, she couldn't even eat.

Meg set out their lunch on the blanket Tye had

spread beneath a walnut tree and fixed places for the three of them.

"You was right, Tye!" Eve exclaimed. "Meg brung milk in a jar."

"Growing girls need their milk," he said with a smile.

"And I'm growing bigger," she said.

"You certainly are," Meg agreed. "You'll be big enough to go to school next fall."

"Will I?"

Tye frowned but said nothing.

They ate their lunch, an ordinary meal made special by Eve's exuberant delight. The sun filtered down through the leaves, speckling their heads and shoulders with golden light and bone-penetrating warmth. Meg couldn't remember being so happy.

Tye had initiated her to physical delights and taught her lovemaking was nothing to be ashamed of. Eve's presence added a cheer and a fullness to their home and their every activity that filled Meg's heart in another way.

And they had money in the bank. For the first time in several years Meg could breathe easily. There was enough for the next note *and* some improvements around the ranch. She could even buy material for dresses and order Eve a doll from a catalog.

What could possibly be better?

After eating, they threw walnut shells that the squirrels had left last fall, seeing who could throw the farthest. Tye let Meg win. He chased Eve across the tall grass and hid from her behind an outcropping of red rocks.

She found him, and they again chased one another. Finally, exhausted, Eve drank the remainder of the milk and fell asleep on the blanket, using Tye's thigh for a pillow.

He finger-combed the girl's hair from her forehead.

"Is something wrong?" Meg asked finally. He'd made exquisite love to her each night. He'd gone about his daily routine each day. But something didn't feel quite right.

"What could be wrong, Meg?" he asked.

"I don't know. You've been sort of quiet."

"Quiet bother you?"

"No." She plucked at the nap of the blanket. "You didn't seem very pleased about me mentioning school for Eve."

"I don't want her to go to school."

She stared at him. "But, Tye! How will she get an education? I know you're not one of those men who think women shouldn't learn reading and arithmetic."

"Not at all." He gazed affectionately on the sleeping child. "I want her to have a better life than I had. I want her to be educated. But you and I can do that."

She studied his handsome face, his blue eyes, letting her gaze encompass his broad shoulders and travel the length of his legs to where they crossed at the ankles.

When he noticed her perusal, his expression grew tender. He took the tablecloth she'd rolled, placed it beneath Eve's head and moved beside Meg. Stretching out, he pulled her down beside him, and she met his supple lips.

Tye stroked her cheek, gazed into her eyes and

kissed her leisurely. She adored his attention. Craved it now. Everything he'd done since they'd ventured into this relationship had endeared him to her. And his love and concern for Eve only reinforced his goodness.

''I'm not a teacher,'' Meg said, touching his sun-dappled cheek. ''And you have your hands full with the ranch. She can learn so much more in school.''

''The only thing more she can learn is how small-minded and cruel other people are—children and adults alike,'' he replied, their noses touching. ''I won't put her through that. I know how it feels to be looked on as something low and dirty. I never want her to feel like that.''

Meg didn't know what to reply. She'd believed people would come around after she'd married Tye, but so far only one or two out of a hundred even spoke to her. She'd been excluded from church activities and women's gatherings, stared at, whispered about and verbally attacked.

And *she* came from a respectable family. Her parents had been married. She had no idea how much worse it had been for Tye all his life. How much worse it could be for Eve.

''Maybe we just need to show them she's as good as they are, and that we're not ashamed of her—or of ourselves.''

''Just like you showed 'em, huh, Meg?'' he said, caressingly threading his fingers through her hair. ''Just like I showed 'em all those years. No. I won't have her hurt like that. And keeping her away from them is the only way I know how to keep her safe.''

His protective instinct was understandable—and endearing, and she knew he meant to safeguard Eve from the same pain he'd endured, but was it right to keep the child hidden away? "I don't know if I have the qualities to teach her all she needs to know. And what about all the time it would take?"

Was she just being selfish?

"I will make this decision, Meg." His tone offered no room for opposition, and being shut out disturbed her…well, *hurt* her.

His vehemence disturbed her. He'd done everything she'd asked of him and never asked for anything in return. If he felt so strongly about Eve not attending school, surely Meg could manage to teach her the basics. He'd said he would share the task. She didn't want anything to change what had been taking place and growing between them. She didn't want to lose this incredible closeness and the delight of his imaginative attentions.

Tye made her feel young and beautiful and alive. He had changed her world. She didn't want to risk losing that for anything. She'd already lost enough.

"All right, Tye. If you feel so strongly."

He ran his palm up her spine, cupped her head and pulled her into a slow, easy kiss. From time to time they spoke softly of inconsequential things. Meg closed her eyes and rested, feeling his touch as he picked grass from her hair or stroked her arm, sensing when he leaned above her on one elbow.

Her face close to his, she smiled into his eyes and he caressed her cheek with a thumb.

When Eve awoke from her nap, she flung herself

over Tye's side with an indelicate flurry of petticoats, and Meg and Tye moved apart to let her rest between them.

"Did you take a nap, too?" she asked.

"Yes," Tye replied with an irrepressible smile. "And now I have work to do, so we'd better get packed up and head back." He sat up.

"Aw, heck," Eve said with a pout, sounding suspiciously like Gus. "Do we have to?"

"Yes, we have to."

"Where's Molly?" Eve asked, glancing around. She got up and searched the blanket.

Meg rose to her feet and straightened her clothing and hair. "Did you bring her? I don't remember seeing her since we've been here."

"I brung her! I did."

Tye and Meg inspected the ground and the basket of food and folded up the blanket. "Your doll's not here," Tye said. "Maybe you left her at home."

"No, I brung Molly. I know I brung her!" Eve burst into tears and crumpled to the ground.

Meg exchanged a startled look with Tye. "It's okay, darling," she said, hurrying to help her up and comfort her. "We'll find her."

They searched again. "Maybe she's at home," Tye whispered.

Meg finally had to agree.

They mounted the horses and rode back to the house, Eve wailing in Tye's lap. By the time they reached the house, Tye looked frantic and Meg felt sick to her stomach. Another investigation ensued without turning up the doll.

By this time Eve was hysterical, and Tye paced the kitchen, running a hand through his hair. "It's just a rag doll," he said and asked Meg over her howls, "Can't you make her another one?"

"Do-hon't want ano-hother one," Eve managed to say between sobs. "I want Molly!"

Meg pulled Eve into her lap and tried to console her.

"Maybe she dropped it along the way somewhere," Tye said.

"I looked as we rode home," Meg told him. "But we may not have traveled the exact same ground."

"I'll go look."

"Take Major," Meg suggested.

Tye nodded and left.

Chapter Fourteen

Meg moved into the other room and settled in the rocker with Eve squirming in her lap. After a while the child calmed down some, but her hiccuping sobs nearly broke Meg's heart.

After a torturous forty-five minutes, hoofbeats sounded, followed by the thud of Tye's boots crossing the kitchen floor. He appeared, holding the much coveted doll.

"Molly!" Eve shot from Meg's lap and Tye bent to hand her the rag doll. She grabbed it in the crook of one arm, Tye's neck in the other, knocking his hat to the floor, and plastered kisses on his cheek. "You found her, Tye, you found her!"

Meg could only shake her head in relief and amazement. She'd never seen anything like Eve's desperation before, and while waiting, she'd wondered if they would ever be able to sleep again if the doll wasn't recovered.

Eve pulled away from Tye, plopped herself on the lion skin and stroked the doll's dress lovingly.

"End of crisis," Tye said wryly.

"Where'd you find it?" Meg asked.

"Major's the hero. He found it in some tall grass we'd ridden through."

"Want a cup of coffee?"

He shook his head. "A cigarette."

Meg grinned at his back as he left the house.

The following week, Tye finished the porch and built chairs and a swing. Meg didn't know who was more surprised and pleased, she or Eve. Eve delighted in having someone with long enough legs sit beside her and rock her. Meg appreciated a place to sit and enjoy the summer air and the view of the ranch. One evening Meg rocked Eve while sewing a cushion from scraps of fabric. She worked and listened to Eve's chatter.

After it grew too dark to sew, she spread a blanket in the yard so she and Eve could watch the stars before bedtime.

Tye finished chores and discovered them lying on their backs, pointing skyward. "What're you ladies doing?"

"Looking at stars," Eve answered. "Did you know they have names?"

He lay down on the other side of her and stared up into the heavens. "I don't remember their names. Does Meg?"

"Not all of them," Meg replied. All the more reason to send Eve to school.

"Is my mama up there?" Eve asked.

Meg cast Tye a sideways glance. He was always

open and willing to talk to Eve. It was Meg with whom she'd begun to think he didn't want to talk.

"Wherever heaven is, Eve, that's where your mama is," he replied softly.

"Is it up there?"

"Maybe."

"Can she see us?"

"I think she's watching over you to make sure you're okay."

"Maybe she helped you find Molly today."

"Maybe," Tye said.

"Do you think she can see the swing?"

"I imagine so," Tye replied patiently.

Eve sat and picked up the doll. "Mama was pretty in this dress," she said.

Not comprehending, Meg sat up, too. "What dress, Eve?"

"This one." She straightened the shiny green fabric of the doll's skirt. "Mama made Molly's dress from one of hers. It was her favorite, she said, and she wanted Molly to have it."

The doll's significance took on a whole new meaning. Meg looked over to find Tye still gazing into the stars, his fingers laced on his chest, his ankles crossed. He did nothing to indicate he was listening.

"Your mama made that doll for you?"

"Uh-huh. She wasn't very sick then. Just sort of. And she didn't go to work anymore. We played together a lot. She told me that someone would come get me before the angels took her."

Meg blinked back the sting of tears.

"And then Tye came," Eve finished.

Lottie had certainly chosen well. Meg had never thought of it like that before. With no one to turn to, the woman had done the very best she could for her daughter. She had to have known Tye would have Eve's best interests at heart. She must have known Tye as well as Meg did. Or better.

The thought disturbed her as immensely as all the others she'd been having. The more she saw Tye and Eve together, the more she noticed the resemblance. Their hair was the same thick, shiny black. Both had a wide lower lip and a softly sculptured upper one. And both had a solitary dimple on the left side of their mouth that winked when they grinned broadly.

That very day while Meg bathed Eve, she had admired her long, slender limbs and her all-over honey complexion. Both Tye and Eve had told her that Lottie had been a redhead. Eve had golden skin like Tye's.

She tried to remember what Tye had said regarding Eve's parentage, recalling only that it had been a comment about the impossibility of knowing who'd sired her. Had Lottie truly not known? Surely once a black-haired infant had been placed in her arms, the possibilities would have been dramatically narrowed.

Mortified at her thinking, Meg listened to the two of them talk softly. A bond had developed between them, a bond as strong as that between a parent and child. Was it possible that Tye actually didn't know? Men were blind to a good many things a woman knew by instinct, Meg had learned.

But Lottie…Lottie had to have known. She'd either used Tye or played on his honor. Or both. Meg chastised herself. She had no business judging anyone else's behavior or character. Rosa had certainly been nice enough. And if Tye had felt something for Lottie, she must have been a good person, too.

Bereft, Meg felt left out of their relationship. She hadn't known Lottie, nor had she experienced growing up without a parent. Eve was simply drawn to Tye and vice versa. Their parent-child bond was a good thing.

Eve yawned and crawled toward Tye. He looped his arm around her, and she curled up against him, the doll beneath her chin.

Meg observed their closeness with a hollow ache in her chest. Who was it she envied? Lottie? Eve? Or Tye?

Several nights later, Tye stood rolling his second cigarette in a row and listened to the distant sound of thunder splintering across the mountains. He stood in the side doorway of the barn, watching Yorkshire Flame. The horse was probably frustrated that his season's work was finished. He pranced along the far side of the fence and took a taunting run past Tye every so often. The high-strung animal had always been placed in this corral at night, the barn door left open so he could either exercise or enter at will. Gus had built a gate so he couldn't get any farther in than his own stall.

Depending on how many of their own foals were males, they might need a second barn in another year. Already they could afford it with the stud fees this horse had brought in.

Tye's feelings were in a quandary. He'd experienced great relief that Meg had saved Joe's things, the papers especially. Otherwise they'd never have known the true value of the Welsh cobs.

And every day he thought about Joe's stroke of luck—or genius—in acquiring the animals and having them sent home. Because of that, their financial difficulties were now ended.

But it disturbed and galled Tye that even in death Joe still managed to provide for Meg. Joe's horses, poker spoils or not, had been their salvation. Tye had pathetically knocked himself out earning the money for Meg's wedding ring, then recovering her father's ring, while faultless Joe had smoothly left behind a treasure trove from which to draw upon.

Tye crushed the stub of his smoke beneath his boot heel. Maybe he was better off not having anything lofty to live up to.

A year after the Welsh mares Tye had bred with Yorkshire Flame foaled, they'd be able to sell them. Add that profit to the stud money and they could build a new house.

And they now had collateral to start *his* project. Somehow he'd been unable to bring up the dream of the slaughterhouse. His insufferable pride held him back. It was still just that: a dream.

In the bright moonlight, he caught sight of Meg approaching the corral fence. She stood and watched the magnificent horse dart across the ground in erratic bursts of energy.

Tye walked through the barn and around the side

to where she stood. "I think the weather has him edgy," he said.

"Me, too," she revealed, acknowledging Tye's company.

"It'll most likely blow over."

"What were you thinking about over there for so long?" she asked.

Had she been watching him before she'd walked over? "The horses," he replied.

"Can we talk, Tye?"

"We're talking."

"No, we're not. We're skirting around whatever it is that's changed."

"Nothing has changed." He still felt the same way about her. She still felt the same way about Joe. Everything was the same.

She released a frustrated sigh. "Something has, yes, it has. And it has to do with one of two things. I imagined it was the horses, but I don't know why you wouldn't be happy about that. Or else it was me suggesting Eve go to school."

He studied the night sky, and Meg studied his face, hating this expanding emotional distance between them. "I hate not being able to discuss it, if that's it. I agreed to teach her, after all."

"That's not it, Meg."

"It's the horses, then."

He rubbed his jaw and raked his hair back with his fingers. "I guess so."

"Well...why aren't you happy about them? We have everything we want now."

He turned and looked her fully in the face. "Do we?"

His coldness frightened her. A sick feeling curled in the core of her already churning stomach. "What more do we need? You can start your packing plant now—"

"Joe's packing plant, you mean."

The disturbing way he said Joe's name gave her pause. "What do you mean?"

"Yorkshire Flame is Joe's horse."

"Well…" *Joe's dead,* she wanted to cry, but the words stuck in her throat—and the fact in her heart. "We agreed," she said. "You help me, then I help you. You kept your end of the bargain. I will, too. It will be 'our' packing plant, won't it? Like it's 'our' ranch."

"It doesn't feel like it's 'our' ranch," he said.

Meg considered his words, gratified to understand them. She understood—because she felt the same. "I don't feel like Eve is 'our' child," she said bluntly.

He turned toward her.

"I have the responsibility of bathing her and dressing her," she explained. "I've sewn her clothes and cooked the meals she eats. But it's you she's crazy about."

"She likes you, Meg."

"Yes, but I have to discipline her and instruct her. You get to spoil her."

"She's not spoiled."

"She will be."

He stiffened his shoulders. "Are you saying I'm doing something wrong?"

"No. I just don't have equal say. And I obviously have no say in her education—you've made that clear."

"I'm sorry, but I can't change how I feel about her schooling. I'm sorry if it makes more work for you, but—"

"It's not the work," she denied. "It's not that at all. It's everything else."

"Like what?"

"Like…" Her better judgment screamed a warning. Her jealousy ignored it. "Like *Lottie*."

"Lottie?" he questioned, clearly puzzled.

"I'm not as ignorant as that fence post," she said. "You were every bit as familiar with that woman as you've been with me. How long ago was that? You never said precisely. Five years? Six? And then she summons you to her deathbed and wrings your promise to raise this little girl. This little girl with black hair and one single dimple on the left side of her smile. What am I supposed to think, Tye? What?"

He stood squarely before her, her momentous words—thoughts he hadn't known words for—groping for comprehension. Five or six years ago, well before the onset of the war…. Yes, the timing was possible, but there'd been so many others… He had no way of knowing with certainty. And Lottie'd been as desperate for someone to take her child as Meg had been for a man to work the ranch. He hadn't been selected to take Eve for any complimentary reason that he could think of.

"Is Eve your child?" she asked.

Elation and doubt clapped around inside his head. Pride and tenderness ebbed and swelled and fought for prominence. Hope quelled them all and calmed his racing heart like a sweet promise.

Elusive thoughts he'd never allowed before came into complete clarity. He'd only been kidding himself about his relationship with Meg. She'd married him for one reason and one reason only. Everyone knew it—no one better than Tye. No matter what he had done and no matter what he could or would do— working, planning, praying—it hadn't been enough. It would never be enough. She was still Joe's wife. She would never really be his.

But Eve, on the other hand...

"I don't know if she's mine," he said at last, his voice steadier than he'd expected. "But I hope like hell she is. I already love her like she's mine. I want her to be."

"Why?" she asked, raising trembling fingers to her mouth.

The reasons ballooned inside of him, filled his head, his will, his purpose. A lifetime of whys rose up and blinded him to her pain. "Why?" he replied tersely. "I'll tell you why. Because *that* is Joe's horse," he said, stabbing a finger toward the corral. "And that's Joe's barn. This is Joe's dirt we're standing on."

Puzzlement silenced her.

Tye snatched her by the forearm and pulled her across the expanse of the dooryard. *"This,"* he said when they reached the front stairs, "is Joe's house."

He led her up the new porch steps, where Major greeted them with a wagging tail. "That's Joe's dog," he said on the way past, the screen door squawking in their wake. He tugged her past the sleeping Eve into the bedroom and gestured with a bitter sweep of his arm. "*That* is Joe's bed."

He released her finally, and she stumbled back a step, alarm straining her lovely face.

Caught up in his explanation now, Tye flung back the trunk lid. "Let's not forget Joe's personal things."

Meg's eyes were now wide and glistening.

"His ring is probably in there somewhere, along with God knows what else." He strode toward her and she stared up into his face, her heart leaping.

"And *you*," he said, pointing with one finger that deliberately didn't touch her chest, "are Joe's wife."

Meg stared from the trunk to Tye's angry face and posture. Stunned, she could think of nothing to say.

"But there's one thing I'm certain could never have been Joe's," he said, his voice changing timbre. He guided her gently to the doorway and pointed at the sleeping child. "That beautiful kid isn't Joe's daughter."

Meg blinked, trying to comprehend, preparing herself for what she didn't want to hear or know.

"I want her to be *mine,* Meg. I want that with all my heart. Just one pure thing in this whole stinkin' world that's mine."

She nodded, tears stinging her eyelids, raw compassion stifling her breathing. That which she'd feared, he desired. That which she envied, he gloried in.

"She sees me as someone I want with all my heart to be," he said hoarsely. "She never says, 'Joe did it this way,' or 'Joe wouldn't have done that.' She never knew Joe—she could care less about who the hell Joe Telford was because it doesn't affect her. For her, there's only me. And I'm good enough for her.''

Heart pounding, stomach turning, Meg bit back a sob. She'd heard others say things like that to Tye—she'd said them herself without thinking. Without knowing the hurt they'd caused.

She understood. Lord help her, she understood. She'd been jealous of Tye's affection for this child, and now that knowledge made her feel smaller than she'd ever felt.

The front door opened and closed and she looked up to find him gone. Wandering into their bedroom, she perched on the edge of the bed and stared absently at the open trunk. Silent tears streamed down her cheeks.

All that hurt and anger had been pent-up inside the man. No wonder he'd never let it out before. If it was her, she'd never have been able to quit releasing it once she'd started.

Her stomach churned. She got up and bolted out the front door and vomited into the weeds beside the house. After the display of nerves passed, she returned and prepared for bed.

She did understand Tye's need for and his attachment to Eve. But she'd been forced to suffer the scorn of the townspeople right along with him. How many of them suspected Eve was his child? Was that why they'd been particularly nasty?

Meg hated her selfishness, but some of it was justified. She had to live her life like this now, too.

Climbing into bed, she thought back over his every kindness, the sacrifices he'd made to get back her father's ring and the unselfish way he gave of himself in all things, and she knew she was the one who wasn't as good as him. But she wasn't sure how to change her feelings.

Especially now that they both believed Tye was Eve's real father. And now that she knew how strongly Tye felt about it. Once again, her world had been shaken. And she prayed she'd find a way to adapt.

A few nights later, Tye came in before dark so he could spend time with Eve before she went to sleep. Meg sat sewing near a lantern and Eve turned the pages of a book, pretending she was reading it aloud.

"I'm just in time for your story," Tye said, settling in the overstuffed chair he preferred.

Eve continued her story, embellishing with child-like details that brought a smile to Meg's face as well as a laugh to his lips. She finished, and he applauded.

Eve brought her trinket box out and chattered about the contents. "This here's the hankie that Meg made me. See, it has my initials in the corner by this little flower?"

"It's very pretty," he said, warmed to think something Meg had made her ranked among her treasures.

Eve withdrew a square-linked neck chain with a dangling locket. She held the round locket in her palm and the light winked from the distinctive rhinestones set in a crescent-moon shape. To the left side of the rhinestone moon was an opal sun.

Tye immediately recognized the piece of jewelry as one he'd purchased from a hawker many years ago and given to Lottie. She'd never had much, so he guessed it wasn't unusual she'd kept it all these years. It seemed strange seeing it again, however.

"This here's the prettiest neck chain in all of the kingdom," Eve said, still in her fairy-tale verbiage. "Meg thinks its pretty, too, don't you, Meg? And she thinks I'll look real pretty when I wear it after I'm big."

Tye nodded his agreement.

"Mama said when I'm bigger and I wear it, I will find my daddy."

Tye's attention riveted on her words. "What did she mean?"

"Mama said my daddy gave it to her, and when I find who gave it to her, I will find my daddy."

Tye could barely breathe around the emotion welling in his throat. Lottie *had* known! Now he could be certain that this child he'd grown to love was really his.

"I gave that to your mama, Evie," he said in a hoarse whisper.

In the other chair, Meg's fingers stilled on the fabric of the dress she held.

Eve looked up at Tye with round and trusting blue eyes. "You gave it to her? You did? Are you my daddy, Tye?"

He worked the lump in his throat so he could speak around it. "I'd be your daddy even if she hadn't said I was the one. You know that, don't you?"

She nodded, and a bright smile lit her angelic features. She got up and stood leaning against his knee. "I can call you Daddy now?"

"If you want to."

"I do."

He lifted her up for a hug and settled her on his lap. She nestled into the warmth and comfort he was glad to offer.

A whole new security washed over Tye. He had a daughter, someone who belonged to him and him alone. Guiltily, he glanced over at Meg.

She placed her sewing on the basket beside her chair and went into the bedroom, closing the door behind her.

The only break Tye took from haying in the next few weeks, other than quick meals and a few hours' sleep, was a previously arranged trip to town that Friday. He and Meg left Eve with Gus and traveled the distance to sign adoption papers at the lawyer's office. Now that Meg understood his feelings regarding her and the ranch, now that she knew Eve was really Tye's child, she took sad-sweet pleasure in watching him sign the documents and receive the certificate that said Eve was theirs.

She knew exactly how he felt about Joe now. Because she felt excluded from the relationship he and Eve were forming.

They stepped out onto the boardwalk, and the summer heat hit Meg full force. A woozy sensation filled her head. She must have swayed where she stood because Tye placed an arm securely around her waist.

"It's so hot," she said, feeling foolish.

"Want a lemonade before we head back?"

"Sure. Let's celebrate." He kept hold of her as they crossed the street and entered a small café populated by the afternoon tea crowd.

Edwina, Wilsie and Gwynn, along with several other women and three little girls, were seated at a table in front of the window. As soon as she and Tye entered, Meg knew the unnatural silence was due to something Edwina had said. Already hot and irritable, Meg swallowed her anger and disgust, gave Lilly a defiant little wave and turned her attention from the gossiping women.

Tye led her to a cloth-draped table. The male proprietor took their order and brought them mugs of cold lemonade. Meg sipped hers gratefully, her head clearing.

"Taking liberties with her in broad daylight," a voice she recognized as her former mother-in-law's trilled.

Meg drank the refreshing liquid and met Tye's stormy gaze, Edwina's words fueling her temper. The insult and injury Tye endured was never revealed on his face or in his actions. She was probably the only person who'd ever recognized Tye's hurt—and she was obviously the only one who'd ever cared.

"Thank God Joe had the decency and the manners to treat her like a lady. And back then she behaved like one."

Tye's jaw twitched and his lips formed an angry slash. But it was Meg who shot out of her chair and crossed to the other table.

"I am sick and tired of your constant harping about a man you know nothing of," she said, leaning over Edwina. "Tye Hatcher is the kindest, most honorable man I've ever known, and he doesn't pretend to be anything he's not. I've had it up to *here*—'' she gestured with her hand across her forehead and saw Edwina flinch ''—with your small-minded, puritanical, hypocritical, judgmental back-stabbing!''

Edwina's face turned purple with fury, and her overendowed chest puffed out like an indignant banty hen's. ''How dare you parade yourself and that man in front of this community. You may not care about your good name, but you could at least consider the rest of us Telfords!''

''I am pleased to inform you that my name is no longer Telford. It's Hatcher. And while the name Hatcher doesn't immediately make one think of a big house with a 'veranda—''' she said the word with an uppity inflection ''—it does make one think of hard work and honesty.''

Beside Edwina, Gwynn's mortification stood out plainly on her pale face. Lilly stared wide-eyed. Another woman, the one who'd spoken politely to Meg and Tye after his musical debut, gave Meg an embarrassed, apologetic look.

Wilsie pulled a bottle of smelling salts from her reticule and cast her mother wary looks.

''You have never cared about my good name, Edwina. Or my feelings or my future,'' Meg went on. A trickle of perspiration itched between her breasts and her vision blurred with the heat, but she had her teeth sunk into the immediate subject, and she wasn't ready to let go. ''All your concern is for *your* name and *your* standing and *your* wants and wishes! You should be ashamed of the example you're setting for these women—*and* for Forrest and Lilly. You're teaching your grandchildren to be just as bigoted and close-minded as you—just like you taught Harley! I'm sorry, Gwynn.''

Gwynn shook her head gently. "No, no, it's true.''

"Joe wasn't like you, Edwina, or I wouldn't have loved him or married him. He saw people as equals. He was never unkind to Tye. *You're* the one he's ashamed of if he's watching today.''

Meg felt herself sway. Gwynn stood and took Meg's arm to steady her, and Meg sensed Tye come up behind her.

"Meg's right,'' Gwynn said to her mother-in-law timidly. "I want my children to grow up loving others, not condemning them. I don't want them to be critical, with no forgiveness in their hearts.''

A commotion on the street outside the window seized Meg's attention, and several men and women ran past the café shouting.

Tye left Meg with Gwynn and stepped to the door. "What's wrong?''

"Fire at the livery,'' Claudelle Parks called loud enough for them all to hear. "Jon Whitaker sent for help.''

"Stay with her,'' Tye said to Gwynn, and shot out the door.

"Harley and Forrest are there with the pony,'' Gwynn said, terror lacing her voice.

Meg clasped her hand and they followed.

Black smoke curled into the bright blue sky, and a scorched scent permeated the air. The group of women and children and the café owner hurried toward the source.

One entire side of the wood structure was in flames, smoke billowing from the open double doors.

Gwynn gripped Meg's hand so hard she winced.

"Perhaps they're out riding," Meg suggested, searching the confusion for Harley and her nephew as well as Tye.

Men shouted and ran in all directions. It seemed to take forever before buckets appeared and the bystanders organized themselves to dip water and pass the heavy containers forward.

"Let's help with the buckets, Gwynn," she said, pulling her toward the nearest trough. They hung their handbags from a hitching post and pushed their sleeves up.

"Cinnamon!" a youthful voice cried in panic. Meg spun to see Forrest racing across the street toward the flaming building, Harley quite a ways behind.

"Forrest!" Gwynn screamed.

A horse whinnied, and Tye came through the smoke-filled doorway into the safety of the street, holding a feed sack over the eyes of a mare he could barely control. Meg's heart plummeted at the sight of him covered with soot. Tye uncovered the mare's head and let her run.

Blinking against the daylight, Tye spotted the young boy tearing past him toward the stable. He turned and bolted after Forrest.

Gwynn screamed, stumbling forward to her knees. Harley helped her up.

"Forrest!" she cried, yanking away. "Go after Forrest!"

Harley turned and took a couple of hesitant steps toward the livery.

The boy's shouts could be heard over the commotion before they saw him. "Cinnamon's in there! My pony's in there! Let me go! Put me down!"

Tye carried him out over his shoulder, the lad kicking and pounding his back. Tye held him firmly until he reached Harley, and then deposited the boy at his father's feet. Harley clamped his hands over Forrest's shoulders and detained him.

"My pony's in there," Forrest sobbed. "Please, mister!"

Gwynn ran and hugged her son. He sobbed and pointed to the building.

Another man, his face and hands blackened, led another panicked horse into the street and released him.

"That it?" Tye called to him.

"Two more in the rear stalls," he gasped. "We'll never get to them in time."

"Cinnamon!" Forrest screamed.

Tye grabbed a bucket from the nearest man and poured the contents over his head and shoulders. Meg's breath left her lungs when she realized his intent. "No! Tye!" she shouted, panic constricting her voice to a croak.

Before she could move forward, he'd darted back into the thick, choking smoke.

Chapter Fifteen

Meg watched the doorway with her eyes burning and her heart in her throat. "It's a horse," she said in shock, weighing the risk. "A horse!"

"Listen to you," Gwynn replied from beside her. "You've made more sacrifices than most people because of your love for horses."

"Not just for the horses," Meg said with a shake of her head and a sob in her throat. "For the dream. So I could still be me."

"He didn't even stop to think about going in there," Gwynn said. "He just ran in."

Harley had come to stand beside Gwynn. He now held Forrest, who still sobbed hysterically. Meg fought against echoing his desperate wail by mouthing a fervent prayer.

Too much time passed. Meg's anxiety increased with each second. An ear-splitting crack signaled the collapse of the barn roof; sparks flew, and a shingled section fell over the open doorway, blocking any further passage.

Meg watched in horror.

Gwynn supported her weight when her knees buckled. Wilsie, too, appeared from the crowd and helped Gwynn ease Meg to sit in the dusty street. Meg could hear Lilly crying behind them somewhere. The stable rolled in undulating heat waves.

Wilsie uncapped the smelling salts and swiped the bottle beneath Meg's nose.

Her nose stung and her vision cleared immediately. "Oh, my God, Tye," she whispered. He couldn't be trapped in that inferno. He couldn't be! He couldn't die! She couldn't go on without him. She wouldn't want to. She brought her hand to her mouth.

And Eve. The new adoption papers were in his vest pocket. Meg couldn't even conceive of going to the ranch and telling the child that something had happened to the man she adored, that she'd lost not only her mother, but the father she'd just found.

The man that Meg, too, adored.

Flames danced across the shape that had once been the doorway. An oppressive panic roared in Meg's chest. This couldn't be! Tye couldn't be dead. She stared in disbelief.

A shout came from the alley side of the livery, where men were digging a trench between the blaze and the nearest building. An unfettered horse shot from between the buildings, his eyes wild and rolling, and men scattered out of his path.

Tye stumbled into the clearing next, his fist securely knotted in the Shetland's mane. The poor animal skittered and flung its head up in panic, but Tye held him securely.

"Cinnamon!" Forrest shouted.

Tye led the pony to his owners, and Forrest immediately kicked out of his father's arms. Harley stared at the tears streaming down Tye's char-smeared face. "Why did you do that?" he asked, astonishment written plainly on his features.

Meg had struggled to her feet to run toward Tye. He reached to embrace her against his side. He smelled of acrid smoke. "How did you get out of there?" she asked in joy and wonder.

"Chopped a hole in the back wall," he said, still breathing hard and coughing. "There weren't any flames against that back corner, but I couldn't see through the smoke." He wiped his eyes on his sleeve.

"Here," she said, leading him toward one of the nearly empty troughs. "Wash your eyes."

He obeyed her, plunging his head into the tank. She kept her hand at the small of his back, not wanting to break contact. She flipped up the hem of her skirt, offering him the use of her white eyelet petticoat to dry his face.

"I got it all dirty," he apologized, standing once again.

"I don't care if my petticoat's dirty. I almost lost you in there, you foolish man!"

"Meg, I'd been in there already, I knew the fire was pretty much at the front and along one side. I just didn't expect the smoke to be so bad."

"Don't ever, *ever* do anything like that again," she demanded, striving for composure. "Promise!"

"I promise," he said with a grin.

She flung herself against him, not caring who saw or what they thought. "Oh, Tye, I was so scared."

He ran a thumb over her cheek and held her securely. "You won't have to be scared like that again."

"I refuse to be scared like that again."

She gloried in his masculine strength, his arms around her and his reassuring words. She loved him.

The realization flitted around her, daring her to take notice. But he pulled away. "Sit over there safely away from the fire while I help the men get the last of the flames out."

She watched him go, a lump in her throat.

Harley, too, joined the men, and the women and children watched in silence as the danger of the fire spreading passed. Eventually the charred remains of the livery stood smoldering in the afternoon sun.

Weary and ash-covered, the firefighters headed for their homes and places of business. Tye came toward Meg, Harley on his heels.

"Thank you, Mr. Hatcher," he said from behind.

Tye stopped before Meg and turned to observe the man's uncomfortable expression. Gwynn stood three feet away, satisfaction on her pretty face. Wilsie hung behind her, her wary gaze darting from Tye to the others and back.

"Thank you, Mr. Hatcher," Forrest seconded in his still-wavering childish voice. He gripped the Shetland's mane securely. "Papa, where are we going to keep Cinnamon now?"

Harley obviously hadn't had time to think about it.

"You're welcome to leave him at the ranch," Tye said immediately. "I'm sure he'd be comfortable there until a new livery is built. There's room in the barn, and he could exercise and graze.''

"Can we take him there, Papa?" Forrest asked, looking up at his father hopefully.

"Well, I...I guess so.''

"Good,'' Tye said. "We have a wagon here, if you want us to take him now. I have to get back to the hay.''

He and Harley led Forrest and the Shetland away. Meg and Gwynn exchanged a surprised look and followed, Wilsie on their heels. Lilly, straining to pull away from Edwina, finally broke loose and ran to her mother. Gwynn hugged her and took her hand.

Edwina gave the women on either side of her a sheepish look and dropped in behind. Meg remembered she'd been in the middle of dressing down her former mother-in-law when this whole nightmare had unfolded.

To her great surprise, Edwina huffed forward and touched her arm as they walked briskly behind the men. "Do you feel well enough to ride back?'' she asked. "You could come to the house and rest for a while.''

"I think I'd feel better going back home,'' Meg replied. "Besides, Gus and Eve will start to worry if we're gone too long.''

"Is that old man able to care for her properly?'' she asked with a frown.

Meg would have laughed if her limbs weren't still trembling from the scare she'd had and if she hadn't been too relieved over Tye's safety to give anything else a second thought. Edwina wouldn't be Edwina if she didn't have something to harp about. "They do just fine."

Tye helped Harley and Forrest tie the pony securely to the back of the wagon.

"Won't he get tired walking all the way to your place?" Forrest asked. "Shouldn't he ride back there?" He pointed to the wagon.

"He might be small, but he's hearty," Tye replied. "He'd get too scared if we tried to put him in the wagon bed."

"When can I come see him?" Forrest asked. His face still bore red blotches from his crying.

"Anytime you like," Tye responded with a tired smile.

"This is quite forward of me," Gwynn said, Lilly close at her side, "but if you don't have other plans, why don't we come for dinner after church this Sunday? I'll bring my butter rolls and a pecan pie."

Meg wondered if she'd heard correctly. She wondered if she'd fainted back there and was having some sort of wild dream.

The looks on everyone else's faces told her she was awake and that Gwynn had taken the initiative and made a suggestion that could breach the hard feelings. Forrest beamed. Harley avoided making eye contact and studied the tips of his once shiny boots. Wilsie blinked like a baby bird, scanning the others' faces.

Edwina's cheeks were tinged with bright spots of pink, but she made no objection. What could she have said when Tye had just saved her grandson and his horse in one fell swoop?

Tye looked at Meg, uncertainty lacing his features.

"I think that's a wonderful idea," Meg managed to reply at last. "Nothing would make me happier than to have company for Sunday dinner. Gus and Purdy eat with us," she added as a warning to Edwina. She wouldn't exclude the men who'd been loyal through thick and thin just because the Hatcher name had gained a sudden speck of esteem.

If they were going to accept Meg again, they were going to accept Tye and Eve and her hired hands in the package.

"It's set, then," Gwynn decided. "We'll see you Sunday."

Tye lifted Meg onto the seat, and she waved to the Telfords as the team drew them away.

"I can't believe you risked your life for a horse, Tye," she said in reproach.

"I've risked my life for more thankless reasons," he replied.

"But you have a family now. You have a wife and a daughter."

She couldn't decipher the surprised glance he cast her way.

"You have to think of Eve first," she declared.

He'd lost his hat somewhere and squinted in the afternoon sun. "I've never had a family before," he said, his meditative gaze touching her face, her hair. Streaks of soot remained under his chin and near his eye. His hair had dried in loose waves. "I'll remember that in the future."

"See that you do."

Meg's obvious fear and relief were a surprise to Tye. He thought over her reactions and her words the next day as he forked hay out of the wagon into an enormous pile near the barn.

This situation was new to him. It had been a long time since his mother had been alive and he'd quit school to provide for the two of them. Even then he'd only taken care of her for a few years until she'd died. After that it had never mattered if he took a daring chance because he'd never had anyone counting on him or anyone who cared whether or not he returned.

Meg had behaved as if she cared. She'd brought him to task verbally, but she'd touched him as if to reassure herself of his safety. She'd cried tears of relief.

And all that had followed her magnificent tirade in the café. Tye was accustomed to ignoring the gibes, even prided himself in his practiced ability not to allow the comments and snubs to provoke him.

He'd never had a defender before. He hadn't needed one, but it had been nice to hear the things she'd said on his behalf. She'd called him a kind and wonderful man. But more amazing than that, she'd declared herself Meg *Hatcher*. In front of a dozen people, she'd denied being a Telford. He could see her now, her face flushed and pink, her lovely tawny eyes flashing sparks, her spine stiff with indignation.

Why that particular announcement touched him above all others, he could only guess. He'd thought of her as Joe's wife for so long, it wasn't conceivable to think of her as his. He wasn't good enough for her. But then, had Joe been good enough?

Having a daughter was wonderful, but his life

wouldn't be complete until he truly had a wife. She'd been hurt by the fact that Eve was his child. He understood that, but he couldn't change it. All along he'd thought he could somehow prove himself worthy of her, and yet he'd never been able to accomplish that.

You have a wife and a daughter now, she'd told him. She hadn't even realized the importance of those words.

Encouraged by her display of concern and that revealing declaration, Tye found the workload light and the tasks a pleasure. He had a purpose now. And just maybe he had someone who cared. Just maybe she was starting to think of him as her husband.

By Sunday the news of the fire and Tye's part in it had swept the town. The tone of the whispers rippling among the congregation had a whole new sound. Tye still played the organ, even though Fiona no longer wore the sling, and the newest rumors were that she hadn't really injured her arm at all, that she and Reverend Baker had devised a plot to initiate Tye to the position of church musician.

Whatever the means, the end result pleased all. Tye's playing added a dimension to the worship service that had been missing before. Smiles and pleasant salutations greeted Meg and Tye after the service, and Meg reveled in the change of attitudes.

Tye, on the other hand, seemed reluctant to trust their change of heart. He spoke politely and smiled, but Meg had the impression that he held back.

But she had the impression he held back with her, too, so maybe that was just his way.

She'd started preparation for dinner the night before, and by the time the Telfords arrived, the trestle table was set with the good china and the kitchen smelled of beef and rich gravy.

Edwina looked the table over and glanced about the room. She'd only been there a few times while Joe was alive, and each time she'd criticized the lack of amenities. This time she held her tongue.

Meg knew there was a world of difference between this functional kitchen and the lovely wood-paneled dining room the Telfords ate in on the Sabbath. But she wasn't ashamed of the difference.

Edwina wandered through the other room and returned. ''Meg, you have a veranda!''

Meg smiled inwardly. ''Tye built it.''

''The chairs and the swing, too?''

''Yes.''

''Isn't it a busy season? I'm surprised he took the time away from the cows and whatever else it is you ranchers do to build something purely for enjoyment.''

Meg stopped mashing the pan full of potatoes for a moment to look up in consideration. ''Yes, it has been busy. He worked on it in between other things. When I asked him why, he just said he'd done it because I wanted a porch.''

The fact that Joe had never built her a porch remained unspoken but not unconsidered.

''Sounds pretty romantic to me,'' Gwynn said with a sly smile.

Meg ignored the teasing comment and whipped her potatoes.

Ten minutes later, she rang the bell, and hungry men and children hurried into the house. Eve scrambled up onto her bench near Tye's chair and, eyeing the strangers, leaned so far toward him Meg thought she'd fall off onto the floor.

She found a stool in the pantry and seated Eve on it so she could be closer to Tye. He allowed her to snuggle his shirtfront while fixing her plate and his own.

Everyone paused while he said a brief and appropriate blessing, and then bowls and platters were passed. Meg was proud to have plenty of food to serve her guests, and pleased that they'd come.

Gus and Purdy had dressed in their best shirts and pomaded their sparse hair. Purdy's handlebar mustache was a work of art.

Forrest accidentally dropped a crockery bowl with green beans and bacon remaining in the bottom. Harley started to reprimand the boy, but Tye held up one hand, stood and strode to the door.

Major bounded in and Tye picked up the unharmed bowl and pointed to the mess on the floor. The dog eagerly licked up the treat, and the adults joined the children in a gale of laughter.

"Is that what you used to do with your food?" Meg asked him, leaning in to whisper.

"Only one biscuit—ever," he replied.

She laughed.

"Gus used to eat part of it when you weren't looking, though," he admitted.

She squeezed his arm…and met Gwynn's twinkling gaze. Heat rose up her cheeks.

After dinner, Gus chased the women onto the porch and took over the cleanup.

"Does Gus always do that?" Edwina asked, wide-eyed with amazement.

"On Sundays," she replied. "He helps with meals every day, though. And does nearly all the cooking on the range during roundup."

"My goodness, it's like having your very own live-in help," Edwina gushed.

"It's more like having another member of the family," Meg corrected easily. "I pay Gus and Purdy so little, I think of them as family. They've been here since Joe bought the place, and stayed with me all through the war."

"How is your garden doing, Meg?" Gwynn asked.

"My beans have grown clear up the poles," she replied.

"Let's go have a look."

Meg and Gwynn excused themselves from Edwina and Wilsie and the children, donned sunbonnets and walked out to survey the plants.

"I didn't know you were interested in vegetables," Meg said with a lift of one eyebrow.

"New growing things always fascinate me," she replied with a secretive smile.

Meg pointed out her beets and turnips and carrots, and the watermelon and pumpkin patches Tye had planted himself.

"How long are you going to keep it a secret, Meg?"

Meg glanced from the wide leaves and vines to her one-time sister-in-law. "Keep what a secret?"

"Come on, Meg. The baby, of course."

Meg looked at her curiously. "What baby?"

Gwynn's entire expression changed. Amazement flooded her fair features. "You don't know."

"I don't know what? Tell me?"

"The dizzy spells you've been having—you've probably been sick several times. How long since you had your monthly?"

Meg's head whirled with the implication. "I thought it was just the heat, but it never affected me like that before. I haven't had it for…for I don't know how long."

"Doesn't your body feel different?"

Meg thought about the heaviness in her breasts. "Yes."

"You're going to have a baby, Meg."

Meg stared at Gwynn until her face blurred. She blinked and glanced at the bright blue sky. A baby? Could it be true? Already she was carrying a baby? "Oh my goodness," she whispered, blinking back tears.

Gwynn hugged her. "He loves you very much."

"Tye?"

"Of course Tye, you silly!" She laughed. "Who else? It's so obvious that even Edwina has to recognize it."

"It is?"

"He looks at you like you're some kind of princess. He's attentive, and he built you a porch. Why,

I almost think I'm jealous of such a love as you have.''

"Harley loves you.''

"Yes, he does now. But he married me because I was from the right family.''

"Tye didn't exactly marry me for reasons of passion,'' Meg replied.

"But he feels it, you can't deny it.''

Meg thought over her relationship with her husband. No, she couldn't deny it.

And a baby.

The growing realization elated her.

The rest of the afternoon passed pleasantly. The children played games and took turns riding the good-natured Shetland who'd immediately adapted to his new surroundings.

Meg showed Wilsie the dress she was making for Eve, and Wilsie asked if she could add a lace underskirt.

Edwina enjoyed the swing and the lemonade and conceded that the fresh air was good for the children.

Tye and Harley spent some time with the horses, and then joined the children in the yard. By the time the Telfords climbed into their buggy and rode off, Meg was glad for the quiet.

On the porch, Eve played with her doll, and Tye and Meg sat on the swing, watching the sunset.

"Thank you for the porch, Tye. I don't think I ever thanked you properly.''

"You're welcome,'' he replied easily. "Did you enjoy their visit?''

"Yes. It pleases me that they've accepted you.''

"I wish they'd have accepted me before the fire."

"So do I. But it took the fire to show them what kind of person you are. Harley has good breeding, but did you see him run in there after his son's horse?"

"He's not as foolish as I am, obviously. Didn't you say that was foolish?"

"It was brave. It was who you are."

"Foolish. I lost my hat."

She grinned. "It was a great hat. But you can buy a new one." She studied the tangerine sphere on the distant horizon. "Let's go into town tomorrow and see about the loan for the packing plant. You have plenty to put down now to get started, and we can use the cobs as collateral."

"Is that what you want?"

She nodded. "It's what I want."

Everything had gone better than she could have hoped. The horses were an asset she'd never hoped for. All her hopes and dreams had fallen neatly into place. The ranch was more secure than it had ever been. The mares carried foals that would make them even richer the following spring.

And Meg had a wonderful secret.

She'd hung on to Joe's ranch, and Tye was turning it into a profitable business. The repairs were done, the stock was healthy. And now she'd have her very own child.

All the dreams she and Joe had started out with had come to pass.

The sun disappeared and the sky wore a dark cloak. A sudden stab of possessiveness startled her. Why did she feel that she didn't want to share any of this happiness with Joe? What had come over her?

Meg studied her shadowed porch with loving eyes. Joe had never built her a porch. He'd thought the stock and the barns more important than their house, and she'd gone along. But had she really agreed, or was it only so she didn't feel slighted?

She'd spent so much of her energy feeling guilty over her passion for Tye that she hadn't appreciated it fully. Joe hadn't set her skin and her body and her mind on fire. Tye had done all that and then patiently taught her it was not wicked to feel that way.

And Tye had given her this baby. This baby was theirs and theirs alone.

She placed her hand on his arm, and in the semi-darkness he glanced over. She smiled. She couldn't wait to tell him.

Eve approached the swing and Tye slowed to pick her up and arrange her on his lap. Meg studied them contentedly, amazed that could she love two people so much. Her heart's desire had changed completely, but it had never been more clear. Her greatest longing was to be a wife to Tye and a mother to Eve…and a good mother to this new child. Tye reached for Meg's hand and held it.

One of the stallions whinnied from his pen.

A whippoorwill called its mournful cry.

"Remember that baby you asked about, Eve?" Meg said softly.

"What baby?" she replied, her head against Tye's chest.

"You wondered when God was going to give us a baby."

"I remember."

Meg's heart fluttered as though she stood atop the barn roof ready to leap. "Well, God gave us a baby just like we talked about."

"He did?"

"Mmm-hmm."

"Where is it?" she asked, her eyes wide and her amazed expression endearing.

"It's in my tummy. It will take a while to grow big enough to be born."

Tye's fingers convulsed on hers. He turned his face to see her eyes.

"Is it a boy baby or a girl baby?" Eve asked.

"I don't know. We'll have to wait and see."

"Meg," he said, his voice hoarse.

She couldn't see him for the tears that filled her eyes.

He pulled her hand to his mouth and pressed his lips against the backs of her fingers. Meg followed her hand and leaned into him, raising her face.

In order to reach her, he crushed Eve between them, pulling Meg close so he could kiss her. Eve squirmed and hugged them both.

"Meg," he said again, his voice disbelieving. "A baby?"

She nodded, her forehead now against his.

"Will the baby be mine, too?" Eve asked.

Meg kissed the top of her head. "It will be your brother or sister since we are your legal parents now."

"But I don't have to call you Mama," she said quickly.

"No, you call me Meg if you like. I know you have a real mama, and it's okay." And it was, it really was. Eve had loved her own mother very much; it was unfair of Meg to think she could easily forget her or not resent the fact that she was gone.

How many times had she been angry with Joe for leaving her life in a jumble? A new mother didn't replace a previous one.

Just as a new husband didn't replace a previous one. But Tye had added a whole new dimension to her life, a dimension she'd never have known if Joe hadn't died.

Perhaps if she was patient, she could be someone special to Eve, too. She'd come to love the child more than she'd believed she could. She wanted to be a mother to her.

Later, when they'd climbed into bed with the lamp still burning, Tye pulled Meg close and stroked her hair. "Are you happy about the baby, Meg?"

Of course she was happy. Was he? "I wonder if the news is less exciting because you've just learned about Eve."

"You're wrong. This baby is special because it's the only thing I gave you that Joe didn't give you first."

Those words cut straight to her soul. But it was so untrue. Tye had given her so much more. "What about you?" she asked, sitting up. "You already have Eve."

"I love Eve as much as I possibly can, but I didn't love her mother. This is as different as can be."

"How is it different?"

He was silent for several minutes. "I've admired you from the first time I ever saw you," he said. "I thought you were the most beautiful girl at school. The kindest, too. When none of the others would talk to me, you always did.

"I spent my whole life on the outside looking in, and you were always in the center of things. I watched you grow up and get prettier and prettier. I saw how happy you were with Joe, and I knew I'd never have a woman as lovely and perfect as you."

"I'm far from perfect," she denied.

He ignored her. "When you proposed the idea of marrying to save the ranch, I couldn't believe such good fortune could fall in my lap. It took a good many others' bad fortune for me to get there, but it didn't matter that I wasn't first choice. All that mattered was that I had a chance to marry sweet Meg."

"And start your packing plant?"

"Too much good fortune for a fella like me to believe. I let it go to my head, though."

"What do you mean?"

"Occasionally I forget the reasons we're married. Joe's the one you love. You never promised me anything different. I had a strong back to offer. It's yours with no regrets."

"You're a foolish man."

"So you've said."

"You've given of *yourself,* Tye. You said Joe had supplied the cobs, but I would have wasted their potential without you. You're the one that recognized their breeding and prodded me to find the papers. I might have sold them for a lot less than they're worth. Because of you, we still have the cobs and now the foals, plus the stud fees.''

''Yeah, well, that was luck.''

''Was my father's ring luck, too? You worked nights for a month or better to get that ring back for me.''

''It was because of me you had to sell it. If I'd have come into this marriage with something, you wouldn't have had to.''

''Hogwash.'' She straightened the quilt. ''What about the porch? You took time from other work to build a porch just because I wanted one.''

''A porch is a far cry from a piece of jewelry or something a woman really likes.''

''I really like the porch. It's personal. It's from you. You give of *yourself,* Tye.''

''I just love you, Meg. I always have. But that's never been enough.''

His words touched her heart and calmed her spirit. *He loved her.* He'd always loved her. ''I'm sorry I didn't know,'' she whispered.

''It wouldn't have changed anything,'' he said. ''You love Joe.''

Yes, she'd loved Joe. She'd loved him with her whole youthful heart and being. But she'd gone on without him. And she'd forged a new life.

''I did love Joe,'' she said. ''That can't change. Just like you being Eve's father can't change. That's

all right. Those things have made us who we are today. But we can go on. We can go forward.''

"I'm tired of being a shadow, Meg," he said, pain
in his tone. "I'll never live up to his memory. I don't
want to try. I don't want to sleep with you with Joe's
things at the foot of the bed."

Meg turned down the covers, got out of bed and
picked up the lamp. "Come here."

He wrapped the quilt around his waist and followed.

She knelt before the trunk and lifted the lid with
one hand.

Tye, with love and remorse scoring his heart,
turned his gaze from her face to the open trunk. It
took a minute for what he saw in the tray to register.
A single dried wild rose. The rose he'd given her the
day they'd ridden the riverbank searching for stuck
cows. Beneath it lay a picture of a horse Eve had
drawn with charcoal.

Meg handed him the lantern. She removed the
liner, revealing pressed tablecloths and sheets.

"What did you do with his things?" he asked.

"I sent them home with Edwina. Everything except
the letters, that is. They're up in the attic."

"Meg, I didn't mean for you to give up the things
that were important to you," he said, regret eating his
insides. "I was angry that day. I said things I
shouldn't have said."

"You said things that were true." She gave a shake
of her head. "And I thought about them afterward.
Those things gave me comfort when I needed them.

But I don't need them anymore. I loved Joe. But he's dead.'' She blinked. ''I've never said that before.''

He'd never loved her more than he did at that moment.

''You taught me to be honest with myself, Tye. I hid from myself all along. I hid from my feelings, and I hid from who I was and who I wanted to be. I hid from the fact that Joe had his selfish qualities, and I didn't even face the fact that he was dead. I thought if I kept his dream alive, I'd keep him alive. But after a while my own dream seemed to be more important.''

''And what's your own dream?''

''A man who loves me more than *his* dream.''

''I love you more than my dream, Meg. I don't need a packing plant if it doesn't make you happy.''

''And I don't need this ranch if it doesn't make you happy, Tye. We could sell it and start over somewhere else.''

''You mean that, Meg?''

''I mean it.''

He thought over her words and the idea only briefly. ''I think we should stay. And I think we should send Eve to school in the fall.''

''You do?''

''I do. I don't think anyone will be giving her a difficult time after this.''

''I don't, either.''

''But if they did, I'd have to hurt them.''

''I'd help you.''

Their lips met.

''I have a gift for you,'' she said.

She'd never given him a present. "What is it?"

"It's not an ordinary gift."

"I'll try not to show my shock."

She turned and pulled an envelope from her bureau drawer.

"What is it?"

"Open it."

He placed the lamp on the night table and opened the envelope. An official-looking piece of paper slid out. He glanced over the document from the Colorado capital, stating the Circle H brand had been recorded. "What is it?" he asked again.

"It's our brand. It's not the Circle T anymore. I drew them a picture of the new brand. See, we can add a bar across this side to change the T to an H."

The significance of the gesture astounded him. "Thank you, Meg. Thank you isn't enough. You make me feel like I'm not on the outside looking in anymore. I don't know what else to say."

"Say you're happy."

He studied the honey hue of her hair in the light, the delicate bow of her lips, and rested his palm along her satin cheek. "There's only one thing that would make me happier."

She didn't reply. She led him back to the bed and adjusted the quilt and the covers, then joined him beneath. He kissed her with all the love he'd harbored for so long, made love to her more gently than he'd done in the past, with a new reverence for her body and his child growing inside.

Meg cried with the release of her pent-up emotions and the joy of knowing Tye loved her. While he slept beside her, she stroked his hair, his shoulder, and listened to the wind in the aspens along the ridge.

All along Tye had thought he had nothing to give, when he'd given the most important thing of all— himself. And all along she'd withheld. Oh, she'd made love with him, but she'd held back that last little bit of herself. Initially she'd been so concerned over what Joe would have wanted for her that she'd ignored what she wanted for herself.

That would have been too selfish. That would have been too revealing. That would have been too risky.

Because what if she gave of herself and the feelings weren't returned? She'd been so sure of Joe. He'd been her safety. Her security. Her friend.

Tye was a little wild. A little naughty. He'd known other women, and he even had a child of his own. Giving all of herself was taking a risk. But then so had marrying him been a risk. He'd never proven her trust unfounded.

Loving Tye was not disloyal to what she and Joe had shared together. Theirs had been a different kind of love, a safe and comfortable kind of love. Loving Tye had seemed anything but safe and comfortable. And he was more than a friend.

But how long would she hide from herself?

"Tye?"

He snuggled closer.

"Tye?"

"Mmm-hmm?"

"I love you."

Tye's hand found his wife's cheek in the darkness.

*   *   *   *   *

Anglophile
('an-glə-fil)
One who greatly admires or favors England
and things English.

+

Dreamer
('drē-mər)
One who lives in a world of fancy and
imagination.

=

MY LORD PROTECTOR
by Deborah Hale
England, 1748 (29052-7)

THE BRIDE OF WINDERMERE
by Margo Maguire
England, 1421 (29053-5)

ROBBER BRIDE
by Deborah Simmons
England, 1274 (29055-1)

**Harlequin Historicals
the way the past *should* have been.**

Coming to bookstores in February 1999
and March 1999.
Available at your favorite retail outlet.

HARLEQUIN®
Makes any time special ™

Look us up on-line at: http://www.romance.net   HHMED3

If you enjoyed what you just read,
then we've got an offer you can't resist!

Take 2 bestselling love stories FREE!

Plus get a FREE surprise gift!

Clip this page and mail it to Harlequin Reader Service®

IN U.S.A.	IN CANADA
3010 Walden Ave.	P.O. Box 609
P.O. Box 1867	Fort Erie, Ontario
Buffalo, N.Y. 14240-1867	L2A 5X3

YES! Please send me 2 free Harlequin Historical™ novels and my free surprise gift. Then send me 6 brand-new novels every month, which I will receive months before they're available in stores. In the U.S.A., bill me at the bargain price of $3.94 plus 25¢ delivery per book and applicable sales tax, if any*. In Canada, bill me at the bargain price of $4.19 plus 25¢ delivery per book and applicable taxes**. That's the complete price and a savings of over 10% off the cover prices—what a great deal! I understand that accepting the 2 free books and gift places me under no obligation ever to buy any books. I can always return a shipment and cancel at any time. Even if I never buy another book from Harlequin, the 2 free books and gift are mine to keep forever. So why not take us up on our invitation. You'll be glad you did!

246 HEN CNE2
349 HEN CNE4

Name	(PLEASE PRINT)	
Address	Apt.#	
City	State/Prov.	Zip/Postal Code

* Terms and prices subject to change without notice. Sales tax applicable in N.Y.
** Canadian residents will be charged applicable provincial taxes and GST.
All orders subject to approval. Offer limited to one per household.
® are registered trademarks of Harlequin Enterprises Limited.

HIST99   ©1998 Harlequin Enterprises Limited

Look for a new and exciting series from Harlequin!

HARLEQUIN

Duets ™

Two <u>new</u> full-length novels in one book, from some of your favorite authors!

Starting in May, each month we'll be bringing you two new books, each book containing two brand-new stories about the lighter side of love! Double the pleasure, double the romance, for less than the cost of two regular romance titles!

Look for these two new Harlequin Duets™ titles in May 1999:

Book 1:
WITH A STETSON AND A SMILE
by Vicki Lewis Thompson
THE BRIDESMAID'S BET
by Christie Ridgway

Book 2:
KIDNAPPED? by Jacqueline Diamond
I GOT YOU, BABE by Bonnie Tucker

2 GREAT STORIES BY 2 GREAT AUTHORS FOR 1 LOW PRICE!

Don't miss it! Available May 1999 at your favorite retail outlet.

HARLEQUIN®

Makes any time special.™

Look us up on-line at: http://www.romance.net   HDGENR

COMING NEXT MONTH FROM

HARLEQUIN HISTORICALS

- **ROBBER BRIDE**
  by **Deborah Simmons**, author of THE LAST ROGUE
  The de Burgh brothers are back! Here, Simon de Burgh finds his
  match in a free-spirited lady who is hiding from her despicable
  would-be husband.

  HH #455 ISBN# 29055-1 $4.99 U.S./$5.99 CAN.

- **THE TENDER STRANGER**
  by **Carolyn Davidson**, author of THE WEDDING PROMISE
  A pregnant widow who runs away from her conniving
  in-laws falls in love with the bounty hunter hired to bring
  her back home.

  HH #456 ISBN# 29056-X $4.99 U.S./$5.99 CAN.

- **RORY**
  by **Ruth Langan**, author of BLACKTHORNE
  In this first book of THE O'NEIL SAGA, an English
  noblewoman falls in love with a legendary Irish rebel as they flee
  from soldiers intent on taking his life.

  HH #457 ISBN# 29057-8 $4.99 U.S./$5.99 CAN.

- **FATHER FOR KEEPS**
  by **Ana Seymour**,
  author of A FAMILY FOR CARTER JONES
  An heir returns to win back the woman who had his child in
  Ana Seymour's sequel to *A Family for Carter Jones*.

  HH #458 ISBN# 29058-6 $4.99 U.S./$5.99 CAN.

DON'T MISS THESE FOUR GREAT TITLES AVAILABLE NOW!

HH #451 JOE'S WIFE
Cheryl St.John

HH #452 MY LORD PROTECTOR
Deborah Hale

HH #453 THE BRIDE OF WINDERMERE
Margo Maguire

HH #454 SILVER HEARTS
Jackie Manning

HARLEQUIN · FIVE DECADES OF ROMANCE · CELEBRATES

In April 1999,
Harlequin Love & Laughter shows you
50 ways to lure your lover as we
celebrate Harlequin's 50th Anniversary.

*Look for these humorous romances at your
favorite retail stores:*

50 WAYS TO LURE YOUR LOVER
by Julie Kistler

SWEET REVENGE?
by Kate Hoffmann

Look us up on-line at: http://www.romance.net   H50LL_L